JACK & STELLA'S STORY

forever love

Printed in Australia
Cover design by Shawline Publishing Group Pty Ltd
Images in this book are copyright approved for Shawline Publishing Group Pty Ltd
Illustrations within this book are copyright approved for Shawline Publishing Group Pty Ltd

First Printing: March 2023
Shawline Publishing Group Pty Ltd
www.shawlinepublishing.com.au

Paperback ISBN 978-1-9228-5016-4
eBook ISBN 978-1-9228-5021-8

Distributed by Shawline Distribution and Lightningsource Global

A catalogue record for this
work is available from the
National Library of Australia

More great Shawline titles can be found here:

New titles also available through Books@Home Pty Ltd.
Subscribe today - www.booksathome.com.au

JACK & STELLA'S STORY

forever love

TRACY-LEE PULLAN

You were so proud of me when I wrote this story. How I wish I could have shown you the published book. Thanks for being the best dad a daughter could ever have had. I will miss you forever.

Love you Dad xx

The universe always unfolds and shows everyone the true path they need to follow to find true happiness. Never doubt that.

CHAPTER 1

We all travel along on the journey that is meant for us, and we pick up and drop off people along the way. They can be in your life for a short time or a long time, but they all leave something behind. Some of the best moments in life are the ones you can't tell anyone about but Jack and Stella decided they wanted to share their story with you.

※

Stella was on her way to McGregor and Bailey, a very well-known web design agency. She had to keep pinching herself, it had been a dream of hers for so long to one day work here, and to think, she had an interview! It would be challenging, she had no doubt about that, but they were looking for a graphic designer who could bring something different and she felt quietly confident this was the role for her. Her recruitment agent had already told her that her fresh ideas and positive attitude had shone in her resume.

Stella had fallen in love with the role as soon as she had read the job description. Her current role had run its course and she wanted something she could really sink her teeth into to stimulate her creativity.

Her confidence on the day of the interview was momentarily rattled when she walked into the interview room and her gaze locked with the darkest brown eyes she had ever seen. Something almost primal stirred deep within her.

'Take a seat,' he said. She sat where he had indicated with a brief wave of his arm. His aftershave wafted between them and she couldn't help but discreetly inhale it. It was spicy and intoxicating.

'I'm Jack Turner and I am one of the senior partners here at McGregor and Bailey.'

As he shook her hand she was startled. It felt like an electrical current was coursing through his fingers. She looked into his eyes to see if he had felt anything but his expression remained neutral, so she guessed it was all in her imagination. She couldn't help but think, *Is it possible to feel instant chemistry when one meets a complete stranger?*

Distracting herself from the handsome interviewer by looking around the room, she noticed that every wall was glass. It felt a little bit like sitting in a fishbowl. There were a couple of big ferns in black pots on either side of the table, but otherwise the room was devoid of decoration. She took some quick breaths to calm herself down. Her hands felt clammy and she surreptitiously wiped them on her skirt.

As she stole another look at her interviewer, Jack, she couldn't help but admire his well-tailored navy pinstripe suit. He had paired it with a tie that had some kind of tiny insignia on it she couldn't quite place. The suit clung to him in all the right places and accentuated his broad shoulders. *Stop it*, she thought, *this is a job interview, not a first date.* But his presence seemed to dominate the room and she couldn't take her eyes off him.

'So, tell me a bit about yourself Stella. What is it about the role and our company that you're most interested in?' asked Jack.

'I've been in my current role for quite a while now and I'm looking for a change. I have a lot of ideas but haven't had the opportunity to use any of them. Your agency has such a wonderful reputation and from what I have read on your website, some of the clients you have— I was impressed. Most people in the web design industry dream about working here.' She took a deep breath, conscious that she had been speaking very quickly.

'But you can see room for improvement?' Before waiting for her to answer, Jack smiled, and leaned back in his chair. 'Don't worry Stella, it isn't a trick question. I just don't believe in beating around the bush,' he said with a laugh.

'Well, yes. If I can speak freely, there is a lot of room for improvement.' She sat up straighter in her chair with a new found confidence surging through her. 'The first thing I noticed was the font you use on your website it is very outdated. I'm not sure how you can expect to design other people's websites, when your own one is very, well, bland.' Jack's eyes narrowed and she paused, wondering if she had gone too far.

'If something as simple as the font we use is deemed as outdated, I am now very interested in the vision you have for the rest of our company.' He was trying hard to suppress a smile but the raised corners of his mouth gave him away. She didn't let this deter her as the cogs turning in her brain spurred her on.

'With a fresh new direction and better layout you would have a much better, user-friendly website. I'm sure you would capture the customers you are currently losing. I imagine they take one look at the clunky website you currently have and move on. I would also love to do something with your Instagram and other social media— it really does need to be dragged into the 21st Century.' Her face turned a very light shade of pink, had she gone too far? She decided to opt for some more tact.

'I noticed most of your clients are from the top end of town. How do you attract other clients in a way that doesn't make them feel intimidated?' Tilting her head, she stared into his eyes.

'What do you mean, what other clients would we want?' His nostrils flared.

'Well, there is a whole other customer base that you are missing out on. Where are the non for profits and other small businesses?' she said, tapping her fingers lightly on the wooden table.

'We haven't really had the resources to deal with small businesses and often their budgets are so tight that we can't really design anything for them they can afford.'

'Really? Surely there can be some kinds of suitably priced packages for these clients—why should they miss out on having a great website just because of their financial status?' Stella could see that she had him on the hop now and once again hoped she hadn't gone too far. But he had asked her opinion and she wasn't going to sugar coat it.

Her hands were still sweaty so she wiped them down her skirt again. She had a vision of her white satin top being completely transparent as she felt so hot and sweaty and she took a quick peek to check. Thankfully all was as it should be, and no outline of her bra was visible.

'Thank you for that Stella. I love the fact that you say it how it is. It's quite uncanny how similar we are.' He raised an eyebrow and leaned back in his chair. Relief washed over her. It seemed her speech had paid off and she'd managed to impress him.

'As you would appreciate, our industry is extremely cut throat. Do you think you can handle it?' he said, bracing his elbows on the table and leaning toward her.

'Absolutely. I am ready for the next challenge in my career and I really feel I can offer a lot to your company.' She braced her arms on her chair and leaning forward, mirroring him. Jack appeared rattled by the confidence she projected and cleared his throat.

'To give you an idea of the chain of command, you would report into me but would also work with other members of the team. At the end of the day, Dylan Bailey, our Managing Director, has the final say on what comes out of the agency. As you would have seen from our website, Dylan started this company many years ago and is still very much involved in the running of it.' Jack steepled his fingers and she fidgeted beneath the intensity of his gaze.

'But you and I would be working very closely together so it is important to me that I hire someone that I feel I can work with and trust to do a good job for the company.' Her ears pricked up when he mentioned "trust". Gosh, if only he knew her views on that small word. Her mind drifted for a moment, but she stopped herself from going down into that dark place.

As the interview wore on, she was liking this company more and more and hoped she had made a good first impression and then wondered if she was trying to impress him for the job or was it because it was important to her that Jack liked her in general? She could feel the lines blurring and then decided firmly that it was going to be a business decision and she wanted the job.

࿊

Jack was excited as the candidate, Stella, ran through other projects she had recently worked on. She was exactly what the company needed to bring some new energy into the team. Their last graphic designer had kept on churning out the same ideas over and over and they were losing clients at a rate of knots. The rest of the team would be impressed with her and their new clients would no doubt enjoy working with her.

He told her that they were just about to start work on a major tender, one of the biggest ones in the company's history. Basically, this was why they needed someone with her experience, to help bring this together. Even though it was an interview, without even realising, the two of them started brainstorming. Bouncing ideas around they both felt so inspired. All of this just from an interview. He wanted her and was going to do everything in his power to convince Dylan that she was the one.

The interview concluded and as they shook hands, he could feel the heat permeating through her and their eyes clashed. Did she feel the spark that he did? He dropped her hand, determined to keep things professional.

Jack was keen to get in her for a second interview and introduce her to Dylan. If he signed off on this, he would get straight back to the recruitment agency and offer her the job. The sooner she started the better as far as he was concerned. He wanted to see her again, she had surprised him in so many ways and it wasn't often that happened.

❧

Stella's confidence faded as she arrived home. She didn't want to get her hopes up. Perhaps she wasn't actually good enough for the role. Did they want someone more senior? Her usual self-doubt seemed to swamp her.

Kicking off her shoes she settled down into her favourite chair and called Jaz. They had been best friends since meeting at primary school and she was her sounding board for everything in her life. They had been through so much together—the good, the bad and the ugly. Her advice always made her feel better.

'Hey, it's me,' she said as Jaz picked up.

'Stella, how are you? I was just thinking about you. So, how did you go?' Her friend had known that the interview was today, had even texted her a string of good luck emojis this morning, so had naturally been waiting for the debrief.

'It went well; I think but—'

'But nothing Stella. You would have nailed it. You're perfect for the role and you know it. Don't go down that path, please don't.'

'I can't help it. Maybe I should have said more, worn a different outfit. I don't know.' Jaz snorted down the telephone line.

'You have all the qualifications and are perfect for this role.'

'I know but maybe I'm not the right fit for the company? Perhaps they had a different type in mind and then I walked in? I don't know—I just feel sick.'

'So, what was the boss like? Male, female, young, old?' Stella knew Jaz was trying to move her thoughts away from the path it was heading in. She was getting good at this; she had been protecting Stella's fragile mind since they were ten years old. Stella's home life had been anything but nurturing and Jaz had made it no secret that she hated Stella's mum, probably more than Stella herself would ever admit to.

'His name is Jack—I really liked him. He was very welcoming and so easy to talk to. He is younger than me though,' she hesitated, wondering what Jaz's thoughts would be on that bit of information, 'but we really clicked and I think we will make a great team.'

'Are you smiling Stella?'

'No,' she said and she forced herself to stop.

'Yes, you are! What is it you aren't you telling me?'

'Nothing, I promise you.' She could feel a smile spreading across her face again.

'Stella Carter, I know you're holding out on me. Spill. What happened?'

'Well,' she started, fiddling with a loose thread on one of the many cushions decorating her couch, 'promise you won't judge me?

Something weird happened with Jack and I, the guy I would be working with closely...'

'What? Did you spill a coffee or something all over him?' Jaz laughed.

'I wish that was what had happened.'

'Now I'm really intrigued, what did you do?'

'Nothing bad. But when I shook his hand, I got this weird feeling and it was quite embarrassing. I hope he didn't notice.'

'What kind of feeling?'

Sighing, she tried to explain to Jaz how she had felt.

'It's definitely a feeling you shouldn't get while in an interview, right?' Stella burst out laughing.

'Probably not, but this is so funny. I hope you get the job so you can see him again.'

After they had hung up, Stella thought about that handshake. She was damn sure she hadn't imagined that charge of energy that passed between them when their hands connected.

❧

A few days later she got the call to say they wanted to see her again. She could barely contain her excitement.

It was the same drill as last time. She even sat in the same seat as the previous interview, which helped to settle her nerves. Jack and her shook hands again and yes, there it was, that familiar jolt. Did she imagine Jack's mouth turning up into subtle smile? She was sure he had felt something this time.

Jack introduced her to Dylan.

'So, you're the infamous Stella Carter, the lady who wants to drag my company into the 21st Century?' He chuckled which made his eyes crinkle. Stella's face went bright red and she turned and looked at Jack with a pained look.

'Don't worry Stella, like Jack here, I appreciate honesty, it really is quite refreshing. I'm sure you will fit in here nicely, as you obviously speak your mind.' She smiled weakly but still felt mortified that Dylan was aware of what she had said.

Stella left the interview still not sure whether she had done enough to impress them and secure the role. Her head was spinning. If she did get this job, she would certainly be asking Jack what else he had told Dylan so she could be prepared. If there was one thing Stella hated it was surprises.

⚹

Jack and Dylan sat in the meeting room—there was always a part of the day where they caught up with each other so they took this opportunity while there were no other distractions.

'So, you like her then?' Dylan asked. Jack felt his cheeks turn pink. Something about her had shaken him more than he cared to admit.

'What do you mean like her?' Jack had a moment of confusion as if somehow Dylan had known what had just gone through his mind.

'Yes, like her, do you want her on the team or not? I liked her and think she will be a great asset to the company.' Thankfully, Dylan didn't notice anything unusual about Jack's behaviour. Jack shook his head to clear the thoughts he had about Stella Carter, while Dylan continued, 'Get on the phone now and get the recruitment people to offer her the role. In fact, don't,' and he flicked his assistant an email asking her to get the ball rolling. 'Let's get her started as soon as we can—we have a lot on as you know so she will be thrown in the deep end.'

'Let's hope she can swim then,' whispered Jack.

CHAPTER 2

Two weeks later, Stella walked in to the lobby of McGregor and Bailey. Nervous energy swirled around her as did her favourite perfume—a light fragrance lingered in the lift as she got out, like a summer garden, floral and intoxicating.

She saw Jack briefly and then Milly, Jack's EA, took her around and introduced her to the rest of the team. Her first impression of Milly was she was a bit of an odd girl. She seemed friendly on the surface, but also aloof and distant, like she wanted to be perceived as caring, but didn't really. The rest of the staff seemed to like her and were quite chatty with her, but still Stella felt that she should be wary—gut instinct told her that something wasn't quite right.

Eventually, she was shown to her desk and she popped her bag down. It was in a great spot. When she looked out the window, she could see Hyde Park and she imagined herself sitting down there on her lunch breaks. From where she was seated, she could see Jack's office. She wasn't sure if that was a good thing or not—it could end up being a bit of a distraction.

Following her gaze, Milly giggled and leaned on Stella's desk, lowering her voice conspiratorially.

'Don't worry, everyone has a crush on Jack.' Milly shrugged and checked her nails. 'But it's pointless to do more than admire. He has a girlfriend—her name is Eleanor. But don't say anything or he'll think I have been gossiping and he'll get annoyed with me.' She giggled again. Stella couldn't help but feel disappointed when she heard Jack was involved with someone. 'None of us think it will last though, he dates them for a while, and then moves on,' continued Milly.

'It's really no concern of mine,' said Stella, clearing her throat and looking pointedly at her computer. She didn't want to get in to any office gossip on her first day, especially with Jack's assistant. If Milly was hoping for something more, she was going to be disappointed. Milly shrugged and left her to it then and Stella spent an enjoyable day settling in.

Late in the day, Jack called for her. She wasn't sure whether to take her laptop or not. In the end she did, entering his office equipped to provide a detailed report on her first day. Jack looked up from his computer and ran a hand through his hair.

'Everything going okay Stella?' he asked. 'Did Milly get you set up and introduce you to the team?'

'Yes, she did thanks. I think I've met everyone now.' It was on the tip of her tongue to say, *except for your girlfriend Eleanor,* so she bit her lip to stop this slipping out.

'Well, if you need anything, just ask Milly.'

'Sure, I will.'

'How about we lock in some time tomorrow and I can bring you up to speed on our current projects?' Before she could answer, he had called out to Milly who sat outside his office. 'Book me an hour with Stella, will you? Tomorrow morning, if possible.'

When she got back to her desk and opened her laptop, the appointment had been booked. Clearly Milly was very efficient. She wondered briefly if she was involved in booking things in for his private life as well. And why had Milly mentioned his girlfriend earlier? It had been a little strange to warn her off him immediately. Had there been problems before with colleagues getting involved with him? She was a little curious, she had to admit.

ᖷ

As the weeks went by, Stella settled into a routine and couldn't help but feel triumphant that she was now working in her dream job, one she had never before felt confident would ever be within her grasp. Her whole life, anything good had been dangled tantalisingly in front of her, only to be cruelly snatched away.

Through all her conversations with Jack, even though they were predominately work related, she started to get a feel for who he was. She watched how he interacted with the staff and she could see that he truly cared about all of them. He always remembered birthdays or other special occasions and took time to walk around every day having a chat to the team.

His working relationship with Milly still baffled her though—clearly, she irritated him and it sometimes felt like fingernails going down a blackboard when he asked her to do something and Stella would watch the frustration pass over his face and see his hands clench tightly by his side as Milly would blatantly misinterpret what he wanted or just outright defy him.

Stella knew without a doubt Milly did this on purpose. It almost felt like she was desperate for some kind of attention from him and this was the only way she could get it. Some days, she felt exasperated watching her behaviour, but her view of Milly softened as she realised just how lonely this girl must be. Stella knew only too well how it felt to be invisible.

Even better were the days when he would pop down to her desk and pull up a chair.

Over these casual conversations they discovered just how much they had in common. Jack loved hiking and so did she. They discussed the walks they had done over the years and, funnily enough, they had even been to some of the same places.

'I can't believe you have done so much hiking in New Zealand, Jack. How do you ever find the time?' They had both done parts of the Abel Tasman walk so shared stories and photos. She told him she had gone on a tour and someone took your pack and at the end of the day you slept in a cabin. 'That's hardly what I would call hiking Stella, if you can't carry your own gear.' He had gone in with the minimum of equipment and did what he told her was "real hiking". The comment was accompanied by a good-natured laugh.

'It is real hiking. I'm just clever enough to realise you don't need to suffer when you can arrange for someone else to carry your gear.'

'I would never do that,' he said.

'Well, I do and I will continue to unless you can convince me otherwise. And I'll tell you now, you'll have your work cut out for you,' she laughed.

'I may need to take you on a real hike then and I will not be carrying your pack.'

'We'll see about that—I'm pretty good at talking people into doing things for me.'

'Hmm, looks like I may have met my match.' He winked.

Her face was still flaming long after he had returned to his office. As she sat there working, she could feel someone staring at her.

She looked up and caught Milly's eye. Milly looked away quickly but Stella saw something cross over her face and it made her wary as she remembered that first day, and Milly's gossip.

Jack and Stella were building up a good friendship. If it wasn't for the fact that he had a girlfriend, she felt like he may want to ask her out. There had been little hints and things said that she'd honed in on.

The other day, she overhead Milly talking on the phone organising tickets for him and she assumed, Eleanor, for the theatre. She had a catch up with Jack that afternoon and when she arrived, he was on the phone and he waved for her to sit down.

'Yes, we are going to see *Phantom of the Opera*. No, I certainly don't want to do that Paul.' He glanced up at her with a smile. 'Anyway, I have to go mate, I have someone with me.' He hung up the phone. 'Sorry about that.'

Damn, she could barely focus on what he was saying. She knew she shouldn't care, but she wanted to know who he was taking to the theatre—was it Eleanor? And who was Paul? How she got through the meeting she would never know but an hour later they were winding up. 'So, do you like the theatre?' he asked.

She hadn't been prepared for this question.

'Yes, I do actually, I've seen so many shows. I don't think I've ever seen one I didn't enjoy.' She grimaced. 'Actually, perhaps *Cats*, I wasn't a fan of that.'

He laughed. 'Funny you should say that, I didn't enjoy it either!'

'Well, enjoy your night out.' She headed back to her desk, once again feeling flustered. She was usually so calm and collected, but he seemed to be able to rattle her so easily and in fact, she sometimes felt like he enjoyed teasing her or asking pointed questions.

Milly came up minutes later almost purring. 'Don't read too much into that. He has season tickets to all the theatres in Sydney and goes all the time. Him and Eleanor love the theatre and the ballet—they have so much in common. I'm always booking things for them.' Milly propped her hip on Stella's desk, crumpling Stella's notes. Jack's assistant tapped a nail against her chin. 'I think he may be getting serious about her. They seem to be spending a lot more time together.'

'Really, how fascinating Milly.' Stella drawled, yanking her papers out from beneath Milly's behind. 'I really need to get back to work.' She turned her back on her.

Milly huffed and headed back to her desk. It was clear she didn't like Stella and she made it her business to try and upset her every day. It was so childish. But if it continued, Stella would have to have a word to Jack as she wasn't going to put up with it for much longer.

Strange things were starting to happen and she knew she wasn't going mad. Things kept disappearing from her desk or she would find her notes in her rubbish bin. She had stopped bringing food into the office, as that was tampered with or thrown out. There was no proof, but she knew it could only be Milly. She had tried to be friendly with her and get to know her but it was hopeless. For some reason, Milly didn't like her and was not happy with the friendship blossoming between Jack and Stella.

Stella wondered if perhaps Milly herself had a crush on Jack. She had watched them closely but that didn't seem to be the case. Whatever it was, it was clear Milly craved his attention and did whatever she could to get it. The only times she was nice to him was when Dylan was around. She played up to him and it made Stella sick. Couldn't he see her for what she was? Manipulative and trying so hard to drive some kind of wedge between Jack and Dylan.

Stella's mind moved back to Jack and the feelings she was having for him. She had been badly burned from her last relationship so was super cautious now. Marcus had been someone she had met at work and, like Jack, was a lot younger than her. She vowed she would never get tangled up with anyone younger than her again, or anyone she worked with after that debacle. Why did she keep falling for these men? She sighed.

Then there was her mother's voice continually in her head: *Don't think this job will last Stella, you just aren't good enough. Jack wouldn't go for a woman like you anyway, clearly he's happy with his Eleanor, so you can forget that. Who could love you?*

CHAPTER 3

She had been badly damaged from the fractured relationship she had had with her mother. Stella would never admit it to anyone but the day she heard her mother had died, she felt like she had finally been released from a lifetime of hell. A huge weight had been lifted from her shoulders. But as things came up in her life, her mother's voice had not quietened over the years and some days, the messages in her head drove her to distraction.

This is why Stella now found herself in her forties and still single. She made no apologies with how she lived her life, what anyone thought of her or the choices she made. She held her closest friends tight and cut loose anyone who was toxic or stopped her living her true life. This was a lesson she had learnt after years of been bullied by a very dominating mother. She trusted no one and very few people ever entered her circle. As long as she could remember, her mother had ruined so many of her friendships and relationships. She had chipped away any confidence Stella had had as a child and it had taken her years to finally be able to let certain people in. She almost tested them to ensure they wouldn't let her down or betray her in some way. Trust was just something that she didn't have with anyone. In fact, this is what had ruined all of her relationships with men, they either betrayed her in some way or she cut them loose as she got scared to let them get any closer to her.

She wished she could go back and tell her younger self that it was okay to follow your dreams and make your own choices. All the chatter, the judgements—they're worth naught in comparison to self-fulfilment.

To try and fill the empty void in her life, she had travelled extensively. Her favourite countries being Africa, South America and Asia. Sometimes she would travel as a tourist, but a lot of the time she would sign up as a volunteer and go help in remote villages. These were her most treasured memories and the smiles and hospitality that these people gave her were so special. Often, they had very little in the way of material things, but they gave her so much more. The short time she had helped out had made a small difference in their lives and that made her so happy.

But something had changed and Stella felt like she was just coasting along and living what, on the surface level, appeared to be her best life, but deep in her soul she was unsettled. Is this it? Why do I feel so empty and incomplete? My life needs to be more than this? There is always someone who is worse off than you, and she would try to remind herself to be happy and grateful for what she had. But this thought continued to niggle away at her and she couldn't settle. She knew there was more, and yet she was still searching for it.

All she had ever wanted was for someone to love her for who she was. Not try and change her or suggest she needed to change in a certain way in order to keep them happy.

She had been told her whole life that no one would ever choose her, love her, or want to marry her. Deep down, she didn't think this was true. She had so much to offer and a small part of her truly believed that one day someone would choose her to share their life with.

Even though she had only just met Jack, she felt such a connection with him. In fact, she had opened up to him more than she had to anyone else ever. She never usually discussed her private life with any colleagues. But he had a way of drawing things out of her and it made her feel safe and enabled her to share without the usual feelings of anxiety and the expected betrayal.

After a lifetime of keeping quiet with her mum, it was hard to break this habit. The only person who really knew her was Jaz and she had been happy to keep it like that. But now, sharing things with Jack made her feel happy.

One day, he had caught her off guard and had asked about her family. She gave him the version she had created over the years that her mother had passed away and she was an only child. Thankfully he hadn't asked her anything else—seeing her shut down knew he had touched on a raw nerve.

Could it be that he made her feel safe and perhaps she was starting to trust him?

CHAPTER 4

Jack's childhood was the polar opposite of Stella's. He had warm, nurturing parents and they had supported him his whole life. He was an only child but had never felt lonely. He had been clever at school and making friends had never been a problem for him. He had never lacked for attention from females and at times found this so annoying. A wife wasn't something he'd been looking for, hell, he wasn't even keen on having a fulltime girlfriend.

In fact, he was quite happy to be in his thirties and still be a bachelor. He had been single for a long time before he had met Eleanor and there were times, he wished he still was. She was hard work and becoming increasingly clingy. He hated that in a woman. As much as he tried to pull back, she seemed to be getting more entangled in his life and he wasn't sure how to extract himself without being cruel.

He was catching up with his best mate Paul. They had met at university and they just clicked. He knew he could talk about anything and Paul wouldn't judge him. And most of the time, he had good advice which Jack usually took. The topic of Eleanor came up in conversation.

'I'm surprised to see you tonight without your sidekick,' Paul said. Jack grimaced and took a swig of his drink.

'Mate, it's a bloody problem and I'm not sure how to get her out of my life.'

'Look, if you're not into this relationship Jack, you can't keep stringing her along. You're just going to have, "the talk," you can't keep avoiding it.'

'I know, I know, but I'm not looking forward to it. It will be full of drama and I just can't deal with it' right now.'

'Did you ask her to the gala dinner? Lindy and I are looking forward to it.'

'Yeah, I had to—especially when bloody Milly told her about it. They are way too close those two. I've warned Milly to stay out of my personal life but she can't seem to do that. I always feel that when I'm out of my office, she's in there snooping around. Nothing I can really put my finger on, but I don't trust her mate.'

'Get rid of her then; you're the boss.'

'Easier said than done. I've spoken to Tyler our HR guy and he says to be careful. It could get ugly if I dismiss her for the wrong reasons. The thing is, some days she actually does her job efficiently, it's just the meddling I can't deal with. It's even worse when Eleanor comes in—those two have become quite friendly. Milly is a completely different person around her. I sometimes feel like she is flirting with Eleanor as she just seems obsessed with pleasing her, and I mentioned this to Eleanor. She blew me off, told me I was imagining things. Funnily enough, most of the arguments I have had with Eleanor are due to things that Milly has told her—it's like she is trying to drive a wedge between us.'

'What's her background? How did she get the job?' Paul asked.

'She came from our usual agency and had a great resume. I didn't see any red flags when I interviewed her.'

'Is she seeing anyone? You don't think she has a thing for you, do you?'

'Oh god no, I hope not and I certainly have never encouraged her.' Jack shuddered at the thought.

'Maybe she is jealous of Eleanor and she is trying to break you up? Just be careful mate, you don't want any trouble like that in your life—it could ruin your reputation.'

'Hey, don't say anything to Lindy about this okay—it is confidential.' Jack loved Paul's wife, but she was prone to gossip and he didn't want this being discussed as it was a sensitive matter.

He had actually been out with Paul, the night Paul met Lindy. She had flirted with him all night, and things just went from there and now they were married with three kids.

'So, how's work going? Did you end up hiring a graphic designer?' Jack had told him a while back that they were looking for someone to replace their current one.

'Yeah, we did and she's great. What? Why did you give me that look?'

'No reason.' Paul smiled. 'So, are you going to tell me why she is so great? There must be a reason why you have, "that look," on your face right now.' Jack was feeling a little flustered now and tried to compose himself.

'Her name is Stella Carter and she's been great for the company and that's it.'

'I feel she has been great for you as well.' Paul nudged his arm.

'We're work colleagues and I'm her boss. That's it. Nothing more. Okay?' The tips of his ears turned a shade of pink betraying him.

'Sure, sure, if you say so.' Paul looked away smugly.

'I do say so. Now, can we drop this whole thing and just enjoy an evening not talking about women?' Picking up his drink and draining the glass was his way of signalling to Paul that this conversation was now indeed over.

Paul pondered over this whole conversation when he got home later that night. It sounded to him like Stella Carter had ruffled Jack's feathers, whether he would admit it or not. All the years he had known Jack, he could not remember any woman having the effect that the mere mention of this one had caused tonight. *Hmm, interesting. I hope she is coming to the gala dinner. I want to meet this lady.*

CHAPTER 5

At least once a week, her and Jack had started having lunch down in Hyde Park which was an easy walk from their office. At the park, she got to see the real Jack. Away from the office, he was such a different person. He seemed to relax with her and they would sit on the grass talking and lose track of time. They never seemed to run out of things to say or things to laugh at. His sense of humour was exactly like Stella's and it had become a competition now to see who could tell the funniest story or who would break first and start laughing.

It had been such a long time since Stella had shared anything with anyone, she could feel some of her mistrust starting to peel away the more time she spent with him.

He had a soothing way of speaking to her and he seemed to sense when she was feeling down and managed to turn her day around. If he planned time with her, he never bailed, a sign of his reliability. He would go out of his way to help her when she got stuck on something, spending his time talking things through, never rushing her. The way he supported her was something she'd experienced from few others. It was becoming apparent to her that she was starting to let him in.

Stella still held out hope that one day he would ask her out on a hike. But they weren't completely compatible as she found out one day when he told her how much he loved scuba diving—that was one thing she would never be able to do such was her fear of putting her head under water.

Skydiving also came up one day to which she replied, 'You don't have a hope in hell of ever convincing me to do that. I can barely travel in a plane let alone jump out of one!'

❧

Through Facebook she saw what he did in his downtime. Eleanor appeared in some of his posts. This light digital investigating (far nicer than calling it "stalking") was Milly's fault, she would tell herself. She had been the one who had told her about Eleanor in the first place and as much as she hadn't been interested in the beginning, she was now. She was hoping for the chance to meet this Eleanor and really check her out. Milly clearly adored her and sang her praises constantly which irked Stella. Seriously, how good could this woman really be? Stella rolled her eyes for what felt like the hundredth time and closed her laptop.

CHAPTER 6

The day had started out badly. She had slept in, then picking up her hairdryer and turning that on, it blew up and tripped out her power. Running out to her car, a heel had snapped of one of her shoes, forcing her to go back inside and grab another pair. She was now officially late.

As the lift door opened, her eyes caught Milly's and she saw the disapproval. Drat the girl, Stella knew that she had it in for her. She seemed to watch every move she made and always had something nasty to say. She had been pleasant enough when she first started but now, it was almost an all out war between them. Stella decided she would keep ignoring it for now but it was getting to the point where she would have to say something soon.

Frantic to catch up, her morning flew by in a whirl of emails and phone calls. It was only when her stomach rumbled well after 1.00pm, she decided she needed to eat and headed out to the local cafe. It was a popular place and being the time that it was, she was pleased she wasn't going to have to try and get a table. She flew through the door and headed straight up to the counter.

A voice beside her started her. 'Stella, fancy seeing you in here. This is a late lunch for you.' She blinked and focused on the man before her, her thoughts had been solely on placing her order and dashing back to the office.

'Jack, ah, yes, it is a late lunch for me today. I've completely lost track of time.'

'I can't have my employees not taking proper breaks, why don't you come and join us?'

Us? she thought as she followed him through the busy shop. They reached a table at the back and she noticed the couple already sitting there.

'I'd like you to meet Stella Carter, my new graphic designer. Stella, this is Paul and Lindy Edwards, two of my oldest friends,' Jack said.

'Nice to meet you both.' She shook their hands and sat down quickly into the seat that Jack offered as she could feel her legs starting to wobble.

She could feel this couple sizing her up—why did she feel like they already knew who she was? It was written all over their faces and they were not doing a good job of trying to hide it. She tried hard to stop the corners of her mouth twitching into a smile.

'So, Stella, what's it like working with Jack?' asked Paul as soon as she sat down.

'It's going well so far. He seems like a great boss.'

'Are you're coming to the gala dinner?' asked Lindy.

'Yes, I will be there and I have to say I'm really looking forward to it.' She was, in fact, a bundle of nerves at the thought of this evening but hadn't been able to think of a single reason why she should not attend. These kinds of functions always made her feel uncomfortable, especially when she really didn't know anyone that well.

'So are we. It will be a great night and a chance to really dress up. Did Jack tell you Dylan went to school with Paul's dad?' she added.

'Um no, I hadn't heard that.' She hoped that would be the last of the questions as she still felt a little uncomfortable interrupting their lunch.

As the group chatted, Stella sat back looking at the three of them discreetly. She could see why Jack and Paul were friends, so much light banter and teasing. From the way he spoke, Paul looked up to him and there was a hell of a lot of respect between them both. Lindy was so friendly and Stella couldn't help but like her too.

'So, I'm assuming that Eleanor is invited as well?' said Lindy. Stella nearly choked on her sandwich.

Was that a grimace or had Stella imagined it? Jack looked a little uncomfortable.

'Yes, she has been invited. Even if I didn't want her there, Milly would have ensured she was. Those two seem very close and one of them is always meddling in my life.' He smiled but it didn't reach his eyes. *What on earth is going on there?*

Nothing more was said about his relationship status, for which Jack was grateful as he really didn't want to be discussing Eleanor in front of Stella; he didn't want it to impact their burgeoning friendship.

Stella was the first to finish her meal. 'This has been great, but I must get back to work.'

'I won't be too far behind you, so see you back at the office,' said Jack. Stella nodded and turned to Paul and Lindy.

'Nice to meet you both and I'll see you at the gala dinner.'

'It was great to meet you too Stella,' said Lindy.

After she had gone, Lindy broke the silence. 'Well, she seems lovely Jack.'

'Yes, she is.' And he smiled.

CHAPTER 7

Eleanor continued to feature in Jack's social media. She was in her thirties, never married and no kids (Milly had told her this). Just how serious were they? It burned Stella up not knowing. But was it fair to try to rob another woman her chance of happiness just because she was interested in him? She knew the answer was no. But, as warm and welcoming as Stella tried to be, her feelings to Eleanor remained petulant.

She often wished Eleanor had never met Jack, and in her darkest moments, never existed. *Why is there always someone else you feel the need to compete with?* Stella asked herself. *Is she prettier than me or does she weigh less than me? Does she have more in common with Jack than me? Does he have a better time when he is with her? Does she make him laugh as much as she did?* The way Milly spoke about them, it sounded like that Jack was going to propose at any minute. If that happened, Stella knew without a moment's hesitation, she would have to resign.

A point of interest for Stella was that Eleanor was actually older than Jack. Such thoughts once again bought up the resounding question: What age gap is too big? Is there an age gap where you think to yourself: no, I'm not going there?

Somehow or another, this question came up one day when they were chatting and it had played on Stella's mind ever since. Jack had made a flippant comment about how he always seemed to date women that were older than him. Eleanor was only a few years older than Jack, but would he be interested in someone who was a lot more than that? She thought that it would be a deal breaker for him and the thought depressed her. The age difference really bothered her and made her so unsure of her feelings for him. *If only he wasn't so young*, she would say to herself as she tried to push the visions of Marcus out of her mind. She had vowed after that break-up that she would never ever get involved with anyone younger than her again. When he had run off with one of their colleagues who was only in her twenties, Stella had been mortified. Her mother had never let her forget it.

She nearly told Jack about Marcus that day but had decided against it at the last minute as she didn't want to have to explain why they were no longer together. Instead, she had made some lame joke about him being a toy boy and he had laughed at that.

Even though there had been subtle flirting between her and Jack, she doubted either of them would ever admit there were any feelings between them. Even if Eleanor didn't exist, Stella was just plain scared to put it out there and potentially be rejected by Jack. She had faced so much rejection and this felt like it would be the worst kind. But her uncertainty, her inability to face rejection, meant that Eleanor would stay in the picture. Her nemesis, for now, had the upper-hand.

CHAPTER 8

Stella had been in the role for three months now and had got quite friendly with one of the other graphic designers. Poor Tim had lost his wife to cancer six months ago. Jack had been wonderfully supportive and had helped find a suitable palliative care spot for her in a highly sought after facility.

Stella and Tim had bonded over their mutual dislike of Milly. They were sitting down in the local coffee shop, as they did most days, catching up on the latest Milly gossip. He had seen first-hand what was going on.

'You have to say something. It's getting ridiculous now Stella. I watched her the other day purposely spill that coffee over your desk. When I tried to confront her, she said it would be my word against hers and I would be sorry if I interfered.'

'What? She threatened you, why didn't you tell me this earlier?'

'I didn't want to drag you into this Stella. If we both say something, it could look like we both have some sort of vendetta against her; she has been here longer.' He waved a hand, getting back to his story. 'Anyway, and then you got your arse kicked by Jack by being so careless—you should have seen Milly's face when you were in his office getting yelled out. She actually looked at me and smiled! She is crazy that one. I'm telling you now, something isn't right with her.'

'Well, at least we have each other's back. If it wasn't for you, I would have gone mad by now,' she said, wrapping her hands around her coffee mug. It was warm and comforting, just like her new friendship with Tim.

'Did you see the guy that came in the other day for the interview?'

'No, I didn't, when was that?' she asked.

'Last Wednesday, he was here for at least an hour with Jack.' Tim tipped a sachet of sugar into his cup and reached for a stirrer.

'Hmm, I wonder what role he is applying for. I didn't think there was anything going at the moment.' She mulled over this as she sipped her coffee.

'I heard from Milly, not that her word is gospel, that they needed another graphic designer to help ease our work load.' His eyes hovered over her muffin hungrily. 'Are you going to eat that?'

'That would be nice, wouldn't it? Some help.' She laughed as she pushed the muffin towards him.

'It sure would. But I guess it depends how experienced this guy is. Hopefully he is up to speed, we don't have time to be training anyone.'

Stella was intrigued about who this new guy was. The one time that she would have been interested in office gossip from Milly and the girl had not mentioned a thing. Milly certainly knew how to push Stella's buttons. She was purposely keeping quiet, Stella was sure of it.

❧

Sitting in the lunch room minding her own business a couple of days later, who should walk in? Damn Milly. The sight of that girl was enough to put Stella off her lunch so she put her sandwich back on the plate, her appetite had gone now.

'That looks nice Stella, did you make it?'

'No, I bought it from the local café.' She nearly added, *so you couldn't mess with it,* but she bit her lip.

Stella was hoping she would just leave but no, she sat down and started to tell her that she had overheard Jack on the phone planning a weekend away and she was sure that this was going to be the time he proposed to Eleanor.

'Isn't it romantic?'

At this point, Stella felt like throwing her sandwich in her face or stabbing in her eye with a fork. *Why won't this girl leave? Perhaps if I close my eyes and open them she won't be here... Nope, didn't work she's still here.* As Milly's voice droned on and on, Stella's mind drifted... She had been having a recurring dream over the past couple of nights and she let her mind drift back to it...

In the dream, Jack had called her and told her it was his sister's birthday. He was stuck for ideas for a present and asked if Stella could suggest anything. She had made a flippant remark saying a cute little handbag would cover it. There had been a slight pause and she could almost hear his brain cranking over as he tried to think about what to say to her next.

Just when she thought the call was going to wind up, he blurted, 'Do you want to go out tomorrow night?'

'What are we going to be doing? It all seemed so random, but then again it was a dream.

'Meet me at my place, around eight.' And with that he hung up.

When he'd opened the door, their eyes met and she felt like she could drown in them. His body had seemed to fill the whole doorway. She could smell his cologne and as he'd moved, his musky aroma encircled her and she'd breathed his smell in deeply. Noticing the cute little dimple on his chin she'd reached out to touch it.

'Come on then, let's go.' He'd taken her hand and led her to his car.

They ended up outside the most gorgeous rustic little cabin. There were three small steps up to a wide porch and on either side of the door were large pots that contained various plants all tangled together.

Jack had left her in the car and disappeared into the cabin. Minutes later, he'd returned and he led her to the steps.

'Do you trust me, Stella? A remote cabin in the woods, alone with a strange man, sounds like the beginning of a thriller.'

She'd told him she did and he produced a blindfold from his pocket. 'Put this over your eyes and I will lead you into the cabin,' he'd said. Feeling a little uncertain, she'd covered her eyes and Jack led the way. 'Right then, now you can remove the blindfold.'

Jack had decorated the room with an abundance of candles and fairy lights. Everything was purple and white. The fairy lights twinkled away and had thrown lovely images up on to all the walls; it looked like they were dancing around the room. He had also placed bunches of purple and white roses around the room and she their fragrance was heady. She felt like she had entered paradise and never wanted to leave.

Looking into those gorgeous brown eyes she'd said, 'I love what you have done and I love you, Jack.'

'I love you too, Stella. I did all of this for you…'

And then, damn it, Milly broke into her daydream, just at the crucial part when they always kissed. *Where is that bloody fork*? She seriously wanted to stab her now.

'I'm sorry, what you were saying? I was a million miles away.' That worked a treat.

'Stella, do you ever listen to what anyone says to you or are you just so concerned with yourself—you're seriously such a selfish person.'

After that parting comment, Milly flounced away, infuriated that yet again Stella had ignored her. Stella sat watching her walk away and laughed her head off.

Milly had heard the laughter and something in her snapped. Later that night, as she added the latest addition to her special collection she muttered, 'You'll be sorry Stella that you weren't nicer to me. You will pay, you all will.'

CHAPTER 9

As each day passed, Stella kept thinking how hard it was having a crush on someone you work with. She tried to keep their relationship professional and to anyone on the outside, they would never have guessed her true feelings.

It's funny how you can work side by side and carry on a normal conversation with someone while there is a completely different script running through your head. This happened on a daily basis for Stella, especially around her feelings for Jack. She'd sit in their meetings thinking, *If only he knew what I'm really thinking!* Especially when some of those thoughts would be, well, X-rated. She would laugh internally, although sometimes a real laugh would escape and he would look at her with a funny look on his face and she would have to scramble to come up with some lame reason for her laughter.

Today had *not* been one of these days—he was tense and so she was on her best behaviour. She's learned there were some days that you just didn't mess with the guy. Even Milly was sitting silently at her desk, not saying a word.

The team were working on the preliminary work for the upcoming tender. Everyone knew that they were going to have put in some long hours to get this finished so there was a lot of tension and terse conversations floating around.

As much as Jack hated to suggest it, he asked Stella if she would mind working over the weekend and she agreed straight away. There was no way she would have answered any other way. She could almost see his face if she had said no. Jack didn't like the word no and it really didn't exist in his vocabulary. There were always work arounds with him—he loved solving problems, especially ones that others had palmed of as being "too hard". He thrived on this kind of thing—in fact it drove him.

'I'm sorry to have to ask, Stella, but we just haven't made the progress I thought we would and I need to get this moving a lot quicker or we will never make the deadline.'

'I don't mind Jack. Did you want to meet up this weekend?'

'You don't mind if we meet at my place, do you? I know it is closer to my place than it is to the office for you so I thought it may be more convenient and I also need a change of scenery to clear my brain,' he laughed. She'd assumed they would meet up at the office but the change of location didn't bother her in the slightest. If she was honest, she was curious to see his home.

'I'm happy to work anywhere. I want to get moving on this as much as you do, some of the hold ups are very frustrating.'

They arranged to meet on the coming Saturday and she swung between being happy to be spending some extra time with him to sheer nerves at the thought of it. But when she arrived all of that was forgotten as she got swept straight into work. There was no chit-chat and they only came up for air at lunch time.

'We need a break,' said Jack as he stretched his arms above his head.

'We sure do.' She stood and stretched; her back was killing her.

'Let's stop and I'll make us some lunch.' He headed towards his kitchen. 'I have some bread rolls and ham and salad, is that okay?'

'Sounds great.' Her stomach growled at the thought of food.

They went and sat outside on his patio and it was so nice to get some fresh air—it rejuvenated them both.

The day was indeed long and stressful and just when she thought that he was going to say they were done for the day and she should head home, he asked her in a very nonchalant way, 'Stella, why don't you stay for dinner?'

It was the last thing she had expected him to say and she nearly fell off her chair in shock—but, adjusting herself to appear just as nonchalant, 'Why not? I would love to and it would give us a bit more time to iron out some of the issues.'

He enquired if she had any other plans and she casually replied, 'No, no, I'm free,' and turned her head so he couldn't see her smiling.

Stella had a closer look at the table they had been working from— it looked like a bomb had hit it as they had papers and coffee cups spread from one of side of it to the other. Stella stacked some papers together and took the empty cups out to the kitchen and then returned to put her laptop and notebook into her satchel so as to make a bit more room. The mess was driving her nuts— she hated working in this chaos. Somehow, their phone chargers had managed to get tangled together and as Stella was working on separating them, she asked her self why everything now days, needs to be charged!

But, despite her bravado, she was actually quite nervous. It was the first time they had truly been alone together (especially at one of their houses) so it was uncharted territory. But after a bit of a moment of freaking out, frantically tapping her foot on the timber floorboards, she pulled herself together and decided just to enjoy herself.

Jack was proving to be quite handy in the kitchen. This irked

Stella a little—it seemed like Jack was good at everything, whereas she was more of a "Jack-of-all-trades and master-of-none," kinda gal. He put together a great platter of cheeses, crackers and all sorts of other interesting bits and pieces and then poured her a much-needed glass of wine.

He pushed the platter towards her. 'What takes your fancy?'

It took all of her willpower to not burst out and say, 'You naked on this kitchen bench.' Wouldn't that have gone down well! Thankfully, she didn't actually say that but her lack of a filter came very close to biting her in the ass. She had quite the vision of licking some of that dip off his chest!

She came back to the present with a start when he said, 'I'm thinking of doing a couple of steaks on the BBQ—is that okay with you?'

Her face betrayed her and turned a very light pink but she managed to stammer, 'S-sounds great—what can I do to help?'

'There is a bag of pre-mixed salad in the fridge. Can you pop that into a bowl while I'm out cooking the steak? There's also a potato salad in there, we may as well have some of that too.'

'Sure, sounds great.' Thank goodness one of his talents wasn't mind reading!

Jack headed out to his patio to light up the BBQ and she followed him out there after dealing with the salad and sat, watching him cook. It felt so natural, like they did this all the time.

They chatted away like two people who had known each other for years. They could talk about so many different things and generally approach topics quite deeply. Even in the deepest of philosophical discussions, something would still come up and amuse them both, causing them to just crack up. Usually, they'd keep on laughing until they were both nearly crying.

Dinner was great and they sat outside watching the sunset until the mosquitoes forced them back into the house.

'We're going to have to go in before we get bitten, this is the only part of being outside that I can't deal with—bloody mozzies.'

They went and sat on his couch and Stella had to fight the urge to kick her shoes off and curl up and never move ever again. She was conscious of the fact that their thighs were touching and their hands kept meeting as they reached for the dessert snacks sitting on the coffee table.

❧

There had been subtle flirting all day long between them both and the longing Jack felt for Stella was getting harder to deny. He had to keep himself in check in the office as well. There had been so many times lately as they sat in his office that he had wanted to reach out and kiss her. As wrong as this was, he couldn't stop these feelings even if he wanted to.

Jack had spent the better part of today wanting to kiss her. Every time she moved his eyes moved to her. He couldn't help but admire her figure, she was his type, so curvy, feminine and downright sexy. And he made her smile. That was one of the things that drew him to her from the very beginning. He didn't have this with Eleanor and knew he never would. It was obvious to him, and had been for a while, he had to end things with her; he was wasting both of their time. Stella and him connected on a level that he had never experienced and it both thrilled him but yet terrified him.

❧

Stella had to stop herself from getting up and leaning in for a kiss. When she was around Jack, these feelings just rolled over her and it was so hard to not cross that line. She knew he was dating Eleanor but still the temptation was there.

They chatted and drank more wine and the conversation shifted to her travels. She mentioned her love of elephants. Stella had always been in awe of these great creatures even before she first started travelling through Africa. Jack had travelled through Africa and he too was fascinated by them.

'I've got some great pieces; would you like to take a look?'

'I'd love to.' She looked around the room, expecting them to be in one of the glass cabinets in his lounge.

'No, they aren't there—no room I'm afraid. Come upstairs and take a look.' He picked up his glass of wine to indicate she should do the same and follow him.

She plonked herself down on the bed as Jack opened the cabinet and started pulling bits and pieces out to show her. He had so many beautiful figurines that it put her collection to shame. He pulled out a miniature elephant and instinctively Stella held out her hand. She turned it around and around, it was exquisite. It was a very pale cream and around each of its ankles, it wore gold bangles that shimmered and rattled when you moved it. It took Stella's breath away and she was loathe to part with it.

Jack offered to show her another piece from his collection. As she stood up to have a closer look she tripped and spilt her glass of wine (thankfully it wasn't full). His glass was on the other side of where he was standing so he managed to quickly move it out of the way with one hand and drop the figurine back onto the shelf undamaged with his other, but somehow or another her arm still got tangled up with his and they both fell back on to the bed. It would have been hilarious to watch this unfold—you could have sworn it was scripted. Stella's heart pounded with anxiety and embarrassment.

'Oh my god, Jack, I'm so sorry, I've spilt wine all over the floor,' she said. He looked deep into her eyes, unblinking, and she stared back for what seemed like hours.

'It's okay. I think that the elephant is my lucky charm as I finally have you in a compromising position.' She sat there stunned, not daring to move and break this moment and he leaned in and kissed her. Stella felt like she was drowning. As the kiss deepened, time simply didn't seem to matter to either of them. His arms tightened around her and she felt like she was safe and at home, where she belonged. When he finally pulled away, she felt like part of her soul had died. She physically hurt, if that is even possible.

She would never forget the range of emotions that passed over his face. It was clear he had felt what she had, and like her, didn't know how to process what they had experienced. Hanging between them both was also the knowledge that he had a girlfriend.

It could have gone so many different ways that night. For better, or for worse. But Jack stood and started putting everything back in the cupboard.

'We should really go back downstairs,' he said, his face emotionless. 'I'm sorry about what just happened.' She couldn't believe it. She had never been so mortified and hurt in her life. Her heart continued to pound, but no longer in anticipation or excitement. It was sheer embarrassment. Her cheeks, already flushed from the wine, felt like they were on fire. Her palms were sweaty and she was shaking. She wished the floor would just open up and swallow her up right now. *How will I ever be able to face him again?* The thought circled around in her brain. It was a truly awful, awkward moment.

She jumped up, straightened herself and said, 'I'm going Jack. I-I-I… don't think I should stay any longer.'

He grabbed her arm and insisted she didn't need to go. His grip felt alien; it felt compromised. No longer as warm and welcoming as it had been during that kiss. The moment was ruined.

She looked at him blankly and replied, 'It's for the best if I go home. I need to leave your house right now, I'm so sorry. So, if you'll excuse me.' She walked to the stairs. He followed as she went back into the lounge to pick up her hand bag and work satchel.

'Stella, please don't go, we need to talk about what just happened,' he begged her.

'Not now,' she said to him. 'I need to leave, please step away from the door so I can.' He opened the door and she brushed past him without looking back.

As she got into her car and drove. At the end of the street she had to pull over and try to compose herself. Her eyes welled up and she started crying. *Oh my god*, she thought. *How humiliating.* Stella put her face into her hands and groaned. It felt like the world had unravelled and fate was pointing and laughing at her misery.

Making this situation feel even worse than it already was, she was expected to attend the company's 50th anniversary gala dinner, tomorrow night. She had been involved in some of the last-minute preparations and up until this point, been excited to be attending.

All the talk around the office had been about what everyone was wearing and as partners were invited as well, who would they be bringing along. Milly had tried so hard to find out if Stella had a date for the night but she had remained tight-lipped.

Milly had had so much delight in telling her all about the dress that Eleanor would be wearing because they had gone shopping together. Stella nearly threw up when she heard that. She tried to get out of Stella what she would be wearing but she gave her nothing.

CHAPTER 10

The screeching cockatoos woke Stella from a troubled sleep. Her head hurt and her mouth was so dry. *Oh god, what a nightmare.* She felt sick about what had happened. *Why the hell did I stay for dinner? Why did I drink that wine?* All these thoughts were ultimately pointless. The damage had been done. As they say, "You can't cry over spilt milk"—or wine, as it was in this case.

Looking at her phone, Stella didn't know if she felt happy, or sad there was no message from Jack. Maybe just relieved. How could she have expected anything really? It was such an ugly situation.

They were work colleagues.

Sure, they had been starting to build up a nice friendship, but after last night, she had no idea what he thought about her now. Maybe she needed to resign and never go back. Or maybe he would suggest she should leave the company. She imagined the glee that Milly would have over that scenario. Such was her humiliation she truly didn't feel she had the power and composure to face him ever again.

But what was done was done. She had to just move forward and be positive that things would work out for her.

She had been through much worse, after all. She closed her eyes and shuddered as some of the memories came pouring in like they always did when she was in a low point of her life.

When had she not been humiliated? It had been happening since she was a child. Her mum had made it very obvious to Stella that she wished she had never been born. She never knew her father and the whole time growing up, her mum never brought anyone home.

Stella's mum had hated her and had great pleasure in never hiding this.

Her days had been filled with cruel comments and taunts which Stella had never fully understood. Anything good in her life was soon crushed by her mum.

Thankfully Jaz had stuck by her. She had witnessed the way Stella's mum treated her more times than she cared to remember but she hadn't been scared away. Coming from such a loving home, Jaz had never understood how anyone's mum could be as mean as Stella's. It gave her the determination to stick by Stella.

As Stella got older and had left home, she felt such a sense of freedom and started making the choices that suited her. She started travelling the world and giving back to the underprivileged people she met. These trips started to heal her. She realised that there was a lot of love in the world and it wasn't just filled with cruel people.

One of the memories that she always tried to push so far down suddenly popped up and she started crying. She had been twelve years old and walking home from school one day she came across a kitten. It was huddled down under a tree and it was a miracle she saw it. Scooping it up she fell instantly in love with it.

When she got home, she found a box and an old blanket and set it up in there and waited to show her mum. The kitten didn't get the response Stella had hoped for.

Her mum flew into a rage and Stella was ordered to get the kitten out of the house. She cried and begged her mum if she could keep it but she would not relent.

'I barely tolerate you living here, let alone this dreadful creature. If only you had been a better daughter. You have been nothing but a disappointment to me since the day you were born. It was bad enough that I fell pregnant and the only reason I kept the baby was I hoped for a boy—and I got you.'

Stella ran all the way from her house to Jaz's and she could barely tell her what had happened when she got there. There was nothing to be said, so Jaz held her until her crying had stopped.

When Stella eventually went home, the kitten was gone and it was never spoken of again.

Coming back to the present, she remembered that damn gala dinner was tonight. As much as she was thrilled to be attending, she was well aware that these kinds of events always brought out the worst in people. Everyone would claim that they wouldn't drink as much as they had at the work Christmas party and laugh as they said it, but yet the same people would drink way too much and embarrass themselves and other colleagues.

Then you had the super skinny model types that basically ate nothing all night and continually mentioned how fat they were. Or the women that went on and on about how much they had dieted just to fit into the dress they were wearing. Stella just couldn't tolerate it and it took all her strength not to just burst out with something inappropriate every time she was in earshot of these people. And don't even get her started on the small talk, oh god, she was exhausted just thinking about how many meaningless conversations she was going to have to get through. And if one person asked where she had got her dress from, she would scream.

The only positive thing was that Paul and Lindy would be there, so at least she had two other people she could speak to, so the night wouldn't be so bad. She really liked them and her and Lindy seemed to click and she loved how down to earth she was. Stella wished that some of Lindy's confidence would rub off on her.

She poured herself a cup of coffee, flipped open her laptop and settled down so as to finish the final report they had not been able to finish at Jack's place. She was soon lost in PowerPoint presentations, graphs and the final touches to the web page they had been building for their client.

This well and truly kept her distracted from the disastrous evening she'd had at Jack's. She cringed every time she thought of it and was still not sure how to face him at the gala dinner. How would she play it? She was pretty sure he wouldn't bring it up tonight so she would just smile and pretend nothing had happened. There would be time to talk about it later and clear the air.

Thankfully Jaz was coming over to help her get ready. As soon as she had heard that Eleanor was coming and was going to look amazing, she had gone all out herself. It wasn't so much that she was dressing for Jack, she wouldn't do that again, not for any man.

After years of being told that she wasn't loved, wasn't good enough, she had come to realise that she had to believe in herself and not get weighed down with what others thought about her. She had, slowly but surely, built up her confidence again and the likes of Eleanor and Milly were sure as hell not going to tear it down. They had no idea who they were dealing with and if they wanted a fight, by god, she would give them one.

The hours flew by and next thing she knew it was 4.00pm and Jaz was knocking on her door. At least she'd managed to take her mind off things—but she needed to get a wriggle on to be out the door by six.

'What are you planning on wearing?' Jaz had actually brought a couple of her dresses over as well because she knew Stella would procrastinate and need more choices. And sure enough… 'No, no, no, nothing seems right Jaz,' said Stella as she frantically flicked through her wardrobe.

'I'm just not feeling it. Oh my god, I feel sick, perhaps I should message Milly and tell her I'm not coming?' *In fact, perhaps that isn't such a bad idea,* she thought, *then I don't have to face Jack and see Eleanor hanging of his arm.* She frowned.

She didn't want to not put in an appearance, as Milly had let it slip that she had been in a meeting with Jack and Dylan where they were discussing hiring another graphic designer and were undecided whether Stella could in fact be promoted to take on the role of the senior graphic manager and this new person could report in to her.

This was the news that Tim had told her and it had excited Stella but she didn't show too much emotion. Part of her wondered if Milly was making this up. She didn't trust anything that came out of that girl's mouth. But on the off chance that it was a real opportunity, she wasn't prepared to waste it. She was hopeful of moving her career up another notch and finally working at the level she felt sure she had earned over the years of honing her craft. Her career was the only part of her life she felt she could actually control.

Last night her and Jack had shared that fleeting kiss and Stella felt sure that the moment she saw Eleanor tonight she would be able to see the guilt written all over her face. She was going to have to put on the act of the century tonight—it would be worthy of an Oscar.

'No Stella, you're NOT going to bail I won't let you. You've been looking forward to this dinner for ages, so come on, we can figure this out,' said Jaz breaking into her thoughts.

'Come on,' and she grabbed Stella's hand and dragged her to the bathroom. 'Now get in there and work your magic girl,' and pushing her in, she closed the door. She could hear Stella muttering something and she banged on the door 'stop your complaining and get ready will you.'

Stepping in to the shower her stomach was a mass of butterflies and every time she thought about what had happened last night, she felt sick. Would he mention it tonight? How was she going to face Eleanor? The whole thing went around and around in her head and she put her hands over her head.

'Please make it stop,' she said to herself.

Getting out of the shower and drying herself off she walked back out into her bedroom and Jaz handed her a glass of wine.

'Here, drink this, it will calm you down.' Stella gratefully reached out for the glass of wine. The first sip hit her stomach and fizzled away.

By the time she had put on her makeup and styled her hair she was feeling a little better, most likely due to the effect of the wine. Slipping into her dress she couldn't help but think how perfect it was. She was ready to face whatever this evening had in store for her.

Six o'clock came around and Stella was ready to leave. Jaz hugged her and said, 'Make sure you get lots of photos of this night and enjoy it. Call me tomorrow and let me know how it all goes.'

Taking a final look at herself in the mirror Stella headed out the door to the waiting taxi. She looked towards the heavens, 'Why do these things always seem to happen to me, can nothing ever be simple in my life?'

The universe just smiled.

CHAPTER 11

'Stella, wait up!' She spun around and arriving at the gala behind her were Paul and Lindy.

'Hi guys, it's so good to see you.' She felt her confidence surge just seeing them. After that lunch where Jack had introduced them, Lindy had asked her out for lunch—just the two of them. They had started meeting up regularly since then and were becoming good friends. Stella knew Lindy had met Jack the same night that she had met Paul and that it had been love at first sight when her eyes had clapped on Paul.

Paul quite often popped into the office and him and Jack would disappear. Once again, it was Milly who would tell Stella where they had gone. Gosh that girl was nosy. For an EA, she had no idea on when to keep things quiet for her boss. Stella couldn't understand how on earth he put up with her.

Stella had started to wonder if Paul or Lindy had started to suspect her growing interest in Jack. She felt confident that she had managed to keep it pretty well hidden, but if anyone was going to suspect anything it would be those two.

'Wow Stella, I love your dress, it is stunning. You look absolutely gorgeous.' Lindy took another look at her. *She looked radiant* she thought.

The dress was a deep violet and had a slit up the left hand side that went mid-way up her thigh. It fastened at the base of her neck with two little buttons. The back was gorgeous and as it was cinched in it made her waist seem tiny. Stella had spent many hours outside fitting rooms watching friends procrastinate because they weren't sure that the back looked just right. Thinking of this brought a tiny smile to her lips.

'You and purple Stella, what is it about you and that colour?' Lindy shook her head and laughed. Stella shrugged, but couldn't help but blush a little. It had become her lucky colour a few months ago, when she'd landed the job and met the man of her dreams in the interview.

Stella felt happy and confident every time she wore something in this colour. Her mum, of course had hated it, so Stella had never been able to have anything purple. So, as she got older, she made up for lost time and everything was purple!

'Have you seen Jack yet?' asked Paul.

'No, I haven't. I expect he'll already be inside,' replied Stella nonchalantly. Deep down she was hoping he had fallen ill and was not going to be able to attend. Wishful thinking, she knew, but perhaps the universe could please arrange this for her? Just for tonight?

Oh, hells bells, there he is and Eleanor is there as well.

Jack looked over at the exact moment Stella had located him through the crowd. There were lots of people hovering around in groups but their eyes had connected and she was once again pulled towards him. What was it about that man? She had never known such a powerful connection with anyone, ever.

He looked gorgeous; he really was tall, dark and handsome and damn he wore that tuxedo well. The black bow tie he was wearing wasn't quite straight and the devil in her wanted to walk up to him and adjust it. But one quick look at Eleanor told her that it wouldn't be a wise move. *I don't think any woman would appreciate that kind of interference from another woman. Adjusting a tie or a bow tie can sometimes feel like quite an intimate moment and not one you would usually share with a man that wasn't yours.* Even so, Stella's eyes travelled down his body and back up to his face. She just couldn't help but stare at him and she noticed his eyes had done the same to her. In spite of her reservations, she actually felt confident and without sounding conceited, knew she looked great. She felt as ready as she could to face Jack and... Eleanor.

Stella could hear the low hum of the music drifting out to the foyer from the ballroom and she couldn't wait to get inside. She was smiling as she walked through the door, followed by Paul and Lindy.

The moment that Jack and Stella had just shared—when their eyes locked, may have been meant to be a private one. But it did not go unnoticed.

CHAPTER 12

Unknown to Stella, Jack had spotted her moments earlier as she stood just outside the door with Paul and Lindy. He was standing with a group of their work colleagues and had seen her through a gap in the crowd.

He'd felt like his heart had stopped beating. The blood had rushed to his cheeks and he'd wished he could slip his jacket off without drawing attention to himself. He felt like he was suffocating. He wanted to rip the bowtie off and open the top button of his shirt but was afraid of who might notice.

Last night had been great. He had wanted to kiss her for so long. He didn't regret that, but did regret how it had ended with her feeling rejected and humiliated. He would never forgive himself for hurting her like that.

Jack prided himself on being a true gentleman and would never normally have done what he did last night, but she affected him in a way that no other woman had ever before. Gosh, she had even made him question his choice to be a bachelor. Perhaps she was the one that would claim his heart?

Why did he kiss her? he asked himself. It felt like so much more than just a casual kiss due to a combination of too much wine and the fact that he had been in close proximity to a pretty lady. Had they both just got carried away in the moment? He brushed any more thoughts away before they truly engulfed him. But regardless, did he want to kiss her again? Damn straight he did.

He could feel Eleanor bristling beside him. She was irritating him already and from the moment when he had picked her up, he had had to bite his tongue. Why had he let things go on so long with her? Paul was right, he should have ended things ages ago. If he was honest with himself, he should never have kept seeing her from the first date. He had known then that they were totally unsuitable but he had just let things coast along. Really, it felt like Eleanor and Milly had more invested in this relationship than he did.

⁂

Eleanor gave her date a cursory glance and wondered what was going on with him tonight. He had been in an odd mood since he'd picked her up and she sensed some kind of distance between them. She followed his line of vision and noticed Stella. She struggled to stifle her gasp. *This is not right. He is standing right next to me and he is obviously staring at another woman. Was this the woman who he had invited to his place to work? What happened when she went to his house?* She had a funny feeling in the pit of her stomach and the looks that were passing between those two certainly weren't quelling her fears.

She wanted to grab Jack and ask him if there was anything going on but she knew that this was not the time or place. Jack hated any sort of public attention of any sort, so she bit her tongue. *It can wait,* she told herself and picked up a glass of wine from a passing waiter.

⁂

Entering the ballroom, they all came face to face and Stella could barely make eye contact with Jack fearing she would blush. As everyone else knew each other already, Jack introduced Stella to Eleanor.

'Lovely to finally meet you, Eleanor,' said Stella, holding out her hand.

'Nice to meet you too,' said Eleanor but the handshake felt limp and the greeting cold. *I bet that's come from Milly getting in her ear about me*, thought Stella.

Looking covertly between Jack and Eleanor and taking in the body language between them, she wondered if they had perhaps had some sort of disagreement before they arrived, but the moment passed before it was tangible and they all took their seats at their table.

Again, Stella's mind drifted to the promotion—gosh if it wasn't for that, she probably wouldn't be sitting here feeling as uncomfortable as hell. Even if she didn't get it, she liked this company and didn't plan on being chased away by the likes of Milly.

Speaking of her—where was she? Stella glanced around and couldn't see her anywhere. Could she be so lucky that she was sick and hadn't been able to make it? They were all at their table now. On one side of her was Paul and on the other was Tim. Having both of them next to her made her feel a lot more confident. But here was the clincher, she was seated opposite Jack and Eleanor, seated beside him. Stella groaned inwardly as she took her seat. The seating plan had to be Milly's doing, Stella could imagine how much joy she would have had working this out. She must have done this so as to send a message to Stella that Jack was very much taken.

Every time she looked up, Jack seemed to be looking at her. When Stella caught his glance, they would both quickly look away and then Stella would look up and see Eleanor looking at her. She felt like she was playing, "the other woman," in some kind of bad sitcom.

Milly came bounding up and it was then that Stella noticed the empty chair at the end of the table. Of course, she would be sitting there, right next to Dylan and his wife Cassandra and Stella rolled her eyes. Listening to her sucking up to him made Stella nauseous and it eventually became so uncomfortable at the table that Stella excused herself and dashed to the closest ladies' room. *Thank goodness,* she thought as she entered; there was no one else in there. She checked herself in the mirror and frowned as she noticed her cheeks were bright red. *Perhaps I can go back to the table and tell them all I'm unwell and escape from this nightmare.*

She steeled herself to return and face Jack and the others, Lindy came through the door. Stella was just about to make some sort of light conversation with her but Lindy held up her hand.

'Stella, please don't bother, I know exactly what is going on with you and Jack.'

'What are you talking about? What's going on between me and Jack?'

'I've suspected for some time you had feelings for Jack, but tonight my suspicions were confirmed,' Lindy replied.

'Based on what? What happened? I really am so confused,' Stella said, brushing a stray hair out of her face.

'When you came through that door tonight, you didn't notice, but Paul and I both spotted you and Jack, well, staring at one another,' Lindy told her.

'We were just checking each other out. He's an attractive guy; so what?'

'Save it. What I saw was not just two people checking each other out,' Lindy said.

Stella toyed with the idea of making up a story, but her resolve withered and the tightness in her chest was worsening the longer she continued this farce. It might feel good to bare her soul, her anxiety.

'What am I going to do? I do like him; he is a great guy, I don't have to tell you that. But it is wrong on so many levels: he has a girlfriend, we work together, then there's the whole, "age thing,"—that's probably the worst part of it all.'

'What about his age?' Lindy's eyes were wide and she cocked a hip and settled on the edge of the vanity. There would be no escape from this conversation.

'I'm a lot older than him, you must know that.' Stella fidgeted around with her hair, trying to ignore the pit of disappointment that had opened in her stomach.

'So? What's that got to do with anything?'

'It has a lot to do with it. I've been down this path before and it was a disaster.' She could feel the familiar prickles running up her spine as memories hit her and she flinched. She ran her hands under the cold tap. That calmed her down a touch.

'So, one disaster means that you can't ever date anyone younger than you again? That doesn't seem right to me,' said Lindy, raising an eyebrow.

'There is just too much of a difference, plus I can't take the risk of getting hurt again.'

'Well, I guess Jack is the only one who can decide whether this bothers him or not. If he likes you as much as I suspect he does, he won't care. Trust him Stella, don't let your insecurities spoil what could be a great thing.

'I don't know, I'm just not sure that I can put myself through this again.' Lindy looked like she was about to protest, but Stella cut her off, '—We should get back to the table.' Lindy nodded and hopped down from the vanity. Stella relaxed a little, the conversation seeming to be over. But Lindy clearly didn't think so.

'Seeing the way you two look at each other, you can't just leave it be. You're going to have to talk with Jack at some stage.'

Stella knew Lindy was right, they did need to talk very soon. Was there something starting between them? She liked him and enjoyed spending time with him, but was she developing stronger feelings? She was so confused and seeing him with Eleanor tonight had confused her even more now. Was he seriously dating her or were they just in some kind of situation-ship? Her mind was spinning as all these questions swirled around unanswered.

'I've kissed him.' She hadn't mean to say it but there was no taking it back now.

'What do you mean? When?' said Lindy, her eyes wide.

'Last night. We were working at his house and it just happened.'

'Oh my god, I can't believe it.'

'Please don't say anything to Paul, promise me.'

'My lips are sealed. You do know I will need more details Stella, I would never in a million years thought that you would tell me this tonight.' Lindy could barely keep the smile off her face.

'And I promise I will tell you, but this isn't the right time. We had better get back to the others or they will be wondering what we are doing in here,' Stella laughed.

CHAPTER 13

S tella managed to avoid Jack for most of the evening. When they did cross each other's path, as was inevitable, they would exchange the usual pleasantries. But it was quite awkward, and missing the playful banter that they usually had when conversing. Talking in such a forced manner was exhausting, especially when the conversations were normally free-flowing and fun.

When Dylan signalled to the room for some quiet, she, like everyone else, took her seat back at her table. He thanked them all and told them how proud he was of each and every one of them.

Listening to his speech, her mind had drifted away and she was thinking about Jack when all of a sudden, she tuned back in and froze. *Surely this can't be right, I must have misheard,* she thought. But when she looked around the room all eyes were on her. Jack was looking at her with a mixture of horror and confusion. She couldn't move but knew that she had to.

What the hell was going on? Then her eyes collided with Milly's and the look of pure evil on her face confirmed to Stella that she had been set up.

'Don't be shy Stella, come on up here.' Dylan beckoned for her to join him up on the stage.

Her mind was blank, and she barely remembered standing up and making her way towards him.

'This is unexpected but when someone told me that you had wanted to say a few words, well I was very touched, being that you're one of our newest employees.' She followed his line of vision towards where Milly was sitting. How her hand ached to slap that bitch across her smug face.

You could feel the air crackle with all of the energy running through the room.

Stella stood there still not believing what was happening and knew she had to say something. They were all looking at her expectantly, waiting for her to start speaking. All Stella could hear was her mum telling her that she was going to blow this, they would hate her and she would lose her job. Just like usual, she was going to fail.

She took a steadying breath and from somewhere deep inside produced the most amazing speech.

'Dylan, thank you for the opportunity to be part of the wonderful company you have created. What a legacy you have given us and all those that will follow. I have never been so proud in my life to stand here tonight as we honour you and your amazing achievements. We are all extremely proud to work here, with you.' When she finished everyone stood up and applauded. Throughout her speech she kept looking between Eleanor and Milly. They had sat there with their mouths open, not believing how once again she had come out on top.

The only eyes she couldn't meet were Jack's. She was so mortified to have been put in this position and wondered if he would believe her when she told him that she had not asked to have a speech. She could hardly go and tell Dylan that she hadn't asked to speak, he would think it odd.

Damn, Milly was good, but Stella knew that she was cleverer and this girl was going down—soon. No one humiliated her like she had done tonight and got away with it.

⁂

Eleanor and Milly ignored her for the rest of the evening. They were huddled together and the mood between them was very tense. As this behaviour continued; Stella started to get a little paranoid. *Why the hell are they staring at me with such loathing?*

One of Stella's favourite songs came on, 'Dancing Queen' by *ABBA.*

'Tim, come and dance with me.' She took his hand and ran towards the dance floor with him in tow. As they spun around, Stella's dress twirling, they caught a glimpse of Jack and Eleanor in some sort of heated conversation. Eleanor was telling him something and her hands were waving around and he looked tense. Tim commented that they didn't look like they were having a great time.

Stella pretended not to hear what he had said as she didn't want to share any of this with him, it was way too private. She didn't mind them sharing their mutual loathing of Milly, but as for her attraction to Jack, that was off the table. They had become good friends but he was still not someone that Stella would open up to discuss their boss and his girlfriend with. She turned the conversation around to how he was getting on without Janice and he was happy to talk about that. He missed his wife like crazy and coming to this event tonight had been so hard, as he knew how much she would have loved it all.

By 10.30pm, the event was starting to thin out. It had been a long night and it really was just the last stragglers left. You know the ones that always need to finish that last free drink. A few people were being helped out by their partners and every second woman had their shoes in their hands. Plenty of blisters already forming as is very usual when you drag that pair of "party shoes" out of your wardrobe. You know the ones, they always give you blisters but you put them on anyway, always hopeful your feet will handle them so much better at this particular event. Hey, they are pretty you think, I can always pop some band aids on tomorrow. Will this crazy cycle ever stop? No, sadly it will not. Every woman on the planet will repeat it until the end of time.

Stella was exhausted and decided she would call it a night as well. She gave Tim a hug and said they would catch up for a coffee in the morning. He had been in a bit of a strange mood lately and she had put it down to him still grieving his wife. But she did want to have a heart to heart and see if there was anything she could help with.

She thanked Dylan for a wonderful evening and he said again how touched he had been by her speech. She was almost tempted to say something about how it had been unplanned but decided to leave it. She didn't want to jeopardise this promotion, perhaps they would think she was trying just a little too hard to win them over.

She wandered over to where Paul and Lindy were chatting to Jack. 'Well, I'm going to head home now.'

'Did you want us to give you a ride?' asked Lindy. As it wasn't going to be too much out of their way, she accepted. She really couldn't face hanging around waiting for a taxi. She just wanted to get home and lie down; this evening had been way more than she could ever have expected.

While they brought the car around, she waited with Jack. They stood there awkwardly until she finally said, 'Good night, Jack, I'll see you in the office tomorrow.'

'Good night. I trust you had an enjoyable evening. And I must admit I was very impressed with your speech.' He smiled, but it didn't quite reach his eyes and that made her stomach lurch. *He isn't happy with me,* she thought. She wanted to say that she hadn't planned it, but it was not the time nor the place to get in to this. He probably wouldn't believe her anyway. She sighed as he retreated, presumably of to collect Eleanor and make his own exit.

The car ride home was made easier by the fact that they all decided to ignore the "elephants," in the car, so to speak. Stella wanted to tell them that she had not planned that speech and her concerns around Milly but wasn't sure if they would believe her. It was the quietest that the three of them had ever been.

When they dropped her off Lindy suggested coming over to their place for a BBQ. She would call Stella next week and book something in. 'Sounds great Lindy, I look forward to it. Good night and thanks for the ride home.'

Walking into her house she had never been so happy to be home in her life. She had a quick shower and took her makeup off and climbed wearily into bed. She was too tired to even try and analyse the evening and was soon fast asleep.

CHAPTER 14

Jack and Eleanor were no sooner in his car when she let loose.

'How DARE you humiliate me like that tonight. Why the hell did you even bother to invite me when you basically ignored me all evening.'

'What the hell are you talking about, Eleanor?' He felt like telling her that it was Milly that had invited her, not him, but that seemed a little cruel. He really was in no mood to get in to anything with her at this moment as he was too busy trying to work out what had possessed Stella to give her speech.

But she continued until he finally snapped, 'Eleanor, enough, please stop. What you're talking about—I really… I genuinely don't, have any idea,' he insisted, palms raised.

'Don't play me for the fool. You must think I'm an idiot for not picking up on this before!' Eleanor yelled.

Jack bristled. 'What the HELL are you talking about? I'm still completely in the dark here.'

'Bullshit, Jack. Bullshit. Stop lying to me and to yourself. You've frozen me out over the last few weeks. There seems to be such a distance between us now and I don't know what I have done wrong. When we first started going out, I felt like we had… that we had so much in common and you liked me. I mean, I really liked you. I… thought… perhaps I was even starting to fall in love with you. And now, well I don't know where I stand.'

'When I first met you, we had some great times together, but then it started to feel like it was moving too quickly for me. I know I should have said something earlier and I'm sorry I didn't.' *God, this was hard*, he thought.

She knew where this was going and she wiped her eyes as they were starting to fill with tears. 'Seems like I have made a fool of myself. Obviously, I have just been some kind of fill in while you looked for your perfect match. How dare you use me like this,' she was livid and actually shaking now.

'That's not true. I haven't used you, so don't feel like that. I know we haven't been out together for…' and he struggled to remember the last time they had been out.

'It was the theatre, Jack—we saw *Phantom of the Opera*.'

Wow, he couldn't believe it—that had been weeks ago. He had planned to take her hiking, then he'd changed his mind as he really hadn't wanted to spend a whole weekend with her. God, he felt like such a bastard.

Eleanor twisted a strand of her hair around her finger. 'I guess I see clearly now. This will never be, will it?'

'I'm sorry, but no, I don't see us having a future together. Perhaps I'm just better by myself, a bachelor?'

Eleanor rolled her eyes. 'Oh, come on Jack. I saw with my own eyes the look on your face when Stella arrived. Please don't insult me by trying to deny it. I know what I saw. You've never looked at me like that—not even once. How do you imagine that makes me feel? I'll tell you. It… bloody well hurts. A lot.' She then burst into tears.

Jack's head swarmed with thoughts and alien feelings. He had liked Eleanor and had enjoyed most of the time they had spent together. Why wasn't it enough? He had thought it was going to be fine, but that night at the theatre, he had sat there wishing that it was Stella sitting next to him. Eleanor was right, no man should ever be on a date with one woman and spend the whole time thinking of another.

Why couldn't he get Stella out of his mind? He had thought by having lunch with her and really getting to know her he could just be friends with her, but it had just made keeping his boundaries in place even harder. The more time he spent with her, the more he realised just how much he liked her.

Jack sighed, defeated. 'Eleanor, I'm so sorry. I didn't mean to hurt you. That was never my intention. I really don't know what to say. I know that anything else I do is only going to hurt you even more and I don't want to do that.' His knuckles were white on the steering wheel. 'Yes, I have feelings for Stella but I don't know… I just don't know. I'm just no good at opening up to people. I guess I'm flawed that way. I'm not good at expressing myself.'

'But somehow you manage to express yourself to Stella.'

※

Eleanor's fists were bunched by her side, to stop herself from striking him. Did he really think she was going to feel sorry for him and his supposed "flaw"? She shook as anger rolled through her in huge waves.

'Are you serious?' She fought to keep her voice calm. 'Do you realise that this is probably the deepest conversation you and I have had in the eight months that we've dated? And you open up to me on the night we're breaking up. I can't fucking believe this—such a cop out. I was always there for you, standing waiting in the wings, hoping you would open up and let me in. You chose not to Jack.

I hope one day you can feel this pain and someone shuts you out. And you know what? I hope it's Stella, because if you are as fond of her as I was of you, then you will feel what I am feeling right now. When that day comes, I won't feel one ounce of pity for you.' She was grinding her teeth together and could barely get the words out.

He glanced at her briefly, guilt flashing through his eyes. *Good,* she thought.

Then he turned away.

'Eleanor, I know I have hurt you deeply and for that I'm truly sorry.'

They sat in silence, if not for the occasional sniff from the passenger seat of the car. There really wasn't anything else to say—it was over.

CHAPTER 15

Stella walked towards her desk for what she thought could be the last time. She was sure she was going to get her arse kicked today after her speech last night. Her eyes strayed to where Milly sat—she wasn't there. Probably just as well, she would have had to control herself not to march over there and hit the girl.

She couldn't see whether Jack was in yet or not and as she was so humiliated, she hoped he had gotten called away to an all-day meeting. Flipping open her laptop and looking at the emails that had come in over the last 24 hours, she had to knuckle down and do some work. Around mid-morning, a shadow fell over her desk.

'Good morning, Stella.' She nearly jumped out of her skin.

'Oh gosh. Jack, you scared me! I didn't see you standing there.' She held her hand over her heart.

'Sorry to sneak up on you, I could see you were deep in thought.' Normally, scaring her would have made him smile but he wasn't smiling today.

'Yes, it is amazing what has come in since Friday.' God, this whole thing felt so strained, not their usual friendly chatter.

'Let's catch up this afternoon, say 1.00pm, my office?'

'Ah, okay. That works for me.' She popped it in to her diary.

'Where's Milly today?'

'She's sick, so I'm fending for myself.'

'Right, okay. I'll get back too it then and I'll see you at 1.00pm.'

After that awkward exchange, Stella struggled to get back into her work. She was so nervous about this meeting. Was it about her work, or was it about the speech? God, she couldn't stand it.

❧

Tim came up to her desk after Jack had left.

'Come into the kitchen and we'll grab a coffee, I have something to tell you.' She quickly followed him and Tim shut the door.

'What's wrong Tim?' Watching him fluffing around with their coffee mugs was unsettling. It wasn't like him to be this nervous and her stomach was in knots.

'I don't know how to tell you this…' His Adam's apple bobbed as he swallowed hard.

'What is it? You're scaring me now.' She could feel the blood draining from her face.

'I've handed in my notice.' He avoided her gaze, staring down into his coffee.

'Oh no, Tim, no, why?' Her face crumpled and her eyes welled up.

'I love working here but I have had an offer with a company in Queensland and I decided to take it. There are just too many memories here. You know this is where I met my wife… I need a clean start.' He held his hands out, imploring her to understand his decision and she took them and squeezed them gently.

'I am going to miss you so much.' She gave him a hug. 'I can't believe you're leaving me here with Milly.' It was meant to be a joke, but her wobbling lip undercut it.

'I feel bad about that, but promise me you will say something to

Jack or Tyler. Don't let her keep bullying you, it's not right.'

'I know, I know, but once you make a complaint, things get awkward and then I may need to consider leaving. I don't want to chuck in a job that I like because of her.' She took a deep breath and tried to shake off the sadness. 'When are you leaving?'

'I gave my two weeks' notice. Jack understood and once again has offered to assist me in any way he can. He's a good man.'

'I wonder if they have hired the new guy then?' Her mind shifted to how that would work.

'Yes, they have. Jack mentioned it when I spoke to him about leaving. His name is Travis and he sounds like he is pretty experienced. You'll hardly notice I'm gone, I'm sure.' Tim grimaced and Stella scoffed and bumped his shoulder with hers.

'Impossible. It won't be the same as working with you.' She hugged him again. 'I was already having a bad day and hearing you are leaving doesn't make me feel that this day is going to get any better.'

'What time are you catching up with Jack?

'1.00pm and I'm dreading it.'

'Just explain to him about that speech and that you didn't offer to say anything. Surely, he can't possibly think that you would do that? Besides, you nailed that speech.' Tim held up his hand for a high five and the sound of their hands touching reverberated around the kitchen.

'Anyway, we've been in here for a while, people will be talking.' He wiggled his eyebrows suggestively which lightened the mood. Leaving the kitchen, she sat back down at her desk and put her head in her hands. Tim leaving was the final straw. Stella struggled on with her work trying hard not to look at the clock that seemed to speed towards the dreaded meeting time.

At precisely 1.00pm Stella knocked on Jack's door (which was closed—very unusual). She waited for him to ask her in and then taking a deep breath, pushed the door open.

'Close the door please.' Her heart jumped a few beats—he sounded so business like and fear roared up her throat. 'Take a seat please.' She did as instructed, and folded her hands in her lap so that he wouldn't notice them shake.

'I'm just going to cut to the chase here,' he said, his brow furrowed. 'What the hell were you thinking when you decided to have a speech at the gala last night? It was highly inappropriate for you to do so, especially without telling me. I have never been so embarrassed in my life. God knows what Dylan really thought and the rest of the staff—I'm half expecting to be dragged into his office and asked why you did it.' The muscles twitched in his neck so knew he was trying to contain his anger.

'Jack, I was set up.' She decided to be blunt with him.

'What do you mean you were set up?' He quirked an eyebrow and leaned back in his chair.

'I know you won't believe me, but I'm telling the truth. I don't lie.' She looked him straight in the eye. 'If I've done something I'll own it, but I'm telling you now, I did not ask to have that speech. Why the hell would I? Do you honestly think, knowing me as you do, that I would even consider doing that?'

'Well, I did think it was totally out of character, but still...'

'I never asked to do a speech, I was set up by Milly.' There, it was out there now and she felt relieved.

'Milly? Why the hell would she set you up? I don't understand.'

'For some reason, she doesn't like me and there have been numerous things she has done and I have just kept quiet.' She shrugged. 'I'm new here, I didn't want to start any trouble.'

❧

Jack didn't know what to think. If he confronted Milly, he knew she would deny it. Stella sounded like she was telling the truth and he had no reason to doubt her as she had been a model employee up until this point.

'Did you want to put in a formal complaint? I can call Tyler in you would like.'

'I would rather not. I know whatever I say she will deny, so it's pointless. Can we just leave it like it is at the moment as an, "off the record," chat?'

'I'm not happy doing this. I would much rather get to the bottom of it now.'

'Well, I'm not prepared to formalise this chat and would prefer we leave it.'

He mulled over her comments and then agreed that they would leave it for now but he would be having a conversation with Milly.

'Is there anything else?' asked Stella. She felt close to tears and just wanted to get out of his office.

'No, that's all. I had better get back to work.' She started heading towards the door.

'Wait, before you go, I have some news,' Jack said. She paused, her hand on the door handle. 'I'm assuming Tim has told you that he is leaving.' She nodded. 'Very unfortunate, as he is such a big part of our team and will be missed. We have employed another graphic designer to work alongside you. I would like you to take a senior lead. He has quite an impressive background and I think you will work well together. His name is Travis Davies. I am hoping he can start here soon; I am just waiting to see what works with him and the notice he has to give at his current job.'

'Okay, sounds great. I look forward to meeting him. Thanks for giving me the senior lead, I won't disappoint you, I promise.'

'Yes, alright, that's it.' He looked down at his laptop signalling that their meeting was over. He had wanted to say she could never disappoint him, but the words never came out of his mouth.

※

Stella hightailed it out of there. She decided to take a quick break and headed down to the park. She wanted to cry but held it in, she would not give him the satisfaction or Milly for that fact. When Milly returned to the office, Stella would decide what course of action she would take. She wasn't going to be pushed in to it by Tyler or Jack.

It was a horrendous week, what with the whole speech thing and hearing Tim was leaving. Milly didn't return until Thursday and by then Stella had decided just to park the conversation. She was emotionally drained and couldn't be bothered getting into an argument with the girl. Milly kept her distance from her as well and made sure she was never alone with Stella. She looked terrible and Stella almost felt sorry for her. Something was going on, she just wished she could figure out what it was.

The only good thing that happened was that Lindy called her and invited her over for a BBQ. She had no plans, so happily accepted. It would help take her mind off all of this. She planned on telling Lindy that there was definitely nothing going on now with her and Jack. Whatever it may have been, was done now.

Her next meeting with Jack was all business. There had been a subtle change with him and it broke her heart to think that their friendship had been damaged. He was so cool with her and she hated that it had come to this. She still continued eating her lunch down in the park, but Jack no longer joined her. The distance between them seemed to be growing and she wasn't sure how to fix it.

By the end of the week, she had pretty much decided that she was going to leave. As much as it irked her, she felt like saying to Milly that she had won—she was done.

CHAPTER 16

Jack too, had the week from hell. Keeping things businesslike with Stella had been much harder than he had thought. That meeting with her regarding the speech had been one of the hardest conversations he had ever had to have.

He knew she was hurt. All he'd wanted to do was get up from his chair and hug her. Bloody Milly, he had no doubt that she'd had a hand in all of this. She had been nothing but trouble and he had let it go too far.

When Milly eventually came back to work, he asked her if she had had anything to do with that speech and, as expected, she denied it. She told him that Stella had it in for her and she had tried to work with her but Stella was impossible. She had no idea why Stella didn't like her. She started crying and Jack had known there was no point in continuing the conversation. Like Stella, she wasn't prepared to put in a formal complaint. *Jesus, it was all too hard*, he thought. He called Tyler in and they put together a file note just in case one of the ladies changed their minds.

※

On Friday just as he was finishing up, Jack's phone rang.

'How's things going, mate?' Paul said. They hadn't spoken since the gala dinner, so the catch up was welcome.

'To be honest with you, things are a bit of a mess right now. Oh, but you will be happy to know I ended things with Eleanor.' Jack gave him a quick run-down on what had unfolded. 'Yeah, it was just as messy as I expected, and no she didn't take it well at all.'

'How's things going with Stella?' Paul asked.

'Oh mate, that speech.'

Paul asked how that conversation had gone when Jack had confronted her.

'She claims she didn't ask to do it and she was set up by Milly.'

'So, did you get it sorted out? Are you working okay together?'

'No, that's a fucking disaster as well.' He laughed, but it felt forced and he knew his friend wouldn't be so easily fooled.

'I don't know what to say. Look, why don't you come over for a BBQ and a few beers—help take your mind of all of the drama you have with these women in your life?'

'Sure, why not, I'd love to.' A night with Paul and Lindy would be great, just what he needed to get over this week.

❧

Arriving at Paul and Lindy's always brought a smile to his face. Their place was always organised chaos; with three kids it was always bedlam. The front lawn was strewn with toys and bikes and the kids were nowhere to be seen. As if upon command, the kids came running out the front door.

'Hi Uncle Jack,' they chorused.

'Hi guys, what sort of trouble have you been into this week?

'Nothing Uncle Jack, we are always good,' said Bree, the older of them. He laughed when he heard that. He'd seen the mischief they got into first-hand many times over the years.

'Where's your mum and dad? I'm assuming out in the backyard?'

'Yes, they are,' replied Bree before running back into the house, followed closely by the other two.

Jack headed to the back yard. Paul and Lindy had a great alfresco area, it even had one of those outdoor kitchens in it. There was a massive timber table that seated about twelve people. Strung around the covered in structure were fairy lights that all sparkled in an array of colours. There were pots full of greenery and palm trees of various sizes and shapes. Lindy was an avid gardener and this really was her pride and joy. He dutifully looked around as no doubt she would have added something new to this area and would be miffed if he didn't identify it and mention it to her as soon as he saw her. And yes, there it was: a massive bamboo wind chime hanging up.

Paul was already out by the barbeque but there was no sign of Lindy. At least he had a few minutes peace before the interrogation he felt was coming his way started.

'Beer?' Paul said by way of welcome.

'That would be great,' Jack said and took the bottle that Paul held out.

'Where's your wife? Inside fine-tuning all the questions she's about to grill me with?'

'I heard that, Jack Turner!'

'Nice wind chime Lindy.'

'Don't try and sweet talk me now,' she laughed.

Jack was just settling down enjoying his beer when he saw someone out of the corner of his eye. *Oh. Holy shit. I have been well and truly set up. Bloody Lindy.*

Shaking his surprise, he turned towards Stella with a smile plastered on his face.

Jack noticed that Stella too was taken aback. She stopped in her tracks upon seeing him, and he half-expected her to turn on her heel and hightail it out of there. In fact, a part of him wanted to do that himself, right about now. By the look on her face, she hadn't expected to see him here either.

Jack glared at Paul and Lindy. He knew they'd got the message.

Jack had to give it to Stella—she had composed herself pretty quickly and kept walking towards them. She greeted Paul and Lindy and then turned to Jack.

'Hi Jack, how nice to see you.'

He replied in kind and thankfully Paul intervened and saved them both from this awkward moment.

'Can I get you a glass of wine, Stella? Paul's question was a welcome rescue and Stella nodded.

'Yes please, that would be lovely.' She felt like saying, *the whole bottle should do nicely, thanks. Oh, and can you just bring a straw as well!*

They settled down around the table and there was so much polite, banal conversation being thrown around. It was hilarious. Not one of them wanted to address the elephant in the room, not even Lindy.

The tension was broken when the kids came running out to the backyard. They all stopped in a hurry when they saw Stella sitting at the table.

'Who's this Mum?' asked Bree. Before Lindy could answer Bree said, 'Is she your new girlfriend, Uncle Jack?'

'Um, this is Stella and she works with me at my office. Are you going to say hello?' The kids walked up a little closer and shyly said hello.

'This is Bree, Mia and Neil.'

'Nice to meet you all,' Stella said and smiled at them warmly.

'Do you want to be Uncle Jack's girlfriend?' Stella almost choked on her wine at Bree's innocent question.

'Kids, that's enough interrogation of poor Uncle Jack and Stella.

Why don't you go inside and I'll call you when dinner is ready,' said Lindy her cheeks flushed.

'Okay Mum,' said Bree and the three of them disappeared back in to the house.

'I'm so sorry about that Stella,' Lindy's face was still pink.

'It's fine Lindy, no harm done,' and she took a sip of her wine, careful to avoid looking at Jack.

❧

The evening passed by pleasantly and was actually a lot of fun. But Jack later realised, after the kids had gone to bed, that was part of Lindy's devious plan.

Just when Jack had finally started to relax and let his guard down, a little groggy from the beer, Lindy abruptly interrupted the table's conversation and asked, 'So, Jack my friend, just what exactly is going on with you and Stella?'

The look Jack sent her could have frozen water. He couldn't believe what she had just done to him. He glared at Paul who just shrugged his shoulders.

Stella and Jack both looked at each other in horror, eyes wide, mouths agape. Neither of them wanted to answer her question. You could have heard crickets chirping with the silence that followed after her question.

Jack recovered first.

'Hey, I came here for a nice relaxing evening with you and your family. While the kids might get a free pass to ask a couple of intrusive questions, you don't. I'm sure you are making Stella uncomfortable as well.' He stole a quick glance at her. She couldn't even look him in the eye.

Paul laughed, 'Relax, she's just playing with you.'

Lindy smiled and widened her eyes in an act of innocence.

'Well, I did see some subtle flirting at the gala dinner and wondered if there was something going on. But being that you work together I'm sure you wouldn't do anything that would raise any concerns and get you reported to HR.'

Jack froze when she said that. Gosh, he had never thought about how this could play out at work. How had he been so short-sighted? He'd already kissed the woman for god's sake.

Stella didn't say a thing—in fact she looked like she just wanted to disappear and never be seen again.

Thankfully, Paul broke the tension and changed the subject.

'Did you watch the rugby league last night Jack—what a cracker, our team are going to have a great season. I'm calling it now, a NRL grand final is coming their way mate.' And he got up to grab another beer out of the outside fridge.

Jack breathed a sigh of relief once the awkward silence had been broken. The crisis had been averted, for now. Jack didn't dare look at Stella though—he could hear her talking to Lindy but couldn't focus on what they were saying. From that point on, Jack figured it all just had been too uncomfortable for Stella because it wasn't long after that she stood up and announced she would head home.

Jack walked her out to her car.

'I'm sorry about tonight. I had no idea that you were going to be here, and I certainly wasn't prepared for all the questions about us.'

'Look, it's fine. No one meant any harm by it. We both know there is no, "us." Nothing is going on, so there is nothing more to be said. How about we just leave it at that?'

'I broke things of with Eleanor,' he blurted. Stella stopped in her tracks.

'Really? I'm sorry to hear that,.'

'I should have ended things with her ages ago and just didn't know how to.'

'You don't need to explain anything to me. I'm only one of your employees, I don't need to know what goes on in your private life, now do I? I'll see you next week at work.' With that, she got into her car and was gone.

Wow, that hurt, he thought as he walked back towards the house.

The three of them sat around the table after Stella had left. Paul and Lindy both tried to apologise but quite frankly all he was thinking about was what Stella had just said to him.

No one had ever hurt him as much before, with one simple sentence, as she had. The words went around and around in his head taunting him.

We both know there is no "us."

CHAPTER 17

Jack was avoiding her, she was sure of it. Milly had told her that he was working from home today and was only to be contacted if something was urgent. Well, that told Stella all she needed to know. He never worked from home, so it had to be that he just didn't want to see her. He was pissed off with her after what she had said at the BBQ.

She just didn't know what to say to him anymore anyway—they just seemed to go from one misunderstanding to another. It was exhausting and she was once again thinking about resigning. Something held her back from doing this and she had no clue why.

The universe decided that she would intervene and throw them another lifeline.

❧

The next morning, Stella half-heartedly looked at her emails. Now Tim was gone she was struggling without him. Milly had ramped up her bullshit and Stella was ready to snap. The new guy, Travis, had started but as he had been so busy with Jack, she really hadn't spent much time with him. Her initial thoughts when she had been introduced was, he was a little cocky, perhaps even arrogant. She wouldn't stand for that, so hoped he would settle into the new role without causing too much disruption. On day one, he had ruffled one of the team's feathers and everyone was wary of him now.

Scrolling down through the hundreds of emails, one of the subject lines caught her eye: Team Conference: Fiji. *Wow, am I reading this correctly?* She opened the email to have a proper look.

Sure enough, Dylan was inviting their team to a conference in Fiji for four days. There would likely be some downtime where she imagined herself chilling out around a pool drinking a cocktail. 'Yes, I would like to attend,' she replied and pressed send. She was suddenly in a great mood.

While basking in the glow of her getaway, a thought nudged at her. It made the hand on her computer mouse start to shake. Who else was attending this trip? She hadn't even looked at the other attendees before hitting that damn button.

She had assumed that even though Jack was part of this team, he would be far too busy. *There's no way in hell he will be able to spare four days for this,* Stella tried to console herself with this thought. *He'll send one of his other assistants in his place without a doubt.* After those first few moments of terrible panic, she settled down, confident it wasn't going to be a problem.

'Ping.' The notification noise buzzed. Jack had just replied to the invitation. Stella felt sick to her stomach.

They had this weird awkward working relationship. It was messy, and if there was one thing Stella hated, it was any sort of mess. But she could be professional. *It's a work thing, it will be fine,* she told herself.

⚡

It was two weeks after that invitation was sent out before they headed away. They were to leave on the Friday and fly home Monday. She had seen Jack briefly at work over that time and he had told her he was pleased she could make the trip as he valued her input. That was it. *Clearly, he was still angry with her,* she thought.

※

Jack was still beating himself up over this whole thing and the reason he stayed away was because of the guilt he felt every time he saw Stella. He fluctuated between wanting to apologise to her yet again or take her in his arms and kiss her. He hoped the time in Fiji may clear the air and they could at least become friends again—he missed her.

※

Stella arrived at the airport in her usual pre-flying anxious state—she hated being airborne with a passion. She said her usual silent prayer as she always did before any flight, begging the universe to spare her from any turbulence.

She checked in and dropped her bag off before heading toward the business class lounge. *A nice glass of wine,* she repeated as a mantra, *that will surely help settle my nerves.* She walked faster towards the lounge before she started thinking too much about the worst part of flying—the take-off and the landing!

She settled down with a drink and then noticed Jack walking into the lounge towards where she was sitting. When he finally noticed her, he hesitated and then continued his approach. What was going through his mind?

'Good evening, Stella, is this seat free?' he asked.

She looked up and smiled, 'Yes, it is, please feel free to join me. Have you seen the rest of the team anywhere?'

'No, I haven't actually. Have you seen anyone?'

'No, not in here.' She had seen a couple of them when she was checking in but they hadn't appeared in the lounge. They must have of gone straight to the regular gate. She felt a stab of guilt; she had a Platinum membership and should have at least offered to bring some of them in here as her guests. Oh well, maybe she would mention it on the trip home and they could join her then.

'Looks like we will catch up with them once we get to the gate then,' said Jack.

'Yes, I guess we will.' They both sat there with a deafening silence settling around them in the otherwise noisy room.

Gosh, I hope we aren't sitting next to each other, Stella thought. She didn't think she could handle four hours of small talk with him. At that moment, Jack had checked his boarding pass, 'So what seat do you have?'

Stella told him she would be sitting in 1C. 'And you?'

'3C.' What a weird coincidence he should ask right then.

She couldn't help but feel relieved that they wouldn't be sitting together—it wasn't just sitting next to Jack that worried Stella, it was anyone at all. Stella was such a nervous flyer, and she didn't want anyone to witness it, especially Jack. It wasn't unheard of for Stella to grab a complete stranger's hand and utter some profanity when they went through any kind of turbulence. She could relax knowing if she was going to panic it would be next to a complete stranger.

Boarding the plane, she settled back into her seat and fell asleep within minutes once they were airborne. That couple of glasses of wine she had had in the lounge had certainly relaxed her. Yet, despite her stress-free environment, a prickle ran down her spine just before she drifted off, knowing that Jack was just two rows back. She could almost feel his eyes boring through the back of her seat.

They didn't see each other when they disembarked; Stella had been swept away with the other passengers heading towards the baggage pickup area. The team was soon assembled and headed towards the transport to their hotel.

Stella watched Jack get into the bus, and their eyes met briefly before he sat in the seat directly in front of her. As he sat down, she felt an urge to lean forward and kiss the back of his neck.

The hotel was only a short, coastal drive from the airport; you could almost smell the beach. Through the bus window, Stella could see the waves crashing against the shore and when she closed her eyes, she could imagine the sound they were making as they roared and swept the sand in and then out again. She hoped she would get a room with an ocean view.

The driveway leading to the hotel was lined with palm trees and there were rows and rows of some kind of gorgeous exotic flowers All the gardens had lights in them that twinkled away and they threw some lovely colours over the flowers. It was very pretty, and quite romantic. *If only Jack and I were here for a romantic getaway… Stop it!*

Even though she kept telling herself they were just here for a work conference, she couldn't help but daydream about how great it would be to spend some time alone with him.

The bus pulled into the main entrance of the hotel and Stella stood up, ready to get out. She was shuffling along, still daydreaming about Jack and much to her embarrassment, walked right into his back when he stopped suddenly. She could have almost put her hands around him and gosh she had been tempted.

'Oh, I'm so sorry Jack,' and when he looked back, he could see her cheeks were pink.

'My fault, bit of a queue getting out.' He smiled at her and she noticed the dimple on his chin. Her traitorous hand itched to reach up and touch it.

Lining up at reception, she lost sight of him and after picking up her key and bag she headed towards the lifts. Just as the door was closing, she heard someone call out, 'Hold the lift,' and the next thing, Jack was there. The door closed and they stood there in silence. Eventually the lift got to her floor and she exhaled with relief. Stepping out of the lift, Jack did the same thing. They walked down the hallway towards their rooms, the clicking of the wheels of their suitcases on the timber floor the only sound.

Stella thought it would be pretty funny if their rooms ended up being next to each other but didn't think it was appropriate to say; he was her boss, and she needed to remember that.

'Well, this is me,' she said.

Jack looked down at his key. 'Looks like I'm three doors down.'

'Oh well then, I guess this is good night then. I'll see you in the morning.'

'How about we have breakfast together? I have a couple of things that I wouldn't mind running past you. I know you have a good handle on what the client wants and I just want to feel comfortable that I fully understand what they want too. After all, you're the expert with all things to do with graphic design, it is certainly not my forte.' He shrugged. Give me a good spreadsheet anytime, but anything creative, well, that's why we have people like you in the company.'

She couldn't help but feel honoured that he had asked for her opinion!

'That sounds great, happy to help,' she replied.

Jack gave Stella a big smile, his teeth shining in the bright hotel lights. 'Well okay then.

I'll see you in the morning. Good night.' He started to walk towards his room.

'Jack,' she called after him and he turned around. 'We've got this.

By the time we send in our tender they are going to be so impressed. There's no need to stay up all night working—you will feel much better after a good night's sleep.'

She knew what pace he worked at, especially when they had a deadline. The current one they were working towards—well, it was ugly and a lot tighter to anything she had ever worked towards in her career. She could visualise it now, he would open his laptop and that would be it. She doubted if he would even sleep.

He was always the last to leave and he got to the office so much earlier than the rest of them. Even that day they worked at his place, it was obvious from the papers strewn everywhere that he spent a lot of time working at home.

Stella had a quick shower then climbed into the king sized bed. It was adorned with a lush, plump mattress and crisp-white sheets and it looked very comfy. She removed the cushions and then lay back on all the pillows. *This is heaven,* she thought.

She set the alarm on her phone for 6.15am—no way was she going to be late for breakfast. Imagine sleeping in, that was so not happening!

Three rooms down the hall, the tapping of laptop keys and a dim screen light would remain illuminated throughout the entire night.

CHAPTER 18

Stella was eating breakfast when Jack joined her.

'Sorry I'm late, I got tied up on a phone call.' He ran his hands through his hair and this made her heart flutter.

'No worries. Go grab something to eat, it's delicious.' Stella caught Milly's eye and could see she wasn't happy that Jack was sitting with her. She had hoped that she wouldn't be invited, but Dylan had insisted to Jack that she come along and take notes as everyone else would be far too busy.

The day she got invited, she couldn't help but come and tell Stella how good it was going to be and how thrilled she was that Dylan had wanted her there. All Stella heard was *blah, blah, blah*. Eventually, seeing she wasn't going to get a reaction from Stella, she huffed and puffed and headed back to her own desk and then continued to give Stella the evil looks all day. Stella wished she could move her desk just a metre so as to avoid looking at Milly. She was starting to loathe the girl. It wasn't like her to take such an intense disliking to someone but this girl rubbed her up the wrong way and she simply didn't trust her.

Jack had got caught up with other colleagues so by the time he re-joined her and managed to quickly eat something, it was time to move towards the conference room.

'We will try and catch up in a break, as I had some ideas last night and wanted to run them past you.' She looked at him and raised an eyebrow.

'Last night? Shouldn't you have been sleeping?'

'Okay, yes, I was working but I did get a few hours of sleep.'

'That would be up until you took that phone call.'

'I do sleep, but not much,' he laughed.

Once the team were seated, Dylan opened the day with a bit of a pep talk. As Stella listened, she took a deep breath to steady herself and clear her head. It was going to be a very busy day, that was for sure. She glanced towards their newest team member, Travis. He was swinging back in his chair, not even really listening which irritated Stella. Catching his eye, he smirked at her and she turned away.

The whole reason behind this trip to Fiji was to brainstorm for the tender they were going to be putting in to one of the biggest IT companies in the southern hemisphere. They had broken tasks up between the team to tap in to everyone's strengths. They weren't going to take any chances. Jack's primary focus was on the branding and strategy. He had handed over the responsibility of social media marketing to Stella. The design functionality—well they were all still throwing some ideas around with that.

It was going to be a huge undertaking for them all but Dylan and Jack were confident they had the manpower and the experience and could pull this off. The two of them had already spent weeks working on this and the rest of the team had been pulled in once they had heard what the full scope was. This was one of the reasons Stella had been hired: they needed her expertise to round out the team.

If they won this tender, it would certainly put McGregor and

Bailey on the map. Stella's heart sang when she thought of how it could boost up her resume—gosh, when potential employers saw this, it would open lots of doors for her. Although she wasn't thinking of leaving (she loved her job), if things got too uncomfortable with her and Jack, she may need to consider it.

The team was already aware of the long hours that were going to be needed and Dylan had likely hoped that it would soften the blow if some of this work was done in Fiji.

❦

Jack had been a godsend since he joined the company. In some ways, he was like the son Dylan had never had, or so his boss kept telling him.

Jack had been offered a really great role in another company a few months after he had started at McGregor and Bailey. It would have been a great step forward in his career but he had turned it down because it was based in New York and they wanted him to sign up for a three year contract.

He had turned it all over in his mind but something just didn't feel right. He just couldn't seem to sign the contract. Everyone thought he was crazy. Paul had tried to convince him to take it and couldn't understand why Jack was procrastinating. It seemed like a very easy decision, one that Jack would have usually made in a heartbeat. One of the reasons he couldn't sign was because of the loyalty he felt towards Dylan. He had taken a chance on him and he couldn't just leave him in the lurch. Loyalty was everything to Jack and without that, well, you had nothing.

Jack tried to explain to Paul, and so many others, that apart from not wanting to run out on Dylan, there was something else holding him back. He couldn't pinpoint what, he just knew he needed to stay where he was.

So, he turned it down and now three years later, couldn't have been happier.

'So, to finish off, it is going to be tight guys but I know we can do it.' Jack returned from his day dream to those final words from Dylan.

༄

As the day wore on, there was plenty of heated conversations but the team eventually agreed on the pitch—well, everyone but Travis. He was causing a lot of tension with the group and Jack was beginning to question the wisdom of hiring the man. Now that Tim was gone, they couldn't afford for Travis to walk right now so had to find a solution for both parties, but it sure as hell wasn't easy with Travis' current attitude. He was trying to see problems where they didn't exist and disrespecting people who had been with the company a lot longer.

༄

Stella was struggling with Travis big time. Why did he have to be so damn negative all of the time it was doing her head in.

'Why can't he just talk to us all and get his ideas across and not be so passive aggressive?' she said to Jack for what felt like the hundredth time that day. They were taking a short break, and had retreated together to the balcony that ran the length of the conference room. 'You are going to have to say something Jack before this blows up.'

'I know, I know,' he said and rubbed his hands through his hair. 'I just don't want to upset him because then we'll get no cooperation from him and I need him, Stella. He is really good at what he does, but just doesn't know how to get his point across. It may come across as arrogance, but I honestly think he is quite shy and this is his way of combatting that.'

'But he is so negative Jack and it is really disrespectful to everything that this company stands for.' She pursed her lips and folded her arms tightly across her chest. There was no way she was backing down from this one. One bully in the company was enough.

'Look, leave it with me and I'll have a word with Dylan and we'll work something out. I promise.' The smile he gave her did funny things to her stomach and uncrossing her arms, she placed one of them across her chest to still her beating heart.

⚹

Dylan called it at 5.30pm and everyone wearily headed back to their rooms. They were to meet back in the lobby at 6.30pm for drinks before dinner at one of the restaurants located at the hotel.

Jack was the last person to leave the conference room having just had a chat with Dylan regarding Travis. Dylan would have a quiet word with him. They wanted to handle this quickly and without Travis feeling like he was being singled out for voicing his opinion. *Perhaps the others had thoughts and they just weren't game to mention them?* Jack pondered. It was going to be a tomorrow problem now as he just wanted to kick back and have a relaxing evening.

Sitting in the conference room alone, Jack's thoughts drifted to Stella and he sat there drumming his fingers softly on the table. He hated to have to bring work into her downtime, but there was no other option, he needed to talk to her before they got started again tomorrow.

At some stage they also needed to talk properly about that kiss at his place. He wasn't sure what to say, or what she thought, but it had continued to hang between them and it was time to clear the air.

As he stood waiting for the lift, one of the other lift doors opened and Stella walked out in shorts and a T-shirt. Jack could tell she had her bikini on—he could see the strap at the neckline of her top.

'Hi. Are you just finishing up now?' Stella asked, surprised to see him standing there.

'Yes, I just had some final notes I wanted to wrap up. I'm pretty sure I won't have time to get them done later this evening,' he answered. 'I've just emailed them to Milly to add into my PowerPoint presentation.' Stella couldn't help but think how thrilled Milly would be when she got that email—served her right though. Stella was being petty but that girl brought out the worst in her.

'Good idea. It could be a late night, so best to get it sorted now,' she agreed as they stood there awkwardly.

'Stella, um, perhaps we could talk later?'

'Oh, I'm sure we will. I think we made good progress today.'

'Yes, we did, but that isn't what I wanted to talk about.' There was a lengthy silence.

'Did you want to talk now? I can delay my swim.'

'No, no, it can wait.'

'Are you sure? I'm happy to chat now.'

'Look, it's about that night at my place.' He blushed.

'Oh. Yes.' She could feel her cheeks turning pink.

'Um…' His mind went blank.

'Look, Jack, let's just park it for now and chat later.' She just wanted to get away from the piercing looks he was giving her and just couldn't get in to it now standing outside the lifts.

He too felt so uncomfortable. 'Oh okay, I had better not keep you then.' The lift door opened. He was just about to walk in when he held the doors open and called back out to her.

'Stella, do you want to head down to dinner together?'

Stella smiled, the earlier tension eased. 'That would be great. How about you knock on my door at 6.20pm? After the day we have had, I'm looking forward to having a nice cocktail,' and before he could say anything else, she disappeared through the glass doors and headed out to the pool area.

Jack got into the lift. 'God, could that have been anymore awkward? I'm sure she must think I'm an idiot,' he muttered.

But lurking in the back of his mind was the fact that they were co-workers and he did not want to cross the line there. Even if they'd already kissed, it didn't mean he had no boundaries. As the boss he needed to set an example to the others. Plus, he didn't want his private life talked about by any of them, especially Milly, He hadn't been pleased when Dylan told him he had invited her. He didn't trust the girl after how involved she had been in his relationship with Eleanor. She had taken an unhealthy interest in him.

CHAPTER 19

Returned from her swim, and freshly showered, Stella stood in front of her suitcase, a towel wrapped around her, debating what to wear tonight. She had brought quite a few different outfits. But what was the dress code for the dinner tonight? She had assumed it was casual but Dylan hadn't specified and she didn't want to stand out.

Should she just throw on something casual with some flat sandals? Or really dress up and wear some heels? Decisions, decisions!

'Oh lord, why is this so difficult?' she said. Where was Jaz when she needed her; she would have known what Stella should wear. Finally, she decided on an outfit and hoped it would be perfect.

At precisely 6.20pm there was a knock at her door. Stella gave herself one last look in the mirror. *It is what it is,* she thought. Once she opened the door, she wasn't thinking about what she was wearing—she was too busy staring at Jack.

It took her all her strength to keep her composure. Her jaw almost dropped. Jack looked gorgeous and the aftershave he was wearing was a spicy aromatic mix. She had to stop herself from stepping forward and sniffing his neck. She could have stood there for hours just inhaling this smell—it was intoxicating. Her mouth went dry as she ran her eyes up and down him. Stella was convinced he was the sexiest man alive. Jack's cute beard suited him and made him look older than he was—but he was still so damn young. She had to tear her eyes away; the effect he was having on her was driving her crazy.

She wished she could pull him through the door and throw him on to that big king-sized bed and have her wicked way with him. How could he stand there looking so cool, calm and collected? Why wasn't he getting hot under the collar like her?

In spite of this internal battle, Stella managed to quash these thoughts. 'Let's head down and get a drink.'

She brushed past Jack to leave her room. As the door shut behind her and they walked towards the lifts, her left hand had gently brushed his arm.

❧

Arriving at the bar, Jack and Stella drifted into conversations with their colleagues. Now and then she would catch his eye and he would smile at her. It was a smile that was hard to ignore. So pure and sincere, laced with optimism and a joy for life. His smile seemed to light up the room and people gravitated to him like moths to a flame.

After a couple of drinks, a light buzz swirled in Stella's head. She needed to eat something. Jack swooped up his jacket and walked towards her, as others began to slowly make their way to the restaurant.

Touching her lightly on the arm he pointed towards a table, set for two.

'How about we sit here? It's right by the window so we'll get a great view and a nice breeze.' It was a hot night and the ceiling fans were doing their best, but the restaurant was still stuffy. The breeze would be most welcome.

'That looks like a perfect spot! Great choice,' she agreed.

Stella was notoriously hopeless at deciding what to choose whenever she ate out and tonight was no exception. Her eyes went up and down the menu several times and she started to panic as she spotted a waiter heading towards their table.

Jack was one of those people who always checked out the menu before he ate anywhere so had already made his selection. She had never thought of doing this until she met him and was starting to wonder if she should take a leaf out of his book and start doing this. It would make ordering meals so much easier.

He was smiling at her.

'What is so funny?' she asked.

'Ahh. Just you. I love watching you try to decide what to eat Stella, it really is quite cute.' Stella blushed.

'For your information, Jack Turner, I have decided what I'm ordering, so there.' When the waiter arrived, she took a punt and said she would have the fish (and hoped that there was indeed fish on the menu!).

When their meals arrived, they looked and smelt amazing. They kept the conversation very light, their other colleagues were seated nearby so this still wasn't the time to talk about anything too serious... like the kiss they'd shared, but never properly discussed, Stella thought.

Bringing it around to work at one stage, Jack told her he would email her through the PowerPoint presentation once he got it from Milly so she could cast an eye over it.

'Sorry to have to ask you, I know it is after hours, but I really want your opinion.'

'Jack, it's fine, I honestly don't mind. This is why we are here it is a work trip.'

'I know, but I still want you to have fun.' The look he gave her, well, it did funny things to her stomach and she couldn't help but blush. Thankfully he didn't seem to notice as it was a warm night and her cheeks were already pink.

When the dessert arrived, she looked down at it and instantly fell in love. She wasn't much of a foodie, but this dessert looked like it was to die for. It was a roasted vanilla and honey crème brûlee. The smell of that vanilla… and the honey drizzled across the top… Stella inhaled deeply and sighed. When she cracked the top of it with her spoon—it was perfectly baked.

'Oh my god. I think I have died and gone to heaven,' she said.

Jack laughed. 'I hope not. There's a lot more work to be done, so please don't leave me.'

'Don't worry, I wouldn't want to miss this amazing presentation you keep telling me about, now would I?'

'Be prepared to be blown away.'

'I'll be the judge of how good it is—perhaps I will rate it out of 10,' she laughed.

'Well, it is going to be pretty spectacular and if I don't get a 10, I'll be disappointed.' His eyes were warm on hers as they chuckled.

She didn't have the words to express it, but the dessert, in all its rich lustre, was only half as sweet as her night with Jack.

CHAPTER 20

They both dawdled over coffee, neither of them wanting the night to end. Finally, Stella said, 'Oh well, I guess we should call it a night.' Jack pulled out Stella's chair and she picked up her purse and they headed for the exit. Glancing into the bar on their way past, they didn't see any of their team.

'Must have all turned in for the night,' said Jack.

'I'd say so, it was a big day,' she agreed and stifled a yawn.

They stood in the lobby waiting for the lift. When it arrived, Jack pushed the button for their floor.

The lift arrived and they rode it in silence. Stella couldn't stand the tension that was building up between them so she burst out, 'I thought I might go for a swim.'

Jack looked at her, 'I thought the pool closed at seven thirty?'

'It does, but when I was down there earlier, I started chatting to the pool man. He said he would turn a blind eye if I wanted to slip in after it closed.'

'Trust you Stella to be able to talk him in to letting you swim outside of the opening hours,' said Jack. 'You could sell snow to Eskimos.'

'It's a curse, but what can you do.' She giggled and Jack grinned. 'What are you going to do now? Do you want to come down as well?

The pool man never said I couldn't bring a friend with me.'

As soon as she said it, panic washed over her. *Why the hell did I just ask him to come down with me for a swim?* At that very moment, if she could just disappear, that would be a great thing. Her annoying habit of just bursting out with the first thing that went through her mind had once again come back to bite her.

Jack appeared a bit taken aback at first, but then his expression softened. 'I need to make a phone call first, but when that's done, I'll meet you down there.' The lift doors opened and they exited onto their level, Stella tucking a strand of hair behind her ear.

'Look, there's no rush, so take your time and if you change your mind, well it really doesn't matter.'

'Stella, when I say I will do something, I always do. I'll see you down there soon.' He walked on to his room and she heard his door close.

They had been standing outside Stella's room and as her door closed behind her, she slid down on to the floor and closed her eyes and groaned. *Oh my god, how embarrassing,* she thought. Why did I ask him? Oh well, now I have made a complete fool of myself, I may as well put my bikini on and go down. So, she got changed, grabbed a towel and headed back downstairs.

❧

As Stella opened the gate into the pool area, she saw Frank the pool man so she wandered over and told him she had a friend joining her. He was relieved as he worried about leaving her there by herself. Thanking him again for letting her in, she dropped her towel and room key on one of the chaises and headed towards the steps of the pool. As she stepped in and her feet touched the water, she couldn't believe how warm it was. *So lovely,* she thought as she waded further in.

It was a huge pool, well actually it was three large pools that had all been interconnected so at any given time, you could find a quiet secluded spot and she loved it. There were little bridges that ran over all of the pools and crossing those you would find yourself in a completely different part of the pool to where you had entered it. It was a little bit like a maze really and Stella had loved exploring it earlier in the day.

She looked towards the spa pool—she must try it out before she went home. Maybe Jack would like to join her, now she had asked him to go swimming.

She headed to the left, away from such dangerous thoughts. The main pool had so many nooks and crannies but she was heading to the far side—this was an infinity pool and the view from the ledge was breathtaking. It looked out over the garden of the resort, out towards the mountains. The garden was lit by hundreds of fairy lights and looked magical.

When she eventually made her way to the edge of the pool, she had lost sight of the hotel. She positioned herself on the ledge and closed her eyes and let out a sigh. This really was heavenly.

'A penny for your thoughts.' Jack had snuck up on her. He'd entered the pool from another direction, so she hadn't even heard him nor had the water moved to warn her he was approaching.

Stella jumped and proceeded to slip off the ledge and went under the water. As she surfaced, spluttering away, her hair plastered to her head, there was Jack, grinning at her.

'What the hell, Jack? God, you gave me such a fright!' she yelled, splashing water around her as if to emphasise her point.

'I told you I would join you. Sorry, I didn't mean to scare you,' he said to her, his impish features betraying that this was not, in fact, the case.

'I thought you would be longer, it must have been the shortest call known to man.'

'The person I was after wasn't available so I left a message and told them I'd call first thing tomorrow.'

'You didn't think to perhaps call out to me so as to warn me you were headed this way? No, you have to swim up in "stealth mode" and scare the crap out of me.' She punctuated her words by splashing him in the face. 'And how is it even possible that someone as tall as you can swim that damn quietly, I ask you?'

'Well, I swam under the water for some of the way and surfaced a little way behind you and then crept up. Sorry, but this was so much fun. You should have seen the look on your face, priceless! I wish I could have taken a photo and shared it in the company newsletter.' He splashed her back.

'You're an idiot and I'm not sure we can be friends anymore. I will pay you back for this Jack, just you wait and see.'

'I look forward to it,' he said, his face still playful. Stella pushed him under the water.

'Hey that's not fair, you play dirty,' he said when he resurfaced.

Stella laughed, 'Don't think that was the payback—there will be more coming, trust me.'

'How did you find me so quickly? The pool is huge, I could have been anywhere.'

'I bumped into the pool guy and he told me you were heading to the infinity ledge.'

'Oh, that's a bit disappointing, here I was hoping you'd stumbled upon me through sheer luck.'

'Aren't I lucky? To be here, with you?' She splashed him again and he pushed his hair out of his eyes, slicking it back.

In the midst of their playful banter, the distance between them had decreased and their arms brushed together as they circled around each other. Stella had to keep checking herself—she couldn't believe that her and Jack were finally alone. Watching him push his hair back had driven her crazy, it took all her willpower not to reach out and touch him.

⁂

Frank was watching from the garden below. He was on his way home and happy that the young man had found her. Watching them together reminded him of how he had felt when he had first met his wife. They had been together for over thirty years now and she was the love of his life. Love like this didn't come around easily and if these two didn't realise that, it would be such a shame. Frank took one last look at them both and turned for home.

The universe smiled—don't you worry Frank I've got this! They will be fine with me watching over them.

⁂

After the water fight, they both treaded water and smiled at each other, not really sure what to do next. It was kind of awkward for a moment. Eventually, Stella resumed her place by the infinity ledge, her arms draped lazily over the edge admiring the garden below and inhaling the perfume of the exotic flowers. Jack leaned next to her and she was very aware of just how close he was as their arms grazed. He had closed the distance between them and his proximity made the hairs on her arms stand up and she was covered in goose bumps.

They sat in silence, observing the wonderous scene below them from the ledge. After what could've been ten minutes or ten hours, Jack broke the moment.

'How about we head back and to make things interesting, race me?'

'I most certainly do not want to race you back. I plan on heading back at my own pace, thank you very much.' As much as she enjoyed a good challenge, she knew she wouldn't be able to keep up with him and didn't want to give him the satisfaction of winning.

'Suit yourself then.' He started swimming back at a cracking pace.

Stella purposely swam slowly and things were going well until she got to the middle of the pool. Her feet still couldn't touch the bottom when she felt the strap of her bikini give way. *Oh god no.* As she began to struggle, she suddenly remembered that this bikini top had a loose hook and that's why she hadn't worn it the last few times she had been swimming. She was trying to tread water and re-hook the strap back but wasn't having much success. If she didn't get it fixed, she would soon be stranded there, topless.

In the meantime, Jack had circled back to see what was taking her so damn long. As he got closer, Stella knew he could see what had happened.

'Is everything okay here?' he asked he swam up next to her. From the grin on his face, he was enjoying himself just a bit too much for her liking.

'Everything is just fine.'

'Um, it looks to me like there is an issue with your bikini strap,' he continued.

'It's just about sorted now but thanks for your concern.'

'You do know that you can ask for my help. I know you can't touch the bottom and it looks like it is proving rather difficult to try re-hook that strap while treading water and nearly drowning,' he said to her, tongue-in-cheek.

'Oh, bite me,' said Stella. God, he was so bloody smug. But despite her reluctance to admit he was right, she conceded she had to do something to fix this bikini malfunction before she drowned or exposed her breasts. She was going to have to ask for his help, damn it.

'You have two options to help me resolve this situation. One: you re-hook the strap for me, or, two: I hang on to you and re-hook it myself,' she told him.

'Hmm now let me think,' said Jack, purposely stalling before answering her. 'I don't have a problem with either of those options so what would you prefer?' She looked at him with daggers in her eyes. 'Okay, okay. Why don't you just hang on to me and I'll re-hook your top for you?' he said quickly.

'Fine then,' Stella replied, huffing and puffing as she grabbed hold of Jack's shoulders. She was so close to him but she could barely look him in the eye due to the sheer embarrassment of this situation. There was a moment of fumbling and she felt his hands graze over her breasts. Was she imagining it, or had he lingered for a moment? This made her blush and her eyes lifted, and connected to his. Neither of them could break away.

'I've been thinking about kissing you Jack,' whispered Stella.

'So why haven't you?' His eyes moved then to her lips.

'I don't know, perhaps you wouldn't want me to?'

'I wouldn't say no. In fact, I am pretty sure that I want to kiss you too.' She wasn't sure if he meant it or was just teasing her so she didn't make the move. Jack looked at her bikini then and made another adjustment, his hands definitely lingering over her breasts this time. 'There, all fixed now.'

Just as she was about to let go of his shoulders and start swimming away, he caught her arms and said, 'Hey, not so fast, I am still thinking about the kiss you just spoke of. I think I need some sort of payment for my assistance. A kiss should cover it.' His voice lowered, and his gaze was intense. 'A kiss just like the one you gave me that night at my place will be a good start.' He winked. Despite the cool water of the pool, she felt like her skin was ablaze with desire. Her voice was husky as she tried her best to flirt in return.

'That kiss was your fault Jack Turner and you know it—you kissed me!'

'Ah, no, I clearly remember your lips touching mine first.' He was enjoying riling her up. Somehow, they'd swum closer to one another again, their limbs brushing against each other beneath the water. She needed to do something to get this situation back under her control.

'In your dreams buddy,' she said and splashed him a final time. Freeing herself, she started swimming away. She didn't get far.

'Hey, that isn't fair,' he said when he caught up to her. He grabbed her foot to stop her.

'Let go of my foot, Jack or I will really drown this time.' She started splashing around.

'Not until you tell me you want to kiss me as much as I want to kiss you.'

'Okay, let me go first.'

'No, I need some kind of guarantee that you aren't just messing with me,' he held her as she still couldn't touch the bottom of the pool.

'Okay, I want to kiss you,' she admitted softly. He moved closer to her, and from the sparkle in his eye she felt sure he was going to try and kiss her now. But as soon as he dropped her foot, she swam off again, getting closer to the side of the pool.

'Stella Carter, you are driving me insane.' She stopped and turned around to him with a huge smile across her face.

'Is that so, Jack Turner? Well, it's not my fault that you can't keep up with me and get this kiss that you think you deserve.' She swam of again, but very slowly this time.

He caught up to her again and before she even had a chance to protest, he had pinned her arms to her side and was leaning in towards her. Their lips touched and Stella couldn't move. She knew she should move, why wasn't she moving? Jack groaned as their kiss deepened and Stella wrapped her legs around his waist and wished this kiss could go on forever.

Eventually, they pulled apart and neither of them knew what to say. There was no wine to blame, not this time. They walked out of the pool and over to the chairs where they had both left their towels and room keys. There was a cool breeze blowing now, so Stella picked up her towel and wrapped it around her.

They got to Stella's door first. *Now what?* she thought. The silence was deafening.

'Look Jack, that kiss just then, I'm sorry about that.'

'Why are you sorry? I wanted to kiss you and I'm pretty sure you felt the same.' Stella hated the look of hurt confusion that crossed his face.

'And that kiss at your place. I didn't plan that. I hope you know that?'

'Look, I realise it was just one of those moments. Let's just write that off to too much wine shall we.' She was happy to do just that as it still made her cringe every time, she thought about it.

'Well, we still have to be careful. We hadn't had wine tonight, and clearly there's *something* between us. But we're away with our colleagues. I don't want everyone knowing my business. I'm a very private person so I expect that you won't say anything.'

He winced. 'Of course I won't say anything. You have my word.'

She opened her door then and said over her shoulder, 'Good night, Jack.'

'Good night, Stella, I'll see you in the morning.'

She had a quick shower and then climbed into bed thinking about what had just transpired in the pool. As much as she was attracted to him sexually, she wanted it to be more than just a casual hook up on some work trip. And she didn't want to give him the wrong impression of herself. That wasn't how she operated—one-night stands were not her thing.

She had to be upfront with him and talk to him. If he was just after a casual thing, then she would tell him that she doesn't sleep around. If she knew that he was wanting to give this a go and start dating, would she be prepared to give him a chance? The age difference still made her so wary—perhaps he wouldn't be interested in anything serious. He was younger than her, and he'd just gotten out of a relationship with Eleanor. For all she knew, he was happy playing the field and not ready to settle down. But he certainly seemed eager, if his physical reactions were anything to go by, she thought with a smirk as she climbed into bed.

Maybe she needed to tell him why she was so cautious with this kind of stuff. She didn't really want to tell him about her ex, but perhaps it needed to be said. She groaned when she thought of her last relationship—such a bloody train-wreck and her mum hadn't helped with that either.

And she shuddered when she thought about what her mum would think about her and Jack. *Didn't you learn your lesson last time Stella? I told you that Marcus didn't really love you and would leave you, but would you listen? No, you went out and made a fool of yourself. You deserved everything that came your way, you stupid girl.* She put her hands over her ears as she could still hear her mum's laughter.

Taking some breaths to calm herself, Stella set her alarm on her phone and eventually closed her eyes and drifted off into an uneasy sleep.

⁂

Neither Stella, nor Jack had noticed Milly as they walked through the lobby. But she had seen them and what had happened in the pool. She had been out for a walk and had stood there watching. Then, when things had heated up and they'd kissed... *Well, well, well*, she had thought and had quickly snapped some photos on her phone. *He's only just broken up with Eleanor and he's kissing someone else?!* She couldn't wait to tell Eleanor this bit of gossip.

CHAPTER 21

Stella watched Jack come in to the room for breakfast and looked away. She still felt so embarrassed about last night. She was sure he must think she was an idiot, playing hot and cold.

Dylan signalled that they all had to make a move into the conference room so they followed him in. The day started out well but slowly deteriorated and the tension started to rise again. The fundamental problem was that the team was almost divided in two and this had been started by Travis yesterday and was clearly still unresolved. The negative energy he was putting out made the room feel heavy. They had agreed on the pitch and how they wanted to showcase their idea, but just couldn't work out who was best to do each of the tasks required. Everyone thought that their idea was the best and Travis being the more vocal of the group, continually talked over the others. All the inflated egos in the room had led to bedlam.

Jack paced up and down and Stella could almost see steam coming out of his ears. Dylan wasn't prepared to budge. 'This is my company so I think I know what is best for it.' His face was red and he clenched his jaw. He eyeballed Travis, daring him to continue on the path he was.

'With all due respect, you need to keep up with the times, Dylan. Yes, we have some great ideas, but could you just try and see where I'm coming from and not just shut me down?' He was trying not to raise his voice but the scowl on his face showed what an effort it was. He looked desperately around the room. No one made eye contact with him which made him alone and adrift amongst a sea of hostility. He looked towards Stella for support and finding none there, turned back towards Dylan.

Travis took a deep, shaky breath and pushed on and they went around and around in circles as he tried to explain his point of view.

'Dylan, you yourself told me when I first started here that this was a cut throat industry and yet to me, it feels like you aren't prepared to take some big risks. If we don't really push some controversial ideas out, we will struggle to get any new clients to sign on with our company. They are trusting us with their business so we need to deliver.'

'I know this Travis, but we have to consider all the ideas the team puts forward, not just yours.' Crossing his arms, Dylan walked over the other side of the room, face red.

'Well, no one else has spoken up, does anyone have anything to say?' Travis threw his arms up into the air. The room remained silent and he shrugged his shoulders. 'Jack, can you please try and back me here, surely you have to agree with me?'

Travis took a seat at the table, still fuming. Dylan needed some space so he left the room, he knew Jack would get things back on track.

'Right, lets sort this out now.' Jack banged his fist down on the table. 'We have a lot more work to do. Travis has just as much right to push back on our ideas as any of you do. Does anyone have anything else to add, any questions? Because if you do, this is your chance to say something.' He looked around the room and made eye contact with them all. No one spoke up, they all just shook their heads.

He was not going to waste any more time. They were getting this done before the end of the day. 'Travis, let's go through the purpose of this website again and give me the list of deliverables. Stella, how are you going with the templates, have you finalised them yet?' Everyone else jumped to attention.

More coffee and snacks were ordered and they went back through the tender documents to try and see where they could potentially reduce their price point. At this stage, they were going to be far too expensive, but weren't prepared to cut corners if it meant what they produced was inferior. Dylan and Jack both refused to do that and would rather lose the tender than make that decision. It just wasn't how they did business.

However, cutting costs was proving impossible and they were really getting down to the bones now and simply couldn't save another cent.

A couple of hours went by and they were making great progress and then the power suddenly went out.

'Seriously? You have to be kidding me,' said Jack through gritted teeth. His face was clenched and his hands were running through his hair at a rate of knots, ruffling it all up. Totally inappropriate moment to think this, thought Stella, but she thought he actually looked like he had just tumbled out of bed and he looked quite sexy when he was angry. She blushed at this thought.

Dylan pushed through the glass doors into the meeting room and Jack drew a deep breath, immediately calmed by the sight of him.

'I have just been informed that the hotel needs to do some emergency work and have had to switch off the power. As frustrating as this is, we have made great progress so it isn't a total disaster. In fact, it is probably time we all stopped for the day anyway as I know you're all exhausted.' He looked to where Travis was sitting. He had calmed down and had apologised to Jack for his outburst earlier. They had met half way and the tension had dissipated. The plan forward was now very clear and mutually agreed on by the whole team.

'I have arranged a dinner cruise, so please meet me down at the lobby at 6.30pm for drinks and then we'll jump in the minibus and head down to the jetty. The boat leaves at 7.00pm sharp—please do not be late, as we will not wait for you! You can start packing up now and go and get ready. I'll see you all back down in the lobby in an hour and a half. Now scoot, all of you!'

⁂

Jack and Stella found themselves waiting for the lift once more.

'Tonight sounds like fun, just what we all need,' said Jack as they walked into the lift. His head was still spinning from all of the tension the afternoon had brought.

'I know, it's going to be fantastic,' Stella said.

'Can I come by your room and walk down with you?' he asked her. He had been unsure about asking after how things had ended last night. He still wasn't sure what had happened but he knew the mood between them had changed.

'That would be great. I'll be ready by 6.15pm so see you then.' The lift arrived at their floor and as had become their habit, they parted company at Stella's door. As Jack walked into her room, he gave himself a little fist pump. The universe smiled and thought about what was in store for them tonight.

CHAPTER 22

Jack knocked on Stella's door. He was both nervous and excited about tonight. He was going to try and get some time alone with her and finally tell her how he was feeling.

From the moment he had met Stella, something had sparked in him, something that had been missing in any of his other relationships. It was becoming clear, there would never be anyone else for him. She seemed to have slowly snuck into his life and he didn't want her to leave. But he was unsure of her feelings. Yes, she had kissed him—twice now—but how serious was she? Did she just see him as a bit of fun?

He worried that he was too young for her, the age gap didn't bother him, but did she go for younger guys? He felt like he needed to prove that he was serious about exploring things with her, but would she trust him? It hurt his head to try and work through all of this. When she answered the door, she looked incredible, as she always did.

'Let's get this night started, shall we?'

'Absolutely.' He followed her towards the lifts.

They had time for a quick drink and then Dylan, with the help of Milly, herded everyone out to where the minibus was waiting to take them down to the boat.

'Come on you lot, the boat isn't going to wait for us,' he said.

As they walked towards the minibus, Jack stole another look at Stella. She looked gorgeous, and the dress she was wearing was beautiful.

It was a mix of so many different colours, vibrant, but restrained. When she walked it swirled around her legs, reaching just below her knees. A row of tiny buttons trailed down the front of the bodice, which opened into a vee neckline. Jack could see a hint of lace from her bra, which drove him crazy.

On the bus, they sat together and were both very aware of their thighs touching. It was a simple thing, but yet felt so erotic. Jack could almost feel the electricity coming off her.

Conscious of the fact that he was taking up so much room, he thought he should try and move slightly so as to put some distance between them, but as he shifted, Stella seemed to as well and he could still feel her thigh. Jack wanted to simultaneously move, and never move again.

Arriving at the marina they saw that the boat had been decorated for the occasion, festooned in twinkling lights and brightly coloured paper lanterns. A band was aboard and had already started to set the scene for the evening by playing a crooning ballad.

Jack and Stella made a beeline for the bar as they wanted to make it to the top deck to watch the sunset. It was a balmy tropical evening, the water was calm. As the boat pulled away from the pier, waiters circulated around, offering canapés.

Jack grabbed another beer and when he turned back, Stella had disappeared. He looked around, trying to see if he could spot her in the crowd. Where the hell could she have gone? One minute, she had been next to him looking at the sunset and the next she had slipped away.

For a moment, a wave of jealousy roared through him. There were a few other members of their team he knew looked at Stella in a way he was not entirely happy with. Hell, he really had no right to get jealous, but it still irked him when he caught them staring at her. But to be fair, no one in the office knew he was interested in Stella. To anyone looking at the two of them, all you would see was two colleagues who got on well and had a great working relationship. *Hmm, perhaps I need to show my cards and actually ask her out.* He took a sip of his drink as he mulled this over. Could he date someone who he worked closely with? Would it change things in the office? He knew he would have to be careful but surely it wouldn't be too difficult. All he needed now was to pluck up the courage to ask her out.

He ran his hands through his hair. It may not be quite as straightforward as that, there was a lot to consider for the both of them. He took a swig of his beer and looked around for her again.

'Ah there you are, Jack. I've just been talking to the captain, what an interesting man he is,' Stella said as she walked up to him from the other direction. He had seen the captain when they boarded and he had to be well in to his sixties, but still, the unexpected surge of jealousy had unsettled him. He knew he had no right to feel like this. Until he showed his cards, she was free to date anyone she wanted. He scowled at the thought.

'Are you hungry yet?' asked Jack. He noticed Stella was about to say something, before swallowing whatever it was.

'Yes, actually, I haven't eaten anything since breakfast. I'm starving,' she told him.

'Let's go and check out the buffet,' he suggested.

❧

They both loaded up their plates and managed to find an empty table amongst the sea of people.

'This looks amazing, doesn't it?' said Stella as she started trying out the various things she had selected.

'Yeah, it's great,' said Jack between mouthfuls. 'I do hope you're going to finish everything on your plate tonight?'

'Don't be smart, Jack,' and she leaned over and smacked him on the arm. 'I was going to eat everything but now I think I will just leave something on my plate just to annoy you.'

'I dare you to eat it all,' replied Jack. He knew Stella could never resist any sort of dare.

'Dare accepted, Jack Turner.' She proceeded to eat everything on her plate and pushed the empty plate towards him with a triumphant look.

'Oh, my god, now I'm so full, I don't think I can even squeeze in dessert!' She glanced toward the heavy-laden dessert table and groaned. Her eyes widened as they watched a waiter position a pavlova in pride of place.

'I'm sure I can tempt you to eat something from the desserts.' His mind drifting to other things he would love to tempt her with. The thought of smearing her with cream and then licking it off nearly drove him to distraction and it was having the undesirable effect of making his jeans feel very tight.

They drifted towards the dance floor and the band was playing an oldie but a goodie. It was one of the best bands Jack had heard in ages and Stella seemed to relish that their set list was mostly music from the 70s and 80s, singing along until she was almost hoarse.

Jack couldn't believe that she knew the words to every song they sang. This was another side to her that he hadn't seen and he loved it. Jack grabbed her hand and spun her around. Her dress swirled around and rubbed against his legs, and he pulled her in close and spun her out again. He didn't want this night to end.

❧

When the band announced it was playing the last song and the boat was heading back towards the marina Jack held out his hand, 'Stella, will you please have the last dance with me?' She took his hand and followed him back out on to the dance floor. As luck would have it, it was a slow dance. Jack held her close and began to sing quietly to her.

Stella whispered to him, 'I didn't know you were such a great singer. You've kept that talent well hidden.'

Jack whispered, 'I have many talents. Singing to pretty ladies just happens to be one of them.'

'I love this song Jack—it is one of my favourites. I can't believe that the band chose to sing it tonight.'

Much later, as Jack and Stella disembarked from the boat, she suddenly felt nauseous and gripped the handrail. 'Are you okay? You look quite pale.'

'I don't know. I feel a little bit dizzy.' She hadn't really had that much to drink so put it down to a big day and lack of sleep the night before. 'I think I'm just tired.'

The thought of getting back into the minivan made her feel worse. To the side of the marina, she noticed there was a sign-posted, well-lit path where you could cut back to the hotel.

'Would you mind if we walked back?'

'Are you sure you don't want to go in the minivan? I'm more than happy to walk, but are you sure you're up for it?'

'Yes, I'm sure. I feel like I just need some fresh air. Now we're off the boat, I feel a little bit better. It was stuffy on the dance floor.' Taking some deep breaths of the cool air had helped steady her again and she was already starting to feel like herself again.

They explained to Dylan that they would walk and they set off towards the hotel.

'I bet your feet are killing you after all that dancing,' Jack said.

'My feet are a bit sore. Do you mind if we stop and I'll just slip my sandals off?'

'Would you like me to carry them for you?' She hoped he didn't notice the way she blushed at his offer.

'No, it's all good, but thanks anyway.'

When they had got about ten minutes down the path, it opened up and revealed the ocean. The waves lapped against the shoreline and the moon cast a lovely light over the water. It looked like fairies were dancing atop the waves.

Stella grabbed Jack's arm, 'Look at this place, isn't it lovely? Can we stay for a while?' Jack headed towards the water with her.

Dipping in their toes in the ocean they were surprised at how warm it was. It was almost like a bath. They walked back up on to the sand and sat down. Stella couldn't stop looking at the waves, enchanted by nature's beauty.

She lay down on the sand and looked up at the sky. It was such a clear night and there were so many stars. The sky at home didn't look like this—this view was simply magical. 'Isn't it gorgeous?' She looked over at him. He was lying down beside her, but his eyes were fixed on her face, rather than the stars above.

'It really feels like the universe is looking down on us, doesn't it? There is always someone watching over us. They help guide us to the path we need to take in our lives,' she said.

'Is that so? And what is it saying tonight?' he murmured softly and caught her eyes.

Stella's chest felt tight with nerves. 'She is saying that she is very glad that I took that job. There are people that come into our lives for a reason and this is why you and I met at that interview; we were supposed to.'

Would he think she was getting a little too deep? What if he laughed at her? She took all of this seriously and it would hurt if he mocked her.

'She?'

'Of course! Who else could manage all of this but a woman?' That made him laugh.

'Well, then I'm glad she sent me you because I couldn't do my job now without you.'

'The universe has always guided me and helped me make the right decisions. It has also sent some amazing people into my life. Some stayed a while, and some passed through, but they all left some kind of impact,' she said.

'I have to agree with that.'

'I have heard it said that the love we cannot have is the one that lasts the longest, hurts the deepest and feels the strongest,' said Stella. 'Have you ever loved like that before Jack?'

❧

Jack thought long and hard before answering Stella. 'No, I must say I haven't.' Surprised at how her question had affected him. *Why* had he never loved like that before? Was it possible to grieve for something he'd never had? he thought. Damn, he wanted true love, someone he could love forever. He wanted her.

'I have, once but it didn't work out,' Stella said. He could hear the sadness in her voice. He wanted to ask her more but didn't want to push her too fast too soon.

'Listen, what's that?' He could hear the tinkle of music carrying over to them.

She sat up. 'I'm not sure.' She turned in the direction it was coming from, as if drawn to the melody.

He pulled her to her feet. 'Let's go check it out.' She followed him back up to the path that led back to the hotel.

There was a little group of locals sitting just out to the side of the hotel. Two of them were quietly strumming a guitar and the other sang. It was a beautiful, moving song and Jack and Stella sat and listened. When the music had finished, they applauded and asked if they would play some more.

Eventually, it was time to head back in and they said goodbye to their new friends.

'See, this is what I mean, for you and I to share that moment was so special. If we had come back with the others, we would have missed that moment.'

'Thank goodness we didn't then.'

Jack hadn't really known her for that long but it felt like they had been together in another lifetime. He wanted to get to know her better, but there was something in her eyes that held him back. She seemed like a deer that would spook easily if he moved too fast; confused and scared. He didn't know the full story of the lover she'd spoken of on the beach, but he sensed that there was some unresolved hurt there. There was still so much he didn't know about her. But would she let herself be vulnerable and let him in?

Jack swiped his card and the hotel door slid open. They headed to the lifts and by the time they were at their floor, neither of them was sure what to do next.

❧

As they arrived at Stella's door, he said, 'Tonight was great Stella.'

'It was a great night.' She wanted to say so much more but thought it was too soon and she didn't want to scare him away.

The minutes ticked by and then Jack slowly stepped away from her and mumbled something about it being best if they called it a night now. 'We have another big day coming up. We should get some sleep.'

Stella had been just about to ask him to come in so they could perhaps chat. God, the whole thing felt awful now and she just wanted to escape into her room. *See Stella, he doesn't want you. I told you that no one could ever love you*—her mum's voice was so clear in her head and Stella put her hands over her ears to shut it down.

'Stella, are you okay?' Jack's voice was concerned and it made the sting of rejection hurt even more. The mood in the hallway had changed into something dark and Stella felt it crushing in on her.

'What the hell is going on Jack? We have just had the most amazing night so why do I suddenly feel like you're trying to push me away like none of it meant anything?' She could feel confusion and humiliation flowing through her body. Her mum was still in her head saying that she deserved this. 'What sort of game are you playing with me? Am I just to be another notch in your belt? Perhaps Milly is right and you're a bit of a player?' Jack flinched and took a step back, to her satisfaction.

'Do you see this as just some sort of fling? Perhaps Eleanor had a lucky break when you broke things off with her.'

She wanted to hurt him, to push him away. He took a deep breath before replying.

'This isn't the right time or place to be discussing this, please try and calm down. I don't like to see you upset like this.'

'Well, just when would be a good time for you Jack?' she spat at him. 'We have been circling around this *thing* between us for weeks now. I'm sick of not knowing where I stand with you.'

'Oh, come on Stella, both of us haven't been sure where all of this has been going and you know that. I'm your boss, it was always going to be tricky trying to separate our work life and private life. Don't try and paint me as the villain here. I would have talked to you anytime you wanted. I tried to talk to you at Paul and Lindy's.' His eyes narrowed. 'You blew me off Stella and left—I remember clearly you saying you didn't want to talk as there was no "us."'

'Bullshit. You could have tried to have a proper conversation rather than hijacking me at Paul and Lindy's and putting me on the spot. You could have called in the evening; you could have even emailed me to try and arrange some time for us to chat. You chose to do absolutely nothing!'

She suddenly felt very tired, and pressed a hand to her eyes. 'Look Jack, we are going around in circles here, this is all starting to feel way too hard. I'm just going to say good night.' She walked into her room and closed the door behind her.

ॐ

She had no idea on how she could face him tomorrow. She felt so humiliated and annoyed with herself that she had let it come to this, had let herself think he was interested in something more serious. She was usually so careful to keep her walls up, especially after what had happened with Marcus.

She needed to speak to Jaz and so she threw herself down on the bed.

Jaz picked up and before she had even had a chance to say hello, Stella burst out, 'Oh my God Jaz, it has happened again,' and burst into tears.

'What has happened?'

'This thing with Jack, it's got weird and I'm not sure what to do.'

'What's happened? I thought things were okay and you were friends. I know you like him, but doesn't he have a girlfriend?'

'Yes, we are friends, or were friends. I'm not sure now after the conversation we've just had. He broke up with Eleanor after the Gala Dinner—did I tell you? —I thought I had told you.' But it was news to Jaz.

Stella caught Jaz up to speed about what had been happening since they had been in Fiji and where it had all landed now.

Stella could imagine the shake of Jaz's head that accompanied her friend's sigh—why did Stella always find herself in these situations, she was probably thinking.

'What am I going to do? I don't want to face him; I really don't think I can.'

'Well, you're going to have to talk to him again eventually and try and explain. Does he know about Marcus?'

'No, I haven't brought that up yet. I didn't want to have to tell anyone about him.'

'From what you've told me about Jack, he'll understand what you went through and why you're so cautious. Promise me you'll speak to him.'

'It seems like Mum may have been right all of this time. I will never have anyone and no one will ever love me.'

'Stella, your mum was a narcissistic bitch. Don't keep letting her into your head. You know nothing she ever said was true. Besides, she's dead now, she can't ruin anything else for you, not unless you let her.'

'I know. But it is so hard to not think of her, especially when things go wrong in my life.'

'Look, why don't you sleep on it, I'm sure you will feel better in the morning.'

Stella knew she wasn't going to feel better and an idea had started forming in her head. Jaz would think she was overacting as usual, but this was Stella's coping mechanism—she ran.

'Okay, thanks Jaz I better let you go. I'll call you when I get home. Love you.'

'Love you too.'

After hanging up from Jaz, Stella got straight on the phone to the airline and after some pleading that she had a family emergency, managed to change her flight to an early morning one.

She called Dylan and explained that something had come

up unexpectedly at home and she needed to get back as soon as possible. He was sorry to hear that she had received bad news but he understood that her family came first and told her to take as much time as she needed.

She felt a pang of guilt that she had lied, but she just wanted to leave Fiji as soon as possible. She thought about all the work that still needed to be done and she felt so bad letting the team down all because she had a personal issue with Jack. It was so unprofessional but all Stella could think about was removing herself from this situation.

She could end up losing her job once Jack found out she had left. Perhaps he would suggest to Dylan that he thought she wasn't doing well or had some issues. After the way she had reacted last night, he probably thought she was mentally unstable. Maybe she was? *Perhaps I'm my mother's daughter.*

She imagined Dylan telling the team that she had had this family emergency come up and wondered what Jack's reaction would be. Probably disappointed. He would think she was weak and pathetic and would be glad that things hadn't gone further with her.

Stella stormed around her room throwing things into her suitcase alternating between hating her mum and Marcus equally. Normally she was a fussy packer but things were going into this suitcase left, right and centre. She kept out the outfit she planned to wear on the flight, packed up her laptop and took a look around the room. Satisfied that everything was sorted, she went and had a hot shower and climbed into bed feeling drained.

But she couldn't sleep and she burst into tears and cried like she hadn't done in years.

※

She lay there until it was time to get up and head to the airport.

As she was walking out of her room, she made a promise to

herself that she would never let anyone in ever again. This was it, she had tried and failed.

When she went into the office again, it would be to hand in her notice. It was the best solution. She could not stay there and work with Jack, it was just too hard. One of them had to leave and obviously it had to be her.

CHAPTER 23

Jack stood there for a moment looking at Stella's closed door. What in God's name had just happened? He had no clue. One minute they had been having a great time on the boat and listening to the music outside the hotel. It had been a great evening, but now he was standing in the hallway outside of her room—this was not how he had seen their time together ending. How on earth had it come to this? And why was she so upset?

Spinning on his heel he marched down to his room muttering a whole lot of profanities. He mumbled to himself that he would never understand women as long as he lived. Looking at his watch and noting the time difference was still acceptable, he hit Paul's number. Advice from his married friend was just what he needed. Perhaps he could help him work out just where he had gone wrong.

'Mate, I wasn't expecting to hear from you, I thought you were in Fiji on that work conference,' said Paul.

'I am, but something has just happened with Stella and… and I need to talk to you about it,' stuttered Jack. He explained the attraction he had for her and how they were building up a friendship. 'I really like her Paul, she's great but I just don't fully understand what is going on. There has to be something else that is causing her to be so hot and cold.' Jack paced the length of his room as he spoke.

'I know being her boss complicates this whole thing, but still, I'm felt sure we could figure something out. But now I'm not one hundred per cent sure that she would want to go out with me. Maybe it's because I am younger than her?' He moved the phone to his other ear.

'Jack, I really can't see the age gap being an issue. From what Lindy and I have seen, she is interested, I wouldn't doubt that for a minute. You guys have intense chemistry—I say just go for it.'

'Hey, don't talk to Lindy about this mate. I know it will be hard as you guys share everything, but until I can sort out what's going on, can we just leave it between us?'

'Are you sure you don't want me to tell her what's happened? Perhaps she can help you.' Knowing his wife, she would know exactly what was going on and how to fix it, she was good at that.

'Look, she probably can mate, but right now I'm still trying to process what's going on for myself. Maybe when I get back and if things are still like they are I'll have a word, but for now, let's just leave it between us, okay?' He hoped that Paul would keep quiet as right now he couldn't face Lindy's questions.

'Well, if you're sure, just keep in touch. I'd better go now anyway; I can hear one of the kids calling out.'

The call ended and Jack felt better for hearing his best friend's reassurance.

Jack had a shower and climbed into bed throwing all of the extra pillows on to the floor. Pushing the doona back, he picked up his phone and brought up Stella's number. His finger hovered over the screen. Gosh he was tempted to call her, but he didn't and placed the phone down on the side table. It sat there taunting him, almost daring him He reached out and pushed it further away so as to resist the temptation. No, he would leave it for now and talk to her tomorrow when they had both slept on it. A phone call wasn't going to help, he needed to speak to her in person and finally get whatever was between them sorted out.

After a restless night, one that had him up pacing around his room at some ungodly hour, he headed down to her room and see if she would perhaps have breakfast with him and have a chat.

Walking towards Stella's room, he could see the door was open and there was a full housekeeping trolley outside. *That's odd*, he thought. The housemaid came out to pick up something from the trolley.

'Excuse me, sorry to bother you, but my friend was staying in this room and I know she was there last night, so why is her room vacant?' he asked.

'I'm sorry sir, I'm not sure where your friend has gone. This room was on my list to be cleaned. It was vacated very early this morning. Perhaps you can check at reception and see what is going on?' She headed back into the room with a pile of towels in her hands.

Jack ran down towards the lift, anxious to find out where Stella had gone. Pushing the button frantically, he willed the lift to get to his floor quickly.

'Come on, come on where the hell are you?' He pushed the lift call button again. The ping it made when it arrived was like music to his ears. Rushing in, he was pleased to see that it was unoccupied; he was in no mood for idle chatter. Stabbing at the button that would take him to the lobby he stood pressed back against the wall. His hands were shaking.

❦

As he headed towards the reception area, his heart was racing. What was going on? How could she be here last night and then gone this morning? There had to be an explanation and he wouldn't relax until he knew where she was.

Before he could get to reception, Dylan intercepted him. 'Good morning, Jack, I'm not sure if Stella had a chance to tell you; she has been called home with some sort of family emergency. She contacted me late last night in a bit of a state saying she had to go and that she would catch the first flight out this morning.' He glanced down at his phone as it pinged and he sighed as he skimmed over the email. 'Damn, more problems.' He rolled his eyes.

'Ah, no, I hadn't heard,' Jack murmured. His heart felt like it was being pressed between a vice and he struggled to take a breath.

'Well, Milly is taking notes so if there is something Stella needs to know, she can catch up with her next week,' continued Dylan, eyes still fixed on his phone. He had clearly moved on and was focused on the day ahead now.

'Of course, I will have a meeting with her as well when we are back in the office and bring her up to speed,' said Jack. In his mind it was going to be more than a "meeting". He wanted to wring her neck.

He couldn't believe that she had up and left. How was this even possible? He raked his hands through his hair.

'Have some breakfast and I'll see you in the conference room.' Dylan left Jack standing there in utter turmoil.

'Yeah, thanks,' muttered Jack, but he knew for a fact that he wouldn't be able to eat a thing the way he was feeling right now. Perhaps he would just grab a coffee.

'Oh, and Jack,' Dylan had stopped and called to him from across the hotel lobby, 'I'm looking forward to your presentation today.' With that, he was off again.

Shit, thought Jack as he went to get a coffee. *Stella was supposed to help me last night with that.* Milly had done her bit but he had been keen for Stella to look over it with him, but in the romance of the evening the presentation had entirely slipped his mind. Oh well, it was too late now to change anything and at this point he didn't give a flying fuck about that damn presentation—his mind was consumed with Stella. What was this family emergency? Was there even one? Or did Stella loathe him that much after last night that she made up this story to avoid him? How on earth was he ever going to fix this? It felt like he had lost her for good.

Damn woman, it's not enough for her to mess up my private life, she is also impacting my work. He pursed his lips, annoyed with himself for being distracted. This was so not him—he usually had tight control over his life and it rattled him to feel it slipping from his grasp.

Later that morning, Dylan made the announcement to the team and explained that as unfortunate as it was to have lost Stella, they must continue on as planned. Watching everyone around the conference room, Jack's eyes stopped on Milly.

Hmm, interesting, he thought to himself. Why would Milly have such a triumphant look on her face? What was to be gained by Stella not being here? He felt prickles up his spine—like cold fingers slowly moving up his back towards the base of his neck. That look was just plain disturbing and it gave him goose bumps.

CHAPTER 24

How Stella got through that flight, and then to her house, she didn't know. It was all a blur. She hadn't even gotten nervous on the flight; she was too numb. When they'd landed she'd gotten a taxi. She remembered pulling up in front of her house, paying the taxi driver and then opening her front door.

Taking her suitcase straight up to her room, she'd stripped off her clothes and climbed into bed. Finally, she could cry again. She sobbed uncontrollably for hours. Thoughts of betrayal, emptiness and sadness pulsated through her mind before eventually, she ran out of tears and fell into an exhausted sleep.

The next morning, she woke with a start and sat up looking around her room in dismay flinching as she spotted her unpacked suitcase.

Yuck.

Usually, Stella was one of those people who unpacked the moment they got home and put on a load of washing, but she didn't have the energy to do either of those things. She rolled over and groaned into her pillow. Quite frankly, she didn't care if the suitcase never got unpacked. Part of her just wanted to throw it out, along with the memories attached to the clothes inside.

Using all the resolve she had left, she dragged herself out of bed and headed for her ensuite. Perhaps she would feel better after a long shower. Her mind wandered to Fiji. What had they all thought when she had left like that? She was convinced that she had made the right choice but still felt guilty leaving the team in the lurch. It really was so unprofessional. How had Jack's presentation gone? She had been supposed to help him with that and felt a stab of guilt.

She still thought she should resign. She couldn't see any other way out of this mess. Any feelings Jack may have had she was sure had diminished after their argument. Not to mention running away home afterwards.

There was no way he would tolerate the kind of unprofessional behaviour she'd displayed. She was pretty sure if she didn't resign, she would be fired.

The only good thing from that morning was her friend Liz calling out of the blue. She was pleased to hear that she was planning on coming for a holiday.

Stella and Jaz had met Liz years ago when she had come to Sydney on a student exchange from the United Kingdom and had been based at Jaz's. They had all kept in touch over the years and Stella had actually flatted with her for a while in London in her early twenties.

'Oh gosh Liz, this news couldn't have come at a better time. When are you arriving?'

'In a few weeks if I can get myself sorted out,' she said shakily. Stella could hear Liz's voice break as she struggled to talk; tears were not far away.

'How are you doing dear Liz? Sorry I haven't been in touch for a while but Jaz has kept me updated. I still can't believe that Colin has gone. It all happened so quickly, didn't it?'

'Yes, in the end he just slipped away. We tried everything but the bloody cancer got the better of him. I miss him so much.' She started crying, the sound slightly muffled by the telephone line.

'Oh Liz, I wish I was there to give you a big hug.' Stella could feel the tears pricking in her eyes as well. Colin had been a good guy and she had been very fond of him. It wasn't bloody fair that he had died and so young. Such a waste. Tears dropped from her eyes.

'You know you can call me any time and Jaz too,' said Stella trying not to sniff. 'We are both here for you. Have you told her you're coming?' She reached for the box of tissues on her nightstand.

'No not yet. I thought perhaps you could mention it. I just can't face making two calls. It took me all my effort to call you. Every time I think about it, I start crying. I'm sure people are steering clear of me as they don't know what to say.'

'That isn't true. We are both here for you Liz and I'm sure your other friends are too. We all loved Colin and we love you too. Please don't ever think you can't call me.'

'Thanks, I love you so much. You really are such a great friend.' Liz's voice was calmer now, and the sniffing sounds had stopped, much to Stella's relief. 'So, to change the subject, what's been going on with you anyway Stella? Jaz said you have a new job.'

'Yes, I do. It's with a web design agency. I love it.'

'I was so pleased to hear you left the other company. You were too good for them. I hope this other company realises just how great you are.'

'Um, yes, I hope so. It is early days but going well.'

This was not the time to get into everything and tell her about Jack. That conversation would be better face to face.

Hanging up from Liz Stella felt better and she felt a moment of guilt for thinking how bad her life was when her friend had just lost her husband. They had only been married for twelve months.

You can be so selfish sometimes, Stella Carter, she said to herself, *just be grateful for what you have.*

She called Jaz later that day and told her about Liz coming for a holiday and she was rapt.

'I still can't believe that Colin has gone, you know? It all happened so quickly.'

'I know, that's what I said to Liz. One minute he was here and it seemed like things were going okay and then he was gone.'

'I feel so sorry for Liz, but coming to see us will do her the world of good. Let's organise lots of fun things while she's here, make it a really special holiday for her.'

'That's a wonderful idea Jaz.' They spent some time discussing what they could do to help cheer their friend up. The first thing would be dinner down at Circular Quay as Liz loved watching the ferries come in and out.

'Now, what I really want to know Stella is what happened with you and Jack, have you talked to him yet?'

'Um, not exactly.'

'Why not, what happened?' Stella screwed up her face and looked at the time. It was late in the evening, but Jaz didn't sound like she'd be willing to let this slide.

'Don't be angry but I'm at home.' Stella waited for the explosion, slowly counting to three in her head.

'HOME?! What the hell? You aren't supposed to be back until tomorrow!'

'I left. I just couldn't stay. I was so humiliated.' Stella mumbled and admitted that she had perhaps overacted and was a little embarrassed.

Jaz sighed into the phone. 'Oh well. I guess you have to face him now at work. That's going to be an interesting conversation. I'd love to be a fly on the wall when you do that.'

'Yep. I'm not sure how it will go. I'm thinking of resigning. It seems the only way out now Jaz, I don't think I can stay there. Things were bad enough and now I've done this; I have to leave don't you think?'

'Look, don't do anything rash. Just talk to the guy first. You owe him that Stella.'

'Okay, I promise I will talk to him. I have to go now; I'll keep you posted.'

Stella hung up. She just couldn't imagine herself plucking up the courage to talk to Jack, she felt mortified at the thought of ever seeing him ever again. She was going to leave.

CHAPTER 25

Stella could no longer avoid heading in to the office and she felt such trepidation as the day approached. In fact, she felt physically sick when she woke up that morning. The team had returned from Fiji and she had emails from Dylan and Milly—even Travis had emailed asking if she was okay. She still felt bad for lying to Dylan and was touched that Travis had reached out, she really hadn't thought he liked her that much.

She'd deleted Milly's email as soon as she'd skimmed over it. The girl was just fishing for gossip. There was no way she gave a flying fuck about Stella and anything that may or may not have been happening in her life. Watching as the email disappeared from her inbox was deeply satisfying. If only it was as easy as that to get her out of her life.

A staff meeting had been set for today (why she had finally had to return to work) and she would have to sit around the table facing everyone. She had no idea how she was going to field the questions on her family emergency. She decided just to wing it and hoped no one would ask for too many details. Perhaps she would just say a relative had passed away, simple was probably best. Besides, she was more concerned about facing Jack. They had so much unfinished business and she had no idea how to talk about what was or *wasn't* happening between them.

There hadn't been any emails from him and his silence made her feel nervous. She was half expecting to be greeted at the lifts by Tyler and told her services were no longer required and could she kindly leave the building. The thought of that humiliation didn't help her current mood. She could imagine Milly would be watching on with such glee.

As luck (or fate) would have it, the first person Stella bumped into when she walked into the office was Jack.

'Um… Good morning,' said Stella.

'Good morning,' he replied. 'I trust your family emergency has now been resolved?' She told him that all was well and thanked him for asking. But she couldn't stop herself from licking her lips. Could he tell she felt guilty? She hoped not.

Jack smiled. 'I guess I'll see you in the briefing shortly then.'

Hmm, she thought, *he isn't happy with me.* Jack had a habit of smiling too much when he wasn't pleased about something.

❧

She's lying to me, he thought as he walked away from Stella. She always licked her lips when she was nervous.

❧

Stella was working when Milly came past her desk.

'Are you coming in for the meeting Stella?' She plonked herself down on the edge of Stella's desk.

Stella fought back the urge to say *would you kindly get the fuck off my desk?* She replied tersely, 'I will be there in a minute. I just need to finish this email.'

Milly stood up and brushed her hands down over her skirt, 'Well okay, don't be late, there is a lot to be discussed today. You know, things you missed out on.' She smirked. 'Well, maybe you don't know this seeing that you had to leave Fiji so abruptly.' Her flinty gaze swept over Stella, searching for some kind of reaction. Not getting a thing, she flounced off, likely annoyed yet again that she hadn't managed to rattle her chains.

'How about you go and fuck yourself?' Stella whispered under her breath as she disappeared out of sight. God, that girl was obnoxious. Who did she think she was?

Picking up her laptop she headed into the meeting room. Glancing around she found an empty chair near the back of the room and sat down.

There were a few comments from a few of the other staff and she thanked them all and assured them that all was well now. Thankfully, they dropped it and she breathed a sigh of relief.

She felt the atmosphere change in the room as soon as Jack walked in, it almost hissed and crackled. Their eyes clashed momentarily and she could see the conflicting thoughts in those brief seconds. Something passed over his face, and before she had time to work out what it was, it was gone and he had his business face on. She swallowed and exhaled slowly. She clasped her clammy hands together on her lap, so tight that she could feel her fingernails digging in.

Oh god, yep, today is going to be my last day here.

Dylan walked in and it was all business. He thanked them all for their contributions and advised that they had just this morning sent in the tender. 'So now we wait.' They all applauded.

Jack paced around the room while Dylan spoke. As he passed by Stella, she could feel the energy pouring from him and she sat up straighter in her chair, nervous that he would inadvertently touch her as he walked by. If he had touched her, she felt sure that she would have leaned back, unable to help herself. He was like a magnet and she was drawn to him, unable to pull away.

The tension and disappointment of the time in Fiji still tugged at Stella. She felt uneasy and so confused about her feelings. Had she read this whole situation wrong when he'd blown her off that night? Did he actually like her in the same way that she liked him? Stella just wanted this day to be over so she could go home and climb back into her bed and hide from the world and from Jack.

CHAPTER 26

The next morning when Jack arrived at the office, there was a glint in his eye. Stella had managed to dodge him after the staff meeting and had left a little earlier than her usual time so he hadn't had a chance to talk to her properly.

He buzzed Milly. 'Yes Jack?'

'Book me some time with Stella—block out an hour.'

'Sure.'

❧

Milly sent the invitation with a big smile on her face. *Here it comes, this is when he will fire her*, she thought to herself. She could hardly wait and she clapped her hands. 'You had this coming Stella; you can't avoid it now,' she whispered. Stella was clearly one of those people who had cruised through life without a care in the world and got everything she wanted. She hated her for it.

Milly was waiting to hear back from Eleanor as she wasn't sure what to do next.

'Just hold off Milly, I'll tell you when to act,' she had said in her last text message. Milly always did what she was told. From the first time that Eleanor had come into the office and Jack had introduced them, Milly had adored her.

No one had ever cared about her, not in her whole life and each time Eleanor smiled at her or asked her to do something, Milly felt warm inside. She had never had a best friend before, but surely this was it? She had fantasised about it for so long when Eleanor had come along, well it had seemed like a sign. To most people she was invisible, and had been for as long as she could remember. But Eleanor saw her. Really saw her. Milly would do anything for her best friend.

※

Stella saw the invitation pop into her inbox and looked up and caught Milly's eye. She could see her smirking. It took her all her restraint not to give her the third finger salute. Instead, she just smiled.

At precisely 11.00am Stella knocked on Jack's door.

'Come in,' he called and she shivered before entering his office. 'Take a seat.'

She sat in her usual chair. For a moment, they both sat there looking at each other and then looking away. *Oh god, will he just get on with it,* she thought. Her palms were sweating and she could feel beads of perspiration running down her neck. She wished she had tied her hair up today.

※

He had been mulling over what to say, or what he should have said in Fiji but the words still didn't come to him clearly.

'Look, Stella, we really need to clear the air.' He stopped and coughed. His throat felt so dry. 'I'm sorry about what happened and how I handled it. I wish I could take it all back, but I can't. It's done now.' He shifted in his chair, straightening the pens arranged on his desk. 'I guess what I need to know is if this has affected you working here. I'd understand if you wanted to leave or you wanted to put in some kind of complaint to Tyler.'

She looked up at him then. 'That won't be necessary.' She had never thought of what had happened in Fiji between them being a reason for her to go to HR. She was a little confused over him saying that and looking down fiddled around with her necklace.

'Are you still happy to work with me?' He half expected her to say no and was braced for it.

She looked up at him quickly. 'Jack, I need to apologise too. Things sort of got out of hand and I'm just as much to blame as you feel you are. Do you think we could try and move forward? I'm happy to stay on and just focus on why I'm here—as an employee.'

He frowned. She was never going to be just one of his employees. But if that was what she wanted, well, he'd take it. The thought of her walking out and him never seeing her again was unbearable.

'Okay, let's leave it here and draw a line in the sand, shall we?' He wasn't sure how straight this line was going to be and felt sure he would cross it at some stage—he just didn't seem to be able to think straight since she had blown into his life.

'I'm happy to do that.' For the first time since coming into his office this afternoon, she smiled. He relaxed and let out a deep breath. 'Right, now let's have a good catch up on what you missed.'

They slipped back into their working relationship, a place that, for the time, was safe and where there was no chance for misunderstandings.

CHAPTER 27

It had been a month now since Fiji. They had starting having lunch together again down in the park and were getting to know each other better and their friendship was strengthening. She had started to open up about her past and had slip a few things about her mum. Jack hadn't pushed but he was getting a fair idea of what Stella's childhood had been like—so different to his own. His parents were loving and warm, he couldn't imagine going through what Stella had as a child.

A couple of days later, she was sitting at her desk eating a sandwich and as she looked up, she could see Jack heading towards her.

'Oh, hi there,' she said, swallowing the last bite of her sandwich. She had a sip of her water to clear her mouth.

Jack stumbled over his words. 'Um... Stella, um, I know this may sound a bit random, but Paul called me a few days ago and he and Lindy and a couple of other friends are going on a hike to Plumpton Ridge. Lindy was going to call you but thought I may as well ask whether you'd be interested in joining us since I see you every day. We have talked so much about hiking so I'm keen to see you put your money where your mouth is and show me just how experienced you are.' He could feel his face going red and felt like he was talking way too fast. He took a deep breath. 'Would you like to join us?'

Now the question had been asked, he felt a little anxious, wondering if perhaps she would think it was weird. After all, they had agreed to keep their relationship professional, yet here he was asking her to hang out after hours, Gosh, he had never felt so uncertain about any woman in his life before—Stella truly got under his skin and rattled him.

You could have knocked Stella over with a feather. She had been speaking to Lindy the other day and she hadn't said a word.

She paused for a few minutes to try and gather her thoughts. *Would she go? Would she not?*

They had just got things back on an even keel, she didn't want to risk it again. Even though their working relationship was fixed, there was still underlying sexual tension between the two of them and that was nowhere near being resolved, *unfortunately*, she thought.

'Look, is it okay if I think about it and let you know?' she said, trying to sound casual as she moved one of her hands up discreetly over her heart to try and slow it down, pretending she was adjusting the collar on her top.

'Yeah, of course, there's no pressure. Paul and Lindy are keen to see you. I hope you can make it.' The look he gave her almost made her say yes on the spot!

After he had gone, her mind was all over the place. Yes, or no? She wanted to go more than anything, but was it the right thing to do? She looked towards the heavens, 'So, what do you think?'

The universe remained annoyingly silent and she sighed.

⁂

That night when she got home, she called Jaz.

'Bloody hell, Stella, of course you should go. You clearly like the guy. Why did you not say yes straight away?' Even though Stella couldn't see Jaz, she knew exactly what her old friend would be doing. She would be curled up in her favourite chair, her eyes squinted, twirling her pony tail around.

'He caught me off guard and I sort of panicked.'

'Well, you need to tell him you're going and if you don't, I will.' Stella could imagine that pony tail getting twirled tighter and tighter.

'Oh, will you really? It's easy for you to sit there and say I should go. What's going to happen if it all goes wrong and we have another argument?'

'And what if it all goes well and you don't argue and you have a fantastic time?' Jaz paused and Stella knew whatever came next was going probably going to sting. The truth always did.

'Stella, you need to give Jack a chance,' Jaz said, her voice surprisingly soft. 'You have to try and trust again and let him in. I know you've probably been thinking about your ex in all this, but fuck Marcus and all of that garbage. That guy was a tool and never deserved you. Even though you were furious with your mum over what she said to him, I think that old bitch did you a favour.'

Stella had never forgiven her mum, nor spoken to her after what had unfolded, but Jaz's blunt response made her smile.

'Yeah, she was an old bitch. You know, I never even cried at her funeral.'

'I know, I was there. I was surprised you didn't spit on her coffin. And you know what, when I looked around at the few people who were there that day, not one of them was crying.'

Stella sighed in defeat. 'Okay Jaz, I will blame you if this all goes wrong... but I'll tell Jack tomorrow that I would love to go on this weekend trip.'

'Yay! Now you do know that I will checking to make sure you do.

Perhaps I will call Milly and ask her if you went. She will know for sure.' She laughed.

'Oh God, the last thing I need is her finding out.'

❦

The next day as she walked past Jack's office the door was open. She popped her head in.

'Sorry to interrupt you.'

'Oh Stella, that's fine, come in. Did you want to sit down?'

'No, I won't keep you but I just wanted to say I would love to come on the hike.'

'That's great to hear.' His smile lit up his whole face. 'I'll give you more details later.'

'Thanks.'

❦

Once Stella had left his office, Jack did a fist pump. *Perhaps there is still hope*, he thought. His whole mood had lifted the moment she'd said yes. He could have literally done cartwheels around the office.

A few hours later Jack passed by Stella's desk and dropped a piece of paper on it.

'Here's all the details you will need regarding the weekend,' he said. 'I called Paul and Lindy and they are rapt that you are coming. The weather forecast looks great so it should be the perfect conditions. It's a top spot, you are going to love it.'

To have some time alone with her was what he wanted more than anything. Away from the prying eyes of the office, this hike would be a great chance to see if what he felt was real and worth pursuing. He wanted time with her to really get to know who she was and if she wanted the same things he did in life.

He knew she was scared of getting close to people and had lost

147

all hope in romance. That much he knew from the conversations they had shared already, but it felt like there was so much he didn't know about her. With time, hopefully she would start to trust him enough to open up. He still wasn't sure how to handle the fact that he was her boss. He didn't want any sort of trouble at work, but had known he was going to cross that damn line in the sand sooner or later. How would this all play out? At this stage they hadn't done anything wrong. Work colleagues can hang out in the weekend—it didn't need to mean anything more than just friendship and the chance to do something that they both liked. This thought made him feel a lot better. Friends, without any benefits, which was all this was at the moment.

Besides, letting Stella know Paul and Lindy had wanted her to come along too made it clear that he himself wasn't inviting her. The last thing he wanted was to make her feel uncomfortable to the point where she felt obligated to saying yes. The power dynamic and potential complications of being her boss was something he was very aware of.

Even so, he wasn't going to give up on her. If he could earn her trust, that was all he wanted.

CHAPTER 28

The best news was delivered to the team just before Stella and Jack's weekend away. The tender had been successful and they had won the contract! Their weeks of hard work had paid off and the team was in great spirits. Stella felt so proud of the part she had played in this and all of the long hours she had put in certainly had been worth it! She messaged Tim to let him know. He had replied back that he was thrilled. She missed him, but was glad he was happy with his sea change and was starting to move on with his life.

She was tidying up her desk and humming to herself when Jack sauntered up.

'Hi. Are you all set for tomorrow?' Stella had spent a few nights getting her camping gear out. She had found her hiking boots and double-checked that her tent had all its pegs and ropes.

'I'm all set. What about you?' she asked, a playful tone in her voice.

'Nah, I'll just get it sorted tonight when I get home. It shouldn't take me long,' he said.

Stella laughed. 'Don't expect me to lend you a tent peg or anything else you forget.' She never left packing to the night before; she hated to be unprepared for anything.

'That's not very nice, is it? What if I'm missing pegs or ropes and I can't put my tent up? Would you let me bunk in with you?' Stella's cheeks turned pink. She knew he was teasing her, but she still took the bait.

'As long as you don't annoy me.'

'Annoy you? Me? How could that even be possible? I'm so easy going.' He held his hand over his heart in a mock pledge of allegiance and his lips twitched.

He wasn't sure if she was joking or serious, but after Fiji he had already decided he wasn't taking any chances to upset her and would indeed be on his best behaviour.

'Well, I gotta go, I must get home and start my packing,' he said to her and winked.

'Something wrong with your eye?' she asked.

Jack shook his head disparagingly. 'See you tomorrow bright and early,' he said and she could hear him laughing as he headed down the hall towards his office.

⁂

Milly had been hovering around and had overheard most of this exchange. God, it made her sick how they openly flirted. Didn't it bother anyone else? She had tried to discreetly check out if anyone else knew about their attraction, but no one had said a thing. How could they all be so blind? She picked up her bag and then when she got down to her car called Eleanor and a plan was formulated between them both.

'Oh Stella, you're going to have a great hike,' and she chuckled to herself. She would be sure to get some photos this weekend for her collection. When she got home she made some room for them, feeling giddy with delight at the thought of the new additions.

CHAPTER 29

The next morning Stella pulled into the car park at Plumpton Ridge. She didn't see Jack's truck so figured he was running late. *Typical,* she thought, *he tells me to get here early and then doesn't turn up himself!* She walked over to the Kiosk, hoping they were open and she could grab a coffee. She was going to need the caffeine hit today!

As she got to the door of the kiosk; she heard a truck pull in to the car park. She didn't even need to turn around to know who it was. She waved and signalled to Jack to ask if he wanted a coffee and he gave her the thumbs up. God must've been smiling upon them, because the Kiosk was indeed open. She ordered two coffees and Jack wandered over and joined her.

'Mm, this is just what I needed,' he said. Stella nodded in agreement. This really was a good coffee.

Stella hadn't seen Paul and Lindy for a while so was pleased they'd organised this hike. Lindy and her had lots to chat about— gosh, where would she even start?

The married couple arrived shortly after along with Andy and Bella, more friends that Jack and Paul had met at university. By the kiosk Jack introduced Stella and they all prepared to leave.

It was a good six hours to where they planned to spend the night so they were keen to head off and arrive before it got dark. Jack asked Paul if he would walk with him as he wanted to get to the campsite before the others to ensure they could find a good spot to set up. He also wanted to have a private chat with Paul, fill him in on what had been going on with him and Stella. Andy and Bella said they would walk together, so that left Stella and Lindy, who straggled at the back of the pack. Their relaxed pace would give them plenty of time to chat without worrying about holding the others up. The six of them set off in high spirits.

'Please put me out of my misery and spill all the details,' said Lindy as they settled into a comfortable pace.

Stella laughed, 'Oh my god, where the hell do I start? So much has happened since I last saw you.'

'What happened in Fiji?' Lindy asked. 'I heard you left early.'

'Fiji was great. The whole conference went really well. We got the business we pitched for.'

Lindy hit Stella on her arm, giggling. 'I'm not interested in that and you damn well know it! Please tell me what happened with you and Jack. Did you get any time alone at all?'

'I can confirm that we did get to spend some time alone in Fiji,' replied Stella, choosing her words carefully. She was having so much fun teasing!

Lindy failed to see the funny side this time. 'Stella! For God's sake, did you guys hook up? Did you kiss? What the hell happened to make you turn tail and run? Spill all the details right this minute!'

'Okay, okay calm down. They'll hear us,' she said, putting a finger over her lips. She then proceeded to tell Lindy everything that had happened on that trip—the good, the bad and the ugly.

Lindy's mouth was wide open when Stella had finished. 'Oh my god. I can't believe it… and then you caught the earlier flight home. Jack must have been livid!'

'Well, I didn't see him before I left, but I could tell he wasn't very happy when I saw him back in the office after the trip. Things were really cool between us and I felt embarrassed. I overreacted to the situation. I tend to do that, when things get too much, I run. I've been doing it my whole life. Old habits are hard to break.' Lindy offered her a sympathetic look, and thankfully let the topic drop.

It wasn't long until they caught up with the others at the first planned rest stop.

Jack wandered over to Stella. 'Are you enjoying yourself?'

Lindy stifled a grin and excused herself to have a cup of tea with Paul.

'I'm having a great time thanks. It's stunning.'

'So, tell me, how are you managing having to carry your backpack?' His lips twitched like they wanted to curve into a smile.

'It's so heavy. I wish I hadn't packed so much. I'm not sure I'll be able to walk much further with it.' Grimacing, she rubbed her shoulders and neck.

'A rookie error. I thought you would have known better.' He raised an eyebrow. 'If you're trying to hint, the answer is no, I'm not taking any of your gear.' He saw a huge smile appear across her face.

'Gotcha.' She burst out laughing.

'Ha-ha, very funny. You'll keep,' he said over his shoulder and he wandered back over to Paul.

Lindy returned to Stella's side, a mug of tea in each hand. 'I have never seen anyone wind Jack up like you can.' She raised an eyebrow and handed Stella one of the mugs of tea. 'He can be quite serious and you can't always be sure what he is thinking. Not many people would be game enough to tease him like you do.'

'Look, I say it how it is. I make no apologies for that. I can be blunt, I know that, but I would never intentionally hurt someone or make fun of them in a malicious way.' Stella sipped her tea and groaned in appreciation. 'Jack gives back what he gets, don't you worry,' she said. 'He's played many a prank on me at work so when I get the chance, well, it's payback time!' The women drank their tea and repacked their bags. Finished, Stella shouldered her bag again. She'd been joking around with Jack, but it seriously wasn't light. 'Let's get moving again before we both seize up.' She could already feel her feet starting to swell and hoped there would be no blisters forming. She had her old faithful boots on, but sometimes they still gave her grief, especially on long hikes.

⁂

The rest of the day passed by without incident and it was around 3.00pm when Stella and Lindy finally arrived at the campsite. They were tired and looking forward to having a rest.

'Over here ladies,' called Jack. Stella looked at the tents and silently wished that hers had been set up too. Not that she'd let that slip to Jack. She'd rather he not know how tired she really was. Any sign of weakness had been frowned upon by her mum, and she'd grown determined to have a wall of protection around herself since then. She straightened her shoulders and pasted on her game face.

'I left this spot for you Stella. It's pretty flat and in the shade so it should keep your tent cool.'

'Thanks, it looks great.' She dropped her pack to the ground and absently put her hand up around her neck and rubbed it.

'Do you want a hand? I'm happy to set it up for you but it will cost you. How much do you usually pay when you go on your five-star hikes for this service?' Smugness oozed off him and she itched to reach out and punch him on the arm.

'Oh, shut up, will you? I'm perfectly capable of setting up my tent,

I don't need your help.' But she did wonder what he would've said if she'd replied, *Yes, by all means, I'll pay you, just set the damn thing up for me.*

Fiddling with the tent, she turned around unexpectedly and caught Jack staring at her, well, her butt to be exact. She knew these shorts made it look awesome and she'd be lying if she said that it wasn't one of the reasons she'd chosen to wear them this weekend. He looked quite flustered seeing he had been busted having a good old perve. She laughed, before stretching up to tie something to the tent. She wondered if he'd be able to help himself from checking out her bum again. Sure enough, a few minutes later she caught him red-faced and sweating—but not from the heat.

Stella got her tent up and then sorted out her mat and sleeping bag. She was pretty pleased with herself; the tent looked perfect.

She was just crawling out of it when Jack said, 'You got a minute?'

'Sure, what's up?'

'Did you bring a swimsuit?'

'I did indeed, I never go anywhere without it!'

'There's a creek up here we can swim in. It will help your tired muscles.' She didn't even attempt to deny her muscles were aching, he must have noticed the way she kept rubbing her neck. 'Grab your towel and whatever else you need and let's go and check it out,' said Jack.

She quickly got her things together and met up with Jack outside his tent. 'Where are the others?' she asked. The campsite suddenly seemed awfully quiet.

'They've already headed off, so we will meet them there,' he replied.

That's a bit odd, she thought. *Why wouldn't we all go up there together? I wonder why they didn't wait for us.* But she didn't dwell on it for long and just started following Jack towards the path.

It was going to feel wonderful to cool off and she put the others out of her mind.

CHAPTER 30

Jack led the way down a path that was obviously well used—thankfully they hadn't needed to put their boots back on. Stella didn't think she could face those boots again today and was grateful to have been able to slip on some flat sandals.

They reached a narrow part of the track and Jack reached for her hand as they climbed over some fallen tree branches. She was thankful for the gesture; it was quite slippery and she didn't fancy falling over.

As they continued, she noticed a fork in the track, to the left and the right. Jack headed to the right and she looked quickly to the left but couldn't see that it looked much different, so she kept following him. He stopped suddenly and she bumped into his back.

'Oh, I'm sorry. I didn't realise you were going to stop so quickly.'

'It was totally my fault. It seems we have a habit of doing this, doesn't it?' he steadied her with a hand on her arm.

'Well, I should have still been paying better attention to where I was walking.'

He shrugged. 'I have a surprise for you and I want you to close your eyes and don't open them until I tell you.'

'You're not going to push me over a cliff or something are you?' She laughed nervously.

'If I was going to do that, hell, I wouldn't bother warning you, you would be over it already.' That made her laugh and the sound echoed in the bushland.

Stella closed her eyes and felt Jack's arms circle around her. She could have stayed like this forever; she felt so safe and wished he would never let her go. Jack walked them down the track a little further and she felt him shift slightly to the left before stopping.

He whispered in her ear, 'Okay, you can open your eyes now.' He hadn't let her go, much to her delight. She opened her eyes and gasped. They stood on the edge of a gorgeous lagoon; an oasis hidden in the bush, complete with a calming waterfall. She walked to the edge of the lagoon. It had the whitest sand she had ever seen and the water was so clear she could see the bottom. Rubbing her feet through the sand, satin was the first thing that came to mind, it felt just like that. She could have buried her feet in the sand and never moved again.

The trees that lined the lagoon were surrounded by an array of multi coloured flowers. Stella had never seen anything more beautiful in her life.

Fiji had nothing on this spot, she thought. There were so many colours such a brilliant array of reds, yellow, orange, white and so much purple! They smelt divine and she couldn't help but breathe in their aroma. When she closed her eyes, a smile lit up her face. It was pure joy.

'Do you like it?' Jack asked.

'Like it? I absolutely love it! I don't think I'll ever want to leave. Can we just stay here forever?'

Jack chuckled, 'Your wish is my command. Come on, I'm pretty sure you're dying to check this place out.' He led the way toward a small outcropping, where they lay their towels and other gear.

She couldn't resist running her hands over the bark on one of the nearby trees. It was so rough, a contrast to the lovely soft leaves overhead. The leaves all swayed in the breeze, it was hypnotising to watch them moving together as one. Occasionally, one of the branches would move in another direction to the others and she would wonder what had happened to the breeze to make this happen. It was odd to watch, almost like these branches were refusing to conform and simply wanted to move in their own direction.

The spot Jack had chosen was close to the waterfall and the water cascaded off the rocks above. When it hit the water below, the droplets looked like they were dancing. The sound of the water as it dropped down into this spot was actually fairly quiet. It wasn't one of those loud waterfalls where the water hit with such force that you could barely hear yourself think. It was tranquil, a bit like one of those tracks they play in day spa when you're getting a massage. So relaxing.

They swam out towards the waterfall and swimming under it, found there was a small ledge big enough for them to both sit on. 'How did you find this place? she asked.

'It's called Jacob's Leap. An old friend of mine brought me here years ago and once they had shown me the spot, they swore me to secrecy. Clearly, I've broken my word,' he told her.

Oh. It was his spot to impress women. Visions of the other women he had most likely brought up here over the years came to Stella's mind and jealousy stabbed at her chest. Noticing the pained expression on her face, Jack touched her hand.

'You're the only woman I have ever brought here.' He leaned over and their lips met. It was their first kiss since Fiji and the passion between them was just as vibrant. How had she ever thought she could be satisfied as just his employee?

As their kissing intensified, he moved his hand up around her neck and she felt him try to unfasten her bikini top. The heat in her stomach cooled and she pulled away putting some distance between them.

'Look, I know you probably think I'm a playboy and have slept around. But seriously, I haven't had many partners.' He blushed.

'You don't need to explain to me.' She felt such a warm feeling in her heart hearing him open up like that. 'I have never felt like you're like that. This is just me and all my hang-ups on getting close to people too soon, okay?' She thought briefly of Marcus and how he had used her.

'I just need you to understand that when I sleep with anyone, it is serious. I'm not the one-night stand kind of guy that a lot of people assume I am.' He looked away then as he had never had this discussion with anyone else before and it made him feel vulnerable.

'Thanks. I really appreciate your honesty Jack, but I have never thought you were like that. This is all about me, trust me, you've done nothing wrong. When we do sleep together, and I have no doubt that we will,' she rubbed his arm as she spoke, 'well, it is going to be epic.' She laughed, trying to lighten the mood. Was she being presumptuous?

'Epic, you say? Mm, I like the sound of that.' Jack put his arm around her shoulders and his fingers trailed over her breast, she smiled and leaned into his touch.

'Look, just because I don't think we should sleep together yet, doesn't meant there aren't other things we can do to fill in the afternoon.' She rolled him on to his back and ran her hands down his chest. There was just enough room on the ledge beneath the waterfall to lie next to each other.

'You're killing me Stella, but what a way to die,' he groaned in pleasure.

When they eventually drew apart, he said, 'Let's make sure there's no misunderstandings… this kiss was no accident.'

'Agreed. We are both responsible for that one,' her eyes dropped to his mouth once more, 'and this one.' She kissed him again.

୬୧

It was getting cold so they left the water and headed back to the rocky outcropping. Lying in the sun they warmed up and could quite easily have fallen asleep listening to the relaxing sounds around them.

'Are you having a good time?' asked Jack.

'Yes, and if the rest of the weekend goes as well as this, then I'll be hassling you to bring me back out here,' she laughed.

'That reminds me, I still need to take you on a proper hike, don't I?'

'Doesn't this one count? I'm carrying my own pack and put my tent up all by myself.'

'Nah, this is too easy—I need to take you somewhere more rugged than here. Perhaps the Snowy Mountains.' Jack propped himself up on an elbow and dug through his clothes to check his watch. It was time to head back.

'I have to say, it feels good to be dressed again. Now that we're out of the sun it's gotten chilly,' said Stella as she pulled her shirt and shorts over her bathers.

'I can't disagree with that. It's bloody cold, isn't it?' Jack quickly got changed too.

Coming out of the track and back into the campsite, hands still entwined, Stella stopped and dropped Jack's hand as though he was on fire.

Jack couldn't believe his eyes. 'You have to be shitting me, what the hell?'

CHAPTER 31

Stella couldn't believe what she was seeing. Standing there chatting casually to Paul and Lindy was Eleanor, along with Milly of all people! For a moment, Stella thought she must have fallen into a parallel universe and couldn't make sense of it. She shook her head trying to clear the image of the two of them smirking at her.

Stella released Jack's hand and glared at him.

He felt her slide her hand out of his, the distance increasing between them as they stood staring in disbelief. No words would come to Jack. All he could think was, *What the hell were they both doing here?* There was only one person who could have told Eleanor and she was standing next to her. He was furious. Milly had to go and in fact, he was tempted to fire here right now. How dare she turn up here in the first place and to bring his ex, what was she thinking?

Eleanor's eyes had been fixed on Jack and Stella as they'd held hands. Anger flashed across her face, but only for a second, almost unnoticeable. She walked towards them with a smile on her face. Jack stepped backwards slightly.

'Hi Jack,' said Eleanor. 'What a coincidence Milly and I should decide to hike here the same weekend as you guys.'

'Quite a coincidence, isn't it?' he replied, attempting to remain cordial. *Bitch*, he thought. This was no coincidence. He looked over at Paul and Lindy who looked just as horrified as he was. Jack saw Lindy try to catch Stella's eye but Stella was too focussed on Jack's and Eleanor.

'So, Eleanor, how did you know we were all coming here this weekend?' Though he was addressing his eye, his eyes burned into Milly's. She was standing there without a care in the world.

'I bumped into Dylan last week when I was out for lunch and he mentioned you were coming up here hiking,' Eleanor replied. 'I remembered you telling me it was such a great spot so I called Milly and convinced her we should come up here this weekend as well.' She gave a tittering laugh, the one that had grated on his nerves, even when they'd been together. 'It's such a big park. I didn't think we would bump into each other.'

Bullshit, he thought, Dylan had been away and didn't even know Jack was coming up here. She knew they would all end up at the same camp site because his fucking EA had known his plans.

He didn't dare look at Stella. He could feel the hostility rolling off her in waves, boring a hole into his head. Things had turned icy between them in the time it had taken to re-enter camp. He wished they could run away back to the waterfall.

Jack asked Milly what the hell was going on and his voice was getting louder. *Ha, let's see you get out of this you little bitch,* thought Stella. She hoped she would be fired over this and if she wasn't, well Stella would have something to say about that. She wasn't going to be harassed in her weekends by work colleagues. If Jack didn't do anything, she would definitely be speaking to Tyler on Monday morning. This was such an invasion of their privacy. There was no way these two were here by accident.

Taking a final look at them, Stella headed back to her tent. She had seen enough and was absolutely livid. She was also still a bit damp from their swim and getting colder so went into her tent to grab her jacket. When she reappeared, there was no sign of Jack, so she headed over to the area they were going to build the fire in hoping someone had started it as she just felt chilled to her bones.

Lindy had been watching out for her and headed over as well. 'Stella, what the hell?' She didn't know what else to say. There was nothing to be said really, it was an awful situation.

She just looked at Lindy and shrugged her shoulders. 'Oh god here we go,' said Lindy and she frantically looked around for Paul for some backup.

Eleanor and Milly were approaching and they both still looked so bloody smug. Stella caught Eleanor's eye. *Bring it on bitch.* She had no idea who she was dealing with. Stella did not tolerate shit from anyone, let alone this woman and Jack's stupid EA.

Lindy grabbed Stella's arm and shook her head and whispered, 'Don't go there, it's not worth it.' The way Stella was feeling right now, she was definitely going to "go there" of that, she had no doubt.

Stella and Eleanor circled around each other. Eleanor told Stella exactly what she thought of her and how it was Stella's fault that her and Jack had broken up.

'Oh, bullshit Eleanor, I had nothing to do with your breakup. If you can't keep a man, that's not my problem.'

'We were perfectly happy until you came along. This is all your fault. YOU took Jack away from me.' This was true to an extent, as once Jack had met Stella, this had probably been the catalyst that had forced him to end things with Eleanor. But thinking back to the night that Jack had told her it was over, Stella knew that they had had problems before she came into the picture. Eleanor just hadn't been prepared to see the red flags he had been frantically waving. Right now, she just needed to lash out at and was happy to direct all of her anger and frustrations on her failed relationship with Jack directly to Stella.

Eleanor sneered at Stella. 'When have you ever been hiking Stella? I bet you just went out and bought that tent and all your gear when Jack invited you on this hike. You're pathetic.' Stella just rolled her eyes, not deigning that with a reply. Eleanor huffed and took another tact as she could see she wasn't getting much of a rise. 'You do realise that you're just another notch in his belt, right? Perhaps it was one of his fantasies to sleep with an old woman. Gosh, looking at you, I'd say you're a lot older than him.' That hit a nerve.

'Maybe that is the case but at least I'm more fun than you, you boring, stuck up bitch. If you're all that's on offer, no wonder he came looking for me.'

Eleanor's face flushed bright red and she fell silent. She looked at Milly, as if expecting her to step in and fight for her as well, but the EA was standing there almost enthralled.

Jack yelled as he jogged towards them, 'What are you two up to?' He had taken a walk to cool down and returning, didn't like the body language from any of them. He had heard snippets of the conversation as he'd approached but had been too far away to hear it all. Stella wouldn't have cared if he had—what she had said was true and she wouldn't retract one single thing.

Stella stood there rooted to the spot. *This can't be happening*, she thought, *I must be dreaming*. She felt her face get redder and redder and she was so close to tears, but somehow managed to get her emotions back under control. She wouldn't give any of them the satisfaction. Her mum's voice roared in her ears, 'Never cry Stella, don't you dare do that, girl. They will come in for the kill if you shed a tear.' When Stella did cry; the condemnation was hard and fast. 'You're pathetic. What did I do to deserve a daughter like you?'

Marching over to her tent, Stella crawled in and started stuffing everything into her pack, rolled up her sleeping bag and threw the pack out of the tent's opening, crawling out after it. Ripping out the pegs and pulling her tent down like a woman possessed, she shoved the pegs into their bag along with the ropes, rolled up the tent and put it into its bag.

Jack by now was beside her. 'Stella, stop, please stop, what are you doing?'

'I'm going to move. I don't want to camp in this spot. Surely you can't expect us all to stay here like one big happy fucking family.' She laughed, but the sound was harsh, broken. He tried to grab her arm and get her to stop packing.

'Please just let me pack.' She shook his arm off.

⁊⋲

Milly watched all of this unfold. God it had gone so much better than she had ever hoped when she had planted the seed in Eleanor's head that they should gate crash the weekend. Jack and Stella had ignored her and showed her no respect, they deserved this.

Watching Stella feel so humiliated, was the ultimate payback for all the times she had ignored her in the office. Who the hell did Stella think she was anyway?

As for Jack, he was her boss and should have had her back. She had been the best assistant to him, yet he never thanked her or showed any sort of appreciation. She had gone above and beyond for him, keeping up to date with all of her work, running his calendar like clockwork. Even organising all the reservations for him and Eleanor when they'd been together, and this was the thanks she got? She had always known he wasn't good enough for Eleanor and she had hoped in time Eleanor would have figured this out, but she hadn't. Stella catching Jack's eye was the only good thing that had happened since Stella started working at the office. From his face it was clear he was hurting and confused as Eleanor confronted Stella. Seeing the almighty Jack Turner faced with something he couldn't fix gave Milly nothing but satisfaction. He had had such a privileged life and had never faced disappointment or hurt. It was all going to change now.

Eleanor would surely turn to Milly for a shoulder to cry on now that she'd exposed just how hurt she'd been by Jack's rejection. She would be there waiting with open arms, ready to show her what a great, supportive friend she could be.

The commotion had attracted the attention of two park rangers who had wandered into the campsite.

'What's going on here?' one of them enquired. They both looked at Stella—despite her efforts to control her emotions, her distress was probably clear if the heat flaming from her cheeks was any indication.

'I'm fine,' she assured them. They looked at each other and raised an eyebrow.

'Can we assist you in any way?' the first guy asked. Stella really didn't know where she had planned on going but she was packed up and she sure as hell was not spending the night at this campsite.

'Is there another campsite nearby I can go to, right now?' she asked them. Jack started to move toward her again, but before he could say anything, Stella repeated her question.

'Well, yes there is actually. It's probably at least a twenty minute walk from here but we can make it before dark, if we move quickly.'

'Okay,' said Stella, 'let's get going then, we're burning daylight standing here chatting.'

'Well, if you're sure…'

'Yes. I have never been surer of anything in my whole life, so can we please just go *now*.'

She put her pack on and shoved on her beanie. Even though her blood was boiling, there was a cool bite to the air.

Without looking back at Jack or the rest of the group, she followed the two park rangers.

Jack caught up with them and asked, 'Where is this camp, what's it called?'

'It's called Green Fields. Like we told your friend, it's about twenty minutes north of this campsite,' one of the rangers told him. They assured Jack that he had no reason to worry; they would make sure she got there safely. The look on Stella's face told Jack he had no choice but to let Stella leave with them.

As soon as they had left the campsite and started heading down the track to her new sleeping area, Stella let out a huge sigh of relief to be getting away from them all. She still couldn't believe that Eleanor and Milly had had the audacity to turn up. Even though she could be volatile, she knew she would never have had the balls to do that herself. She stood up for herself but still didn't like confrontation. It reminded her too much of the years of having to stand up for herself with her mum's constant allegations and criticism.

The two park rangers introduced themselves—Ray and Steve. They had been working in the park for around a year and loved it. She felt safe with them and settled in for the walk to the new campsite. It gave her some comfort that Jack had enquired where she was going so she didn't feel totally alone out here now she was to be separated from them all.

⁂

Twenty minutes later, Stella, Ray and Steve arrived at the campsite. There were three other tents set up and a fire was going. It looked so peaceful! Thanking them both she assured them that she would be just fine now, so they headed over to the other side of the camp and started setting up their own tents. It was going to be dark soon, so they would be staying the night too.

Dusk fell, the bush looked lovely and Stella started to relax a bit. All the birds were out having their last feed before night fell. The calls of the kookaburras and cockatoos were almost deafening. She took some photos of them and got some great shots of the sun setting.

Shoot, she thought. *I had better get my act together and get my tent set up again before it gets any darker.* She opened her pack and spread the tent out on the ground.

As she worked her way around the tent, she stopped. *Damn, where the hell is the last peg?* She searched through her pack again but couldn't find it. What the hell was she going to do? She would just have to leave it out and hope the tent didn't fall down overnight. She was crouched down trying to put the main poles together and they wouldn't join up at all. After letting out a string of expletives she tried again.

'The poles are back-to-front and they won't go together until you turn them around. Oh, and you also seem to be missing this.' The missing peg was dangled in front of her over her shoulder.

CHAPTER 32

Stella's heart dropped. She knew exactly who was standing behind her, there was no mistaking the deep timbre of that voice. What the hell was he doing here? My god, Jack had some nerve showing up here. She turned around slowly to face him.

'Thanks for the helpful tip,' she said and reached for the peg. She flipped the poles around and they clicked together nicely. *Damn him.* She continued to put her tent up, conscious that he was watching her every move.

She could feel his eyes boring through the back of her neck. Her face was bright red and her heart was racing. She was supposed to be angry with this man, so why could he still stir up these feelings?

'You look like you're done now, so do you want to put my tent up for me?' he asked.

'I'm pretty sure you can manage all by yourself—on the other side of this campsite,' she replied, not looking up at him.

'Ouch, you cut me deep,' he said, sticking out his bottom lip in a dramatic pout. Stella had to stifle a laugh.

One of the park rangers wandered over, his eyes narrowed as he looked at Jack.

'All good?' he asked Stella. Jack looked at Stella and raised an eyebrow. She briefly wondered what the ranger would do if she said no. Clearly, he was concerned that Jack had followed them here, uninvited.

'All good,' she replied. Although she was still annoyed at Jack, he didn't pose any threat—other than perhaps to her heart.

'Okay then, I'll leave you both to it. Have a great evening.'

⁂

Jack still hadn't even started putting his tent up and she was nearly finished with hers. After the ranger had left, he'd wandered over to the fire pit and started chatting to a couple sitting there.

Ha, he better not think by stalling that I'll let him sleep in my tent. She would help him set his up if he asked again, but bloody hell, she didn't want to let him stay with her out of principle. Childish though it might be to hold Eleanor and Milly's appearance against him, he hadn't exactly responded how she'd hoped.

'Okay?' said Jack appearing suddenly by her side. He had startled her and interrupted her thoughts. 'Sorry, do I make you nervous, you are awfully jumpy?' A huge smile spread across his face.

'Okay, what?' replied Stella, trying to sound like she didn't give a damn whether he was standing there beside her or not and she shrugged her shoulders to show her apparent disinterest.

'Have you thought anymore about perhaps helping me with my tent?' asked Jack.

Stella paused. 'Can't say that I have—not interested.' If he was trying to wear her down, he was going to have to work a lot harder than that.

'Oh, come on, don't be like that. I came all the way here to make sure you were okay and spend the night with you and this is the thanks I get?'

'I didn't ask you to. You could have stayed at the other campsite with your ex and your EA.' She was still fuming over them turning up. He hadn't invited them on the hike but nor had he asked them to leave.

'You should have set up your tent earlier instead of chatting to them.' She gestured over her shoulder to the couple sitting by the fire.

'Ah, I knew there would be plenty of time, especially if you were generous enough to help me.' His lips broke into a tiny smile and she was momentarily distracted by the dimple on his chin.

She glanced at the gear he had brought with him. Something didn't seem right.

Hang on, oh my god.

'Where is your tent, Jack Turner?' Hands on hips she faced him squarely.

'My tent? It's here somewhere, I'm sure.' He made a show of searching for it.

'You didn't bring it did you?' Her lips twitched as well.

'Oh, damn, I was so sure I had. I must have forgotten it in the rush to catch up with you.'

'Well then, you do have a problem, don't you?' She had to bite her lip to stop herself from smiling. No way was she going to let him assume that she would let him sleep in her one. The nerve of the guy.

'Guess I will have to sleep by the fire then, won't I?'

'Not really my problem.' Turning her back on him, she bent down and started looking through her back pack. She couldn't find her plate and cutlery. Surely she hadn't inadvertently left it behind at the other campsite. She bit her lip in annoyance. *Ah, there they are.* Relieved, she set them aside and focussed on getting everything back into the pack.

'So, are we going to talk about what happened back at the other campsite?' She stopped her organising for a moment and then continued to fiddle around with her back pack, zipping it up.

'What's there to say? Your ex and your EA turned up and insulted me and I left.'

'Surely you have to know I would never have invited them.'

'Of course I know that, but it doesn't make me feel any better.' She didn't like to tell him that Eleanor's barbs about her age had made her feel unsure. The whole age thing had crossed her mind once or twice before, but now she felt like a bloody cradle snatcher. Did everyone who looked at them think that too?

'I'm going to deal with Milly next week but I need to talk to Tyler first. She is not going to be easy to get rid of. I want to be sure it is handled correctly so HR doesn't have to get involved.' He stepped closer, his eyes searching hers. 'Has she done other things to you?'

'Um, well yeah, but I didn't want to turn it into a big deal.'

'Oh, my god, why the hell didn't you say something?'

'Look, I was new in the role and didn't want to cause any trouble.'

'So, you just put up with it?' He clenched his fists together and his surge of anger took her by surprise. 'You're coming into my office on Monday and putting in a complaint. It'll go to Tyler as well. It may help the case we can build to fire her.'

'I don't really want to but I guess I will have to say something now.'

'I'm afraid you don't have a choice. I won't stand for this.' A muscle ticked in his jaw, he had his boss face on now that was for sure. The mood was bringing her down. She was here to have a relaxing weekend, she wasn't going to let Milly and Eleanor ruin what was left of it.

'Anyway, enough of that. Let's just enjoy the weekend, shall we?' Stella had finished setting up her tent and still hadn't answered Jack on where he would be sleeping. *Let him stew over it for a while,* she thought.

'Did you by any chance bring any food with you?' Stella asked, she still had all of hers, thankfully she hadn't put it with the others or she would have been feeling stupid now. He opened his bag, and from what she could see there looked like there was plenty. She reached over his shoulder and grabbed the bag of chips. 'What you have looks a lot more interesting than mine.' Her eyes landed on a large block of dark chocolate nestled in his cool bag, as well as what looked like some premium steaks. Her traitorous stomach grumbled at the sight. Jack smirked and tilted his head.

'Perhaps if I share my food, you'll let me share your tent?'

'Let's just see how good it is before I promise anything.' She opened the bag of chips and popped a couple into her mouth.

'Okay, be prepared to be amazed then.'

They headed over to the firepit and joined the other campers. Jack introduced her to the couple he had met earlier and she sat beside them. They were there for the weekend and it was the first time they had been here too. The group bonded quickly over how they all couldn't get over just how beautiful the spot was.

❧

Darkness had fully engulfed the campsite so she couldn't see Jack smiling. He was pleased to see how happy she was now and he was relieved. All of that business earlier had rattled him more than he liked to admit. It had hurt him to see her so distressed. He still couldn't understand what Milly had hoped to gain by coming here with Eleanor.

They all started cooking their food. To Jack's relief, his steak turned out to be just as good as promised, marinated with a tasty honey and soy glaze. He cut it into small pieces and once cooked they were tender and delicious. Later, as they all felt like something sweet, they charred some marshmallows over the fire. Finishing her first one quite quickly, Stella reached over and grabbed another marshmallow and pushed it on to her stick. It was soon charred to perfection and she sat there licking the sticky marshmallow from her lips.

Stella was feeling so relaxed now, admittedly, the couple of glasses of wine she had drunk may have also helped with that. At one stage she was up dancing around the fire with their new camp mates, having the time of her life.

But she had forgotten what happened that night at Jack's when she had drunk too much wine. Wine and her wasn't a good combination, especially when Jack was around.

CHAPTER 33

It was close to midnight when Stella decided it was time to call it a night. *Oops. That wasn't the one*, she thought as she stumbled trying to stand up. She giggled at her sloppiness.

'Be careful Stella,' warned Jack. She'd felt his eyes on her all night.

'Umm. I think I'm going to need some help. I can't seem to get my balance,' she giggled and Jack grabbed her just before she toppled over. 'Thanks. You're a good guy. I've always liked that about you. You're a good guy,' she slurred before proceeding to wobble again. He managed to get his arm around her and guided them in the direction of her tent.

'Do you know where my tent is?' she asked. 'I can't remember where I put it.'

'You don't "put" a tent, you pitch it,' answered Jack poking her in the arm, almost causing her to fall over, so he quickly grabbed her again before she ended face down in the dirt, taking him with her.

'Yeah, whatever smarty pants. You're always right about everything, aren't you?' Weaving as she walked, she reached out to him so as to steady herself. 'You don't know everything though. I know something you don't know and I'm not going to tell you!' She could barely walk in a straight line and Jack sighed before picking her up in his arms.

'Yeah, I'm always right. I'm a smart guy.' Jack was enjoying joking with her. He liked this happy and carefree Stella.

'So, what do you want to tell me?' he asked her, curiosity piqued.

'I'm not telling you and you can't make me!' she said, her voice fluctuating in pitch. The way she was acting, he didn't think it would be long before she spilled her secret and he couldn't wait to hear what it was.

'Put me down this minute, I can walk, I'm fine,' she said, squirming in his arms.

'Bloody hell, woman, would you just keep still? We're both going to end up on the ground.'

Jack struggled to keep hold of her. Dear lord, she was very drunk. Thankfully they were close to the tent—he didn't think she would be very impressed if he dropped her. Though given her state, perhaps she wouldn't even notice if he did.

'Here's my tent, I knew I would find it,' she said to him.

'No, that isn't your tent, your tent is red and this one is green.'

'Really? Oh, my god, is it? I can't actually remember what colour it is. Are you sure it's red?' she laughed her head off and Jack couldn't help but start laughing as well.

I was going to tell him something, thought Stella, *but I can't remember what it was. What was it? I know it was something important.* It had slipped her mind. She'd had too much wine. Way too much wine.

Arriving at her tent, Jack was puffed and seemed more than happy to put her down.

'Sit here while I unzip the tent. Do. Not. Move,' he said.

'Okay, cross my heart I won't move, not even one little bit.' She didn't think she could even if she wanted to and she felt herself tipping over to the right and put her hand out. Unzipping the tent, he picked her up again and carried her in, closing the zip behind them before any mosquitoes managed to find their way in.

❧

Before Jack knew what was happening, Stella had managed to sprawl herself across her sleeping mat, on the verge of passing out.

Now what? he thought.

'Okay Stella, you're going to have to help me out here, I need to take your boots off. She tried to sit up to help but flopped back down again with a breathless giggle.

'It's too much effort. Please just leave me alone, I'll sleep like this.'

'I'm pretty sure you won't want your boots on when you get into your sleeping bag.'

'Fine then.' She held out her feet and he quickly unlaced the boots and popped them near the door. When he turned back to her, she was wrestling with the zip on her jacket, he helped her with that and she slipped it off and threw it over her shoulder. 'It's so hot in here,' she mumbled. She pulled her shirt over her head and was sitting there in a tank top before flopping back down on to the sleeping mat.

There was enough room in here for him to sleep, but she hadn't asked him to stay and he didn't want to overstep any boundaries. He sat crouched beside her, conflicted.

'You got enough room?' she asked, blinking up at him. She tried to move over towards the wall of the tent but really made no progress.

'Are you sure? I don't mind going back to the camp fire, I can sleep there if you would prefer?'

'I don't mind if you want to stay, just lie down and go to sleep, will you?' Her words were fuzzy around the edges and she blinked sleepily at him. He removed his boots and put them next to hers. Slipping out of his own jacket he crawled into the space she had left for him. He left his merino undershirt on as he didn't want her to wake in the morning concerned to see him bare chested.

'Are you okay, do you have enough room?' She tried to move further towards the edge of the sleeping mat, failing miserably.

'I'm fine Stella, but for God's sake can you please try and keep still?' Even in the dimness of the tent, he could see the grin she flashed him.

'I don't want to. I like to wriggle around when I'm in bed,' she said. As if to illustrate her point, she wriggled a little more.

'Well can you please not move around so much when we are sleeping together?' he groaned softly. *Couldn't she feel what all this wriggling around was doing to him?*

'Fine. I will turn over and you can just look at my back,' she huffed and proceeded to turn over. This was even worse, as her bum jutted out. Jack longed to reach out and cup her cheeks with his hands or press himself up against her.

She was killing him.

Ignoring his previous request, she turned back over and wriggled over to him, draping one of her legs over his and snuggling up close. Jack held his breath. He tried to move her away from him so as to give them both some space but every time he shifted, she seemed to inch back towards him. It was driving him crazy. If she wasn't so drunk, he would have sworn she was doing this on purpose!

Jack thought that she was settling down for the night and had just closed his eyes. They flew open when she leaned over and kissed him. She tasted of wine and marshmallows and he groaned as the kiss deepened. He pulled away as she leaned in again, trying to distance himself from her. Being this close to her was driving him crazy. She found his lips again and he was hard pressed not to kiss her back; he just couldn't help it. It felt so natural and he had been desperate for more of her kisses since they'd left the waterfall.

'Do you wanna know my secret?' she whispered when they finally pulled apart. Her face was inches from his and their eyes locked.

'Only if you want to tell me.' He took both of her hands in his—his heart beating hard, whether from the kissing or anticipation of her secret, he wasn't sure.

She leaned in close again and said, 'I love you, Jack Turner.'

Before he could process this information she yawned. 'I'm tired, I think I need to go to sleep now.' She rolled over, facing the wall of the tent again. The next thing he knew, her breaths had deepened. She was indeed asleep.

Jack stared up at the tent ceiling, his mind racing. She loved him? Would she remember any of this in the morning, when the wine had worn off? The kiss and her words would be certainly be burned into his mind.

He rolled onto his side and gathered her in his arms, where he wanted to keep her forever. He couldn't remember ever being this happy. Dropping a kiss on her shoulder, he soon fell asleep too.

CHAPTER 34

Stella woke to what seemed like every bird screaming their heads off. It seemed like there was thousands of them. She put her hands over her ears momentarily, before moving them to her forehead. Boy, she had a killer headache—a monster actually.

'Bugger off!' she yelled. Beside her, a large body grumbled at her to keep it down. Jack. Jack was in her tent with her. And he was still trying to sleep it would seem. She muttered an apology and tried to be quieter as she reached for her bag, hoping she had packed painkillers. 'Please let there be something like that in my pack,' she groaned.

What the hell had happened last night? How much had she drunk? Bits and pieces of the evening prior floated back to her. There had been singing and dancing. She looked down at her tank top and saw the remains of something sticky. *Ah, that'd be the marshmallows.*

She had no recollection of getting back to the tent but she vaguely remembered taking her boots and jacket off. Glancing around, she saw them lying near the door of the tent. Her shirt was there too, all crumpled up. Glancing at Jack, she noted that thankfully, he seemed to have most of his clothes on. But still… had they slept together?

No. I would remember, she thought. But her memory of last night was still rather foggy so she couldn't be entirely sure and anxiety crept over her.

Jack opened his eyes. 'Morning, how are you today?'

It turned out, Jack looked gorgeous in the morning. His hair was rumpled from sleep and the stubble on his chin looked so sexy she longed to run her fingers over it. Gosh it was distracting.

'Like I have been pulled through a hedge backwards and I have a killer headache,' she replied, wrapping her sleeping bag around herself. In the light of the day and feeling like she did, she was most certainly out of her comfort zone. She ran her hands over her hair and it felt greasy and limp. She could only imagine what she looked like. How can he look so damn sexy this early in the morning? She alternated between wanting to grab him and kiss him or hide under her sleeping bag as she felt such a mess.

'I'm not surprised. You hit the wine pretty hard last night!' He lay on his side so close to her that she had to fight the temptation to reach out and press her fingertip against his cute little dimple. He smiled and drew her attention to his lips. Was she staring? She felt like she couldn't look away from his mouth.

'Oh god, please don't mention wine. I swear I'm never going to drink ever again.'

He grinned. 'You'll survive I'm sure, but I've noticed you seem to have a bad track record with wine.' He propped himself onto one elbow and had the audacity to wink at her.

'What do you *mean I* have a bad track record?' she asked him. 'I most certainly do not have a bad track record.'

'Well, there was the kissing last night and—'

'What kissing? I'm pretty sure I didn't kiss you,' she cut him off before he could finish his sentence. She frowned at him. A vague memory flitted at the edge of her mind, but just out of reach for her to grasp it.

'Oh yes,' he told her. 'There was kissing, just like that night at my place when you had a couple of wines and we kissed in my spare bedroom. I must remember to always have a supply of wine whenever you come over,' he said and playfully nudged her.

'We've been through this before, I didn't kiss you that night, you kissed me!' protested Stella.

'No, pretty sure you kissed me first,' he said, his eyes sparkling with mischief.

'Well, if it was that horrible for you, I won't be coming over ever again, even if you beg me,' she said crossing her arms. Her protest was undercut by her current state of undress.

Jack's expression sharpened and his eyes were hot on her skin. 'Trust me Stella, you will be the one begging to come over,' and he smiled which infuriated her even more.

'You can dream on buddy, I won't be coming over to your place again in this century.' She was confident she had had the last word and was feeling quite smug and pleased with herself as she reached over to grab her back pack and rifled through it, looking for some clean clothes she didn't much fancy wearing the marshmallow coated top she currently had on.

'But you told me last night you loved me.' Jack's voice was soft behind her. She froze. 'Surely if you love me as much as you say you do, you'll want to come over and see me again. Perhaps even have a sleep over?' She looked down at him and he winked again—which made her feel like punching him in the eye.

'I... said I loved you? No, you must have misunderstood. I wouldn't have said that. You're making it up just to wind me up,' she said, trying to convince herself as much as him. But then, the fog cleared in her mind and she had a vague recollection of telling him something. Surely, she wouldn't have said that though—she didn't think she had been that drunk!

What could she say, really? She flipped her hair and chose to ignore his accusations and changed the subject. *Very mature*, she thought, but there was no way she was going to have this conversation with him now.

'You had better get up. I'm pulling the tent down in about five minutes. We have a big day ahead of us so we need to get cracking.'

Jack took her mood shift in his stride.

'Okay boss. Let me know if you would like me to help.' He got up and slipped his shoes and jacket on, exiting the tent, presumably so Stella could have some privacy to get changed. It was irritatingly considerate of him.

Stella bustled around, she quickly changed her top and packed her pack again. They both ended up pulling the tent down as she had to concede that she just couldn't cope doing it solo today, not with the hangover pressing behind her eyes. Jack rolled the tent up and popped all the pegs and ropes into the bag.

Sitting under a tree, they had some breakfast. All Stella could stomach was an apple and it made her feel marginally better. Their campmates from the night prior were nowhere to be seen; they must have had an even earlier start to try and beat the heat. It was already 7.30am and it felt like it was going to be a warm day. They filled up their water bottles and with a final look around to check they had gathered all their stuff, they headed off.

They soon fell into an easy rhythm and walked along in companionable silence.

The hours passed by and Jack checked his watch. 'There's a nice clearing up ahead and we should be there in about ten minutes. Are you happy to take a break?'

In her hungover state, she was more than happy to take a break and agreed. She would kill for a coffee but knew there was no chance of that.

❧

They soon came across the spot and found some shade to sit in. It felt good to get the backpacks off and Stella stretched her legs out and closed her eyes. *God I really don't want to move from this spot,* she thought, *I could quite easily fall asleep right about now.*

She felt a nudge on her leg. 'Here eat some of this, it will make you feel better,' said Jack.

'What is it?' She sat up to take a closer look, not sure if her stomach could take any food.

'It's leftover sandwiches and some cake. I assure you they are quite edible.'

'Mm, the sandwich is actually still quite fresh,' she said, biting in to it.

'I'm glad it meets your approval, ma'am.' *So smug,* she thought, but she could forgive him; he was just so damn cute! Looking at him out of the corner of her eye her heart raced.

Stella groaned as she stood up and put her backpack back on. It felt heavier. *How can that even be possible?* she thought.

Time flew by and they hadn't seen a single person, which Jack told her was quite unusual for the time of the year, but also really nice as the track was quite narrow in places and it always posed a problem squeezing past others. They stopped and had a quick lunch break— both of them were starting to feel tired now and Stella nearly cried with relief when they reached the car park.

Unlocking the car, she threw her gear into the boot and was ready to head home for a long shower and sleep.

'Thanks for the interesting weekend.'

Jack laughed and replied, 'Any time Stella.'

Monday was just around the corner and they both thought of what had happened over the weekend and the conversations that had to be had with Milly and Tyler.

❦

Stella drove into her driveway and the relief was strong as she took in the comforting sight of her home. There had been so many ups and downs over the weekend, but overall, it had been great. Something had changed with her and Jack and she hoped they could spend more time together. *Perhaps even go on a proper date?* But there was still the issue of him being her boss. Maybe it wasn't such a good idea, them exploring whatever this was between them, especially with all of the trouble Milly was currently causing. Imagine what she could do to them both if they were dating and she shook her head. She certainly wouldn't want Milly organising their dates like she used to when he was dating Eleanor. If she wanted to go to the theatre or out for dinner with Jack, she would make the arrangements thank you very much. Though she was probably getting ahead of herself there, as she had when she told him her feelings. Even though she'd been drunk, she couldn't deny the truth.

She mulled over this as she unpacked, she glanced in her mirror on her way to the bathroom. Yuck, her hair looked dreadful. She was dying to get into the shower and wash the dirt and sweat from her skin.

Now showered, but too tired to cook, she ordered a pizza and lay on her couch.

She'd tried to set the events of the weekend aside, but looming over her was the upcoming meeting with Jack and Tyler regarding Milly. She still couldn't believe the audacity of her and Eleanor, just showing up like that. How dare they intrude on her private life.

CHAPTER 35

Walking into the office she glanced towards Milly's desk, as had become her habit. She wasn't there. Perhaps she had taken the day off? If it had been Stella, she would have.

She sat at her desk trying to get some work done. Every time she heard a voice, she would look up but still there was no sign of Jack or Milly.

Two hours later, her phone rang and it was Tyler. His office was down the end of their floor and her legs wobbled as she walked towards it. The door was open and he gestured for her to come in.

'Just close the door behind you, thanks,' he said. As it clicked shut, she felt her nervousness increase.

It was an awkward conversation as she told him all the things that Milly had done to her since she started working with the company. The messing with her lunch, putting her on the spot at work functions and meetings (though she hated admitting that her speech at the gala was a set-up), and the invasion of privacy this weekend.

'Are you prepared to put this into writing?' he asked when she had finished.

'Look, I really don't want to make any fuss but I will put something together if I have to.'

'I think that would be best. Hopefully we can resolve this swiftly.' He stood, signalling the meeting was over. 'I know you must be wondering where Milly is today,' he said as he showed her to the door. 'She is on leave while we work through everything, I trust you won't discuss this with anyone else.' Stella nodded, desperate to return to the safety of her desk.

A couple of days later, Jack was called away on a work trip. He had come past Stella's desk and told her he was going to be a way for a week but they would catch up when he got back. She wasn't sure if he meant for work or for personal reasons and she wasn't sure if it would be overstepping to ask.

'Well, have a great trip. I'll see you when you get back.'

'Sure.' He hurried back to his office still with a million things to do before he left.

Two days later and he hadn't called or sent her a text. She tried not to let it get to her, but maybe he was cooling things off? Or was she just reading too much into it? She thought about calling him but just couldn't bring herself to do it. She didn't want to look desperate or clingy. A nasty, niggling voice at the back of her mind reminded her that although she'd confessed her love on the weekend, he hadn't returned the sentiment.

She had some very long days and nights. She checked Facebook, hoping he might have put up an update, but there was nothing.

Her mind went into overdrive every time she thought about what he could potentially be up to—she couldn't wait for him to get back. It wasn't that she didn't trust him, but she had no idea what they actually were and she needed to talk to him and define their relationship. Were they just work colleagues? Friends? After the weekend, she'd felt sure they were more than that She wasn't sure what their handful of kisses and intense conversations added up to yet.

❧

She had a late meeting a few days into the second week he had been gone and had rushed into the meeting room.

'Sorry I'm late,' she said and looked around for somewhere to sit.

'Why don't you sit here next to me?' said a familiar voice to her right. She turned and there, looking just as gorgeous as ever, was Jack! She met his eyes and then dropped her gaze to his mouth and that cute little dimple. Her lips quivered and she ached to kiss him.

Gosh, imagine what Tyler would think if he knew what she was thinking. She had to watch herself. She certainly didn't want the spotlight back on her after the whole Milly thing. Milly had come back to the office, and the outcome of Stella's complaint was unclear, but they had moved Milly to another floor at least, so their paths had not yet crossed.

'Hey, welcome back you. How was the trip?' She was proud of herself for sounding so nonchalant, like she hadn't been counting down the days until his return.

Jack motioned for her to sit down next to him and the look he gave her really made her want to reach out and touch him. The rest of the team poured into the meeting room then so there was no time to chat much to her disappointment.

It was a long meeting, a debrief of what the client had thought about their new website and there were some small issues that they had to nut out, just the typical things: drop down menus not behaving and some of the graphics weren't quite the right colours, small stuff but still tiring. When they all finally came up for air it was 6.00pm. Jack and Stella started packing up as the rest of the team filed out of the room.

'Great meeting, but I'm exhausted now.' She stretched and yawned, working on a crick that had developed in her neck somewhere around the second hour of the meeting.

'Same, I've had way too many long days and nights recently, they're starting to take their toll on me,' replied Jack.

'Hey, I don't suppose you would like to go and grab some dinner with me? After keeping you back at the office, it's the least I can do. Plus, it would be nice to have some company after so many solitary meals while I was away.'

She was thrilled. She had missed seeing him every day and the office just wasn't the same when he was gone. 'Sure, sounds good, plus I'm starving.'

⁂

Since it was a nice evening, they decided to walk down to Chinatown, which wasn't far from their office. They stopped and looked at the menus displayed out the front of various restaurants and eventually decided on the Golden Temple. Once they were seated and had ordered they both settled back and waited for their drinks.

Jack looked at Stella and quirked an eyebrow, 'No wine tonight? I always enjoy dining with you when there is wine involved.'

Stella laughed. 'No, I thought I'd play it safe tonight and order a spirit instead. I've given up drinking wine; it gets me into far too much trouble.'

'I'm disappointed to hear that,' said Jack.

'So, tell me about your trip?'

'I was pretty much doing business 24/7, so not much down time,' Jack replied. He picked up his chopsticks and put them down again as their drinks arrived. He swirled his whisky in a slow circle, clearly in no hurry to answer.

The food came out then. 'These honey prawns are to die for,' moaned Stella. Though the food was undeniably good, most of the enjoyment was from sitting there together.

'So, did you miss me then?' he asked coyly.

'Well things were pretty quiet while you were gone.' She kept her reply light and breezy, two could play at this game.

'I missed you.' Jack said, leaning forward, elbows braced on the table. 'I was looking forward to coming back to see you. Please tell me you missed me at least a little bit?' The expression on his face was so earnest, it warmed her heart.

'Okay, I did miss you, just a little.' She shrugged and took the last prawn.

'Did you miss me enough that if I was to ask you out on a proper date, you'd say yes?'

She very nearly choked on the prawn and took a sip of her drink to collect herself.

'It would depend on where you wanted to take me. Would it be worth my while?' she said.

'Definitely worth your while.' He was purposely increasing the tension now between them and their eyes clashed. 'What are you doing next Saturday?'

'I don't think I have anything particular planned, why?' Even if she did, she would've cancelled it within a second.

'Come out with me?'

'Just to be clear, come out on a date?'

'Yes, would you like to come out with me on a date, Stella Carter?' She waited a moment just to make him sweat a little before replying,

'Yes, I would love to go on a date with you.'

Once the meal was finished, Jack walked Stella back to her car, in the office carpark.

'Thanks for dinner, I guess I'll see you at work tomorrow?' She stood next to her car unsure what to do ncxt.

Jack edged closer, putting his arm around her waist and drew her in to him.

'Don't I get a goodnight kiss?'

Her heart did a little flip-flop.

'Well, since you asked so nicely,' and their lips touched.

As Jack drove home, he racked his brain on where he could take her. It had to be something special. He was confident he could come up with something. But the clock was ticking.

CHAPTER 36

Stella was intrigued. *How creative is he?* she wondered. She hoped it wasn't going to be one of those cliché dates with posh food and classical music playing and waiters floating awkwardly around. She hated that kind of thing. It just wasn't her. She always felt so out of place and clumsy and she never knew which cutlery to use first.

It was a long week as she alternated between thinking about the date and what was going on with Milly. They still hadn't spoken and Tyler hadn't given her any kind of clue on what was going on, it was almost like it had all been forgotten and brushed under the rug.

On Wednesday, Jack messaged her to check she hadn't forgotten their date (as if that were possible). Then she saw him before she left the office on Friday and he was all smiles. She couldn't wait to see what he had organised.

❧

Saturday evening finally arrived and there was a knock on her door. Answering it, she found Jack standing on her front porch with a huge smile on his face and holding a beautiful bouquet of sunflowers.

'My favourite flowers, they are gorgeous, thank you.' She took them from his hands and ushered him inside. Should she give him a kiss? She decided just to go for it—it was a date after all, so why not?

'This is a great way to start our date,' he murmured, holding her tight.

'Yes, it is perfect if you ask me.' She rubbed her hands over his back.

The air between them felt charged, like they were suspended in time. She had to stop herself from suggesting they head to her bedroom. She wanted him so badly, but perhaps he would think it was too soon? They were approaching a cross road and a decision would have to be made, but what would it be?

'Um, I need to pop these flowers into some water.' She took his hand led him to her kitchen where she got out her favourite vase and busied herself arranging the blooms.

She stepped back to admire her work. 'They really do look beautiful.'

'Beautiful flowers for a beautiful woman,' Jack said and looked deeply into her eyes.

The chemistry between them was swirling in a heady aura as they headed out to his car, hand in hand.

'So, where are we going?' she asked coyly.

'You'll find out soon enough.'

'Can you give me a hint? Are we going north, south?'

'Not saying. It's a surprise, remember? Usually when people tell you they have a surprise, they don't tell you what it is!' He held up his hand to ward of any further questions.

Stella rolled her eyes. 'Fine, I won't ask you another thing,' and she looked out her window. Two seconds later she looked back at him and he was smiling at her.

She poked her tongue out and he laughed.

They started talking about their favourite bands and found they actually liked a lot of the same kind of music. They had even been to a few of the same concerts and both commented how weird it was that they could have bumped in to each other. They were like two halves of something long-lost that had finally found its other: twin-flames.

'Well, here we are,' he said.

Stella couldn't really see much that excited her. They were in a carpark. It didn't scream romance, that's for sure.

'Come on then, let's head in.' He took her hand in his, his thumb rubbing over the back of her wrist in a way that sent flutters through her stomach.

Head in? Where exactly are we heading to? She couldn't see any signs or any tracks. Though uncertain, she obliged and followed Jack. As they got closer to the tree line, Stella could make out what looked like the entrance to a restaurant… yes it was a definitely some sort of restaurant.

It wasn't often that Stella was lost for words, but at this moment, she just stood there taking it all in.

'It's… so pretty. It's just so perfect Jack.' He just watched Stella's face and the wondrous joy spread over her eyes and mouth. Stella looked around again, determined to burn the image of this place into her brain forever.

How could I ever describe it? It was like nothing she had ever seen before.

Tables had been set up outside, in a semi-circle and all around the edge of the property were beautiful Eucalyptus trees, delivering a lovely fresh smell that delighted Stella's senses.

She could hear so many different birds; the cockatoos were flying around screeching their heads off and she had also spotted a couple of kookaburras who seemed quite happy to sit on their branch watching her. There were wattles, banksias and grevilleas, and their dark green and bronze foliage and striking burgundy flowers took Stella's breath away.

The ground was covered in such soft moss it was like walking on carpet as they made their way to their table. She closed her eyes and succumbed to the world around her, breathing in the sharp, clean air. Jack smiled at her and encouraged her to take a lap around the clearing, while he sorted the rest of the arrangements.

While she took in their surroundings, Jack ordered some drinks and a platter of nibbles and by the time she returned to him, everything was being placed on the table.

Filling their glasses Jack turned to her and made a toast. 'To a great night.'

'Well, it's started out pretty nicely already, Jack—cheers.'

⅗

It was dark now and the candles on their table flickered as a light breeze whispered through the trees above. Stella felt like they were in their own special paradise and she was loathe to ever leave this place—it was simply magical. The staff were attentive, but not intrusive, taking their meal orders with efficiency and wide smiles. After the waiter had delivered their food, they settled back taking in the ambience. The meal was superb and after finishing dessert Jack asked, 'Are you ready for your surprise?'

'I thought this was the surprise, are you telling me there is more?'

'Come with me and I'll show you.'

'Where are we going, won't the staff wonder what we are doing?'

'Never you mind about them.'

He picked up the lantern that had been left for them beside their table and she followed him as he headed towards a small side track.

What on earth can he be showing me now?

Jack stopped and switched off the lantern. 'Hold my hand and I'll lead the way.' He switched the lantern off and as her eyes adjusted to the dark, she saw them.

'No way,' she whispered. She was transfixed and leaned into Jack as he put his arm around her. 'Oh Jack.' Everywhere she looked there were hundreds of glow-worms. She hadn't seen glow-worms for years, not since she had been a child. The whole bush seemed to be full of them. She didn't know where to look first. It was like they were completely surrounding her and Jack. It was such a surreal experience. There was nothing she had seen that eclipsed this moment in time. They stood there for ages, watching them flickering.

She hated to leave but it was getting late so eventually they returned to the open-air restaurant. Over coffee she thanked him again for such a wonderful evening. She knew that she would never forget this—their first actual date.

As they walked back towards the car, she wondered if perhaps he would ask her to stay at his place. The question seemed to hang in the air but who would give in and ask it—that was the million-dollar question.

CHAPTER 37

Stella leaned back in her seat. Should she ask Jack to stay at her place? They would get to her house first, so it made sense, but was it too early in their relationship? It had been so long since she had invited a man to stay the night, and she'd forgotten the required protocol. She had no idea what to say. Do you just ask, do you drop some hints? The awkwardness was getting to her.

The universe once again intervened, pulling them out of their stupor. At exactly the same time, they turned to one and another and asked, 'Do you want to stay the night at my place?' Two seconds later they were laughing hysterically.

'Oh, my god, how weird was that!' exclaimed Stella.

'I know, right!'

'My house is closest, so come and stay?' she said, the nerves fluttering to life in her belly again. He nodded.

When they pulled up to her place, her heart was pounding with anticipation and she put her hand over her chest to try and calm down.

Walking in to her lounge room she flicked on the light. 'Make yourself at home.' Spotting her comfy lounge, Jack made a beeline for it. She sat next to him, perched on the edge of the sofa. *Now what?* she thought and her hands trembled.

'Do you feel like another coffee?' she offered and went to stand up. He put his hand on her arm and she sat back down.

'I don't feel like one, do you?' His voice was low.

'Well, not really, but I feel like I should offer.'

Jack put his arm around her and she snuggled up next to him.

'Do you want the TV on? S-should I put on a movie?'

'Do you want to watch a movie, Stella?' He moved even closer to her, their faces only inches apart.

'Um, not really.' She laughed nervously as she fidgeted with the thread hanging of one her cushions.

'Neither do I,' he whispered against her lips. Time stopped when he took her in his arms and started kissing her.

After a few breathless moments, Jack pulled back, his eyes pinched with concern. 'Are you sure you want me to stay, I'm happy to go home if you have changed your mind?' She knew he meant it, that he'd stop if she wanted to, but that just made her love him more.

'I haven't changed my mind, Jack.' She stood up, the nerves now gone and reached for his hand.

Everything in her bedroom was white, so it made the room feel crisp and cool. A huge picture of an elephant hung on the wall behind her bed. She saw him looking at it and told him, 'It's a photo I took while travelling through Africa.' The windows were covered with plantation shutters and she had lots of pot plants placed around the room as well. The king-sized bed was covered with an inordinate number of cushions and pillows. The scent of her perfume lingered.

'I'm just going to jump in the shower.' She poked her head out the door, 'Do you want one as well?'

'Are we showering together?' he asked, hope and something more primal stirring in him. She answered his question by grabbing his hand and dragging him into the ensuite.

They fooled around in the shower but Jack really wanted to make love to her on the bed. Turning the shower off they quickly dried themselves and ran towards the bed.

Pulling the blanket over them, he held her tight in his arms. They were lying face to face and they could feel their hearts beating together.

'I love you,' he whispered.

His heart felt like it would burst with happiness as she whispered back, 'I love you too.'

They felt so connected in this moment, neither of them wanting the moment to end.

They made love and as they lay there afterwards, they knew there could never be anyone else. They belonged together.

CHAPTER 38

Stella looked over at Jack who was still soundly sleeping. Gosh, he looked gorgeous. She moved some of his hair that had fallen across his eyes and her hand strayed to the dimple in his chin, finally touching it the way she'd longed to for all these months.

Surveying her room and seeing their clothes and the cushions from her bed strewn across her floor, memories of the night before made her blush and a small smile touched her lips as she remembered. She still couldn't believe he was actually in her bed!

She was still smiling when Jack awoke and wrapped his arms around her.

'Good morning, gorgeous.'

'Good morning yourself. I hope you slept well.'

'The bed is pretty comfortable I must admit, but the highlight for me is having you in it.' He kissed her and she felt warm down to her toes.

'We should get up and get motivated,' she said. Stella wasn't one to lie around in bed, even with a gorgeous man next to her. Would he want to leaving now? She was under no illusions as to what most men were like, the morning after the night before, so she wanted to give him an out if he needed it. Maybe it wouldn't hurt as much that way.

'Well before you get up, let's do something I feel quite motivated to do.' Jack grinned and pulled her closer... that took up a significant amount of their Sunday morning. All thoughts of getting out of bed completely vanished from Stella's head as she enjoyed exploring more of Jack.

Sometime later, they got up and showered together. She wasn't sure how she was going to be able to shower by herself anymore, it was so much more interesting when Jack was in there with her.

They decided to head out and grab some breakfast and swung by Jack's first so he could get changed. They managed to christen his bed and shower before any thought of clean clothes crossed either of their minds.

⚡

Just as they were getting dressed yet again, Jack's phone rang. It was Paul. Jack hadn't spoken to him for ages and he felt bad. They had been supposed to get together last week for a drink and Jack had to cancel and hadn't got around to calling him back to reschedule.

'What the hell have you been doing mate?' Paul asked. 'Have you met some hot lady that's keeping you tied to your bed or something?'

Jack looked across at Stella who was sipping her coffee and said, 'Now there's an idea, I'm pretty sure I have some cable ties somewhere.'

Stella laughed, and glanced around the café they'd finally made it to. Satisfied she wouldn't be overheard, she said, 'Well, if you don't, I always carry some in my handbag, just in case! A girl's got to be prepared for these kinds of things,' and they kept laughing.

Jack hadn't said he had his phone on speaker but Paul noticed the new voice immediately.

'Just who the hell are you trying to tie up Jack? I know that particular female's voice,' said Paul slyly. 'Do you need help, Stella? Do you need me to come over and rescue you? I'm pretty sure I have some side cutters in my tool box,' he added and laughed.

'No need, I'm good,' she giggled.

'I can indeed confirm that she is good, well, *very good* actually,' said Jack. Stella smacked him on the arm.

The conversation took the direction down into the gutter as these kinds of discussions usually do. This resulted in them sending pictures of weird and wonderful sex toys to each other. It was quite the competition!

Paul asked them for dinner and they agreed to meet at his place later that evening.

❧

After spending a relaxing afternoon together at Jack's they headed to Paul and Lindy's, stopping quickly at Stella's and she grabbed some wine and cheese to take with them.

When they arrived at Paul and Lindy's Stella went to get out of the car, Jack reached out for her arm and stopped her.

'Are you happy?' he asked, his face serious.

Taken aback, she paused for a second before looking at him.

'I'm happier than I've ever been in my life,' she answered honestly, punctuating the statement with a kiss. He deepened the kiss and slipped his hand down her top.

'Um, we need to stop now Jack,' she laughed.

'I may not want to stop. In fact, I was thinking of pulling you over into the back seat!'

'As tempting as it sounds, I'm not sure that having sex outside your friend's house is a good move. Imagine if the kids came outside!' He looked up then to check that they weren't standing there, thankfully, the coast was clear.

Walking through the side gate into the backyard, Lindy spotted them. 'So good to see you,' she said and walked over and hugged them.

It seemed extraordinarily quiet and out there and he looked around, 'Where're the kids?' Normally by now they'd be screaming around the place wanting him to play with them.

'They're having a sleepover at their grandparents tonight.' He looked at Stella and gave her a wink which made her blush.

'That's a pity, I haven't seen them for ages...' An idea hit him. 'Why don't we all go away camping one weekend? The kids would love it,' said Jack.

'That's a great idea. You'd be up for that Stella? You wouldn't mind spending the weekend with us and three rowdy kids?' Asked Lindy.

'It sounds like fun.' Stella loved the idea of them all going away.

'What's this I hear about camping?' said Paul. He had been getting them all drinks and had just joined them in the backyard.

'We are going to take the kids camping with Jack and Stella,' Lindy told him.

'That sounds great, just let us know when you're both free.'

Relaxing around the BBQ the four of them had a great night.

※

A few weeks later, they went on the family camping trip and as much as Stella had wanted to go back to Plumpton Ridge, Jack decided that Blackwell Park would be better as it was more kid-friendly there was a great lake and some easy trails that they could take the kids walking on.

The only thing he hadn't seen coming was when Paul's eldest daughter Bree (God love her) decided it would be a great idea to have a 'girls-only' tent. His heart sunk as he realised, he would be bunking in with Paul and Neil.

Jack and Stella shared a glance that reflected both of their disappointment with the sleeping arrangements. To make matters even more frustrating, Stella whispered in his ear that she would be thinking of him and all things she would have done to him if they had been in their tent alone with each other! Poor Jack didn't sleep a wink that night.

The next morning, they all headed down to the lake for a swim. The kids had noticed the pontoon floating out there and hounded Paul and Jack to take them out there. The girls could make it out there easily and Jack offered to tow Neil out there on his boogie board.

Stella couldn't believe it and she looked at Jack with daggers. 'What the hell? I thought we were going to sneak away for some alone time,' she whispered in his ear.

'Look, I'll go out for a swim with Paul and the kids. You sunbathe with Lindy and then I'll think of an excuse and come back in. I can't help but notice you have that troublesome bikini on. That is the top that had the malfunction in Fiji, is it not?' He was rewarded by her blush. 'This time I won't be helping you fix it, I will be taking it off you.'

She punched him lightly on the arm. 'Oh, go away and start swimming.'

He was having so much fun jumping off the pontoon and being silly with the kids but it didn't take took long before the sight of Stella lying on the beach sunbathing, tempted him back to shore. It looked like Lindy had popped back to the campsite for the time being, so Stella was alone.

'Mate, I think I'll head in are you right with the kids?'

'Yeah, no worries, I can manage.' Jack slipped off the pontoon and into the water and struck out quickly and quietly towards the shore. He crept towards Stella, the sand muffling his footsteps. As luck would have it, Stella was now lying on her back with her hat over her eyes.

Jack stood there for a moment, admiring her body and then shook himself like a dog. The cold water rained down on her and Stella screamed her head off and sat up shaking the droplets from her warm body.

'You nearly gave me a bloody heart attack—you know how much I hate cold water!' she said to him crossly.

Whispering in her ear, 'Well, how about you let me warm you up.' Before she could protest any further, his mouth found hers and he kissed her.

Jack had originally thought this was a good idea but now he realised he was pressed up against her and he felt himself grow more aroused by the minute, but he couldn't do anything about it. Why the hell didn't he think this through properly?

Stella's screams had attracted the attention of the kids and Jack saw them swimming for shore. It looked like his plan for a bush walk alone with Stella was not to be.

Meeting them at the water's edge he spent more time splashing around with the kids and Stella and Lindy joined them. After a little while, the kids grew tired and collapsed on the beach, eating the snacks Lindy had gone back to camp to collect.

'So, who's up for a bush walk then?' asked Jack as they finished eating and wandered back towards camp.

'We are Uncle Jack,' said the kids and they ran off to get ready. Once they had shoes on, sunhats and sunscreen, all six of them headed off. When they returned sometime later, hot and tired, Paul and Lindy took their kids for another swim.

Jack and Stella excused themselves. Nothing was going to thwart their plan this time.

Disappearing down a track Jack had noticed ran along the side of the lake, they walked further down it. They could no longer hear the others and the silence swept around them.

Finding a secluded spot, they lay their towels down and stripped off. Stella did not mind one bit when he removed her bikini. Jack proceeded to kiss her and do so many other wonderful things to her that she completely lost track of time. They were in their own world, just the two of them and it was wonderful.

Sometime later, Jack made a move to indicate that perhaps they should head back and she pushed him back down and straddled him. She could feel him getting hard again.

'And where do you think you're rushing off to?' she asked him and he grabbed her hips as he entered her. God, she made him crazy. They sure as hell weren't going anywhere now.

CHAPTER 39

Paul had started to light a fire and the kids were helping find wood.

'Where are the marshmallows?' asked Neil.

'Yes Mum, can we please have some?' the girls chimed.

'Dinner first guys.' She gave her kids "the look". They had no choice but to do what they were told.

Stella laughed. She had been tempted to say yes and go and grab the marshmallows herself—but she was thankful she hadn't when she saw Lindy's face. Lindy meant business. No one was eating anything before dinner, that was for sure.

Watching them all, Stella felt so grateful they had come into her life and she couldn't imagine going back to how things had been. She hadn't realised just how lonely she had been before she had met Jack and all of them. The only family she had ever had was Jaz and Liz, but it was nice to feel that she was now a part of another family. Watching Lindy with her kids was an eye opener too. She had never witnessed love like this and she wondered how different her life would have been had her mother loved her like Lindy loved her kids.

After dinner, they lazed around the fire and the kids got some sticks and charred their marshmallows. It was the perfect way to end a perfect day.

The kids had decided that actually they were going to all sleep in one tent by themselves, so Lindy helped them get settled. As they were all exhausted, the three were soon asleep.

Jack had been thrilled when he heard this and had already put his sleeping bag in Stella's tent—he wasn't prepared to have his sleepover with her railroaded again.

'So, what's happening with Milly, Jack?' asked Paul as Jack returned to the fireside.

'Not sure, it's still with Tyler. He messaged me yesterday to say there had been a development and he needs to see me next week.'

'That's interesting. You didn't mention that,' said Stella.

'No, I meant to and then we got side tracked.' He smiled at her.

I wonder what's going on. Perhaps it had all been sorted? She really hoped so as she wanted to put it behind her.

Eventually, Paul and Lindy yawned and stretched. It had been a big day and they knew their kids would be awake early so they should get to bed.

'How about we have a big cook up for brekkie? There's heaps of leftovers and it'll save us having to take it home,' suggested Lindy.

'Sounds great,' said Stella. Jack nodded in agreement. He hoped Lindy would make her famous hash browns, as they were to die for. He had tried to replicate them many a time but just couldn't get the taste right.

After they left, Jack and Stella stretched out in front of the fire on a blanket. Jack took Stella's hand and squeezed it. 'Are you warm enough? Do you want your jacket?'

'No, I'm fine, lying in front of the fire is so lovely and cosy.'

'I love being here with you, I've had the best weekend. But I do have one regret.'

'What?' she asked and he could see the fear behind her eyes.

'I wish I'd had the courage to ask you out earlier than I did. You walked into that interview and as soon as our eyes met, I was completely lost. When I shook your hand, I felt like I'd had an electric shock. They say when you meet your soul mate, you know it and you can't imagine going through life without them—that was exactly how I felt that day.'

⁂

Stella could feel her eyes welling up and then the tears rolled down her cheeks. Jack's brow furrowed. 'Have I upset you? I didn't mean to.' He sat up and took her in his arms. When she could speak, Stella fished a tissue from her pocket and wiped her eyes, almost ruining the romantic moment.

'No, what you said was perfect. I just can't believe that you just told me what I have been keeping from you. I also had quite a reaction that day when we met as well. Like you, I'd never experienced anything like what I felt for you that day,' and she smiled.

'I'm so pleased that you did turn up that day. Our paths might never have crossed otherwise.'

'You never know, I might've gotten a job at one of your client's businesses and came in for a meeting or something. Wouldn't that have been funny?'

⁂

The universe smiled, as she knew that it was because of her that Stella did turn up that day. But bloody hell, humans were determined to make their love lives as complicated as they could and waste so much time searching for each other.

'I have something else to confess,' Jack continued. 'Remember that day you came to my place to work and you stayed for dinner?'

Oh god, Stella remembered it all too well. 'We shared that kiss and then you bailed. Do you know how much I wanted to drag you down the hallway and into my bedroom? I regretted letting you leave that night.'

'Do you know how much I wanted you to do exactly that?' They lay there laughing as they thought about how stupid they had been that night.

'We have come a long way from that day. Perhaps one day we can spend some time in your spare room again… you know, for old times' sake,' she teased. 'I'm sure you have more of your elephant collection to show me.'

He pulled her close. 'Right now, all I'm thinking about is kissing you and then heading to our tent where I can assure you there won't be much sleeping. In fact, why don't we head there now?' Stella took a last look at the starry night and silently thanked the universe for sending her Jack.

⁊

After dropping Stella back at her place late on Sunday afternoon, Jack noticed a couple of missed calls from Tyler which made him feel uneasy. What was so important that it couldn't have waited until Monday? He called him back, pacing around his living room as the phone rang. Finally, Tyler picked up.

'Oh Christ Tyler, you can't be serious? She told you all of this?' Jack shook his head and hung up. *How on earth was Stella going to deal with this latest development?*

CHAPTER 40

Arriving at the office on Monday, Jack had hoped to grab Stella and tell her what was going on but Dylan intercepted him and said she was already meeting with Tyler. Jack regretted his decision not to call her last night, but he'd thought some things were best shared face-to-face. *What the hell is going on?* he thought. Why was Dylan waiting for him? He had a horrible feeling in the pit of his stomach.

'Sit down, Jack,' said Tyler.

'You and Stella are both aware that we have been looking into the allegations you have laid against Milly.' They both nodded. 'Well, it has come to light that something more serious may have been going on.' Tyler looked at Dylan. Jack looked at Stella and she could see she was just as confused as he was.

'Milly alleges that you and Stella have been acting inappropriately. She has said she confronted you Jack and you threatened her.'

'What the hell?' Jack went to stand up. He'd known about Milly's allegations of inappropriateness from Tyler's call last night, but not the threats.

'Jack, please,' Dylan held his hand up. 'Sit down, I haven't finished yet.' He sat but fear was circling around him now.

'You and Stella were seen cavorting in the swimming pool while on the work trip to Fiji,' said Tyler, his expression grim.

❧

Stella's face went from pale to red in seconds and she felt physically sick. Who could have seen them? She flashed a quick look at Jack and he looked just as horrified as she did.

Tyler pushed a photo towards them both and they blanched. It showed the two of them kissing in the pool. A second photo followed, showing him with his hand on her breast while he fixed her bikini top.

Jack stood up and pushed the offending photos back towards Tyler.

'Jesus Christ Tyler, are you trying to tell us that Milly took these photos? This is such an invasion of our privacy,' he roared. 'She has gone too far. I want her gone.' He was pacing around the room running his hands through his hair.

Dylan continued, his voice calm. 'Once this came to our attention, we had no choice but to investigate. You must see that, Jack.' His boss sighed, rubbing a hand over his face. 'There has also been an allegation laid that you and Stella have been having sexual relations here in the office.'

Stella stood up then. 'That is simply not true!' She looked between Dylan and Tyler.

'We only have a verbal accusation of that, but based on these photos and what we've been told, we have to take this seriously. It's not a good look for the company,' said Tyler.

'How can you even *think* there is truth in any of this? I've worked here for over three years without any incidents. The Fiji photos—we swam, we kissed. One kiss in the pool that no one else saw but Milly hardly warrants this kind of complaint being raised. Why was she lurking around and following us, that's what I'd like to know! And why the hell did she take a photo? It's none of her business what either of us do outside of work hours.' Jack slammed his hand down on the table. 'And as for Stella and I having sex in this office—'

Dylan held up his hand. 'Jack I really don't want to hear any more. You're both to go on leave while this investigation continues.'

Jack was already on his feet and started to leave the room, but he paused by the door. 'You know what I can't believe Dylan, is after all of our history you are treating me like I've done something wrong. You can go to hell.' He spun on his heel and walked out, the glass door reverberating as it slammed behind him.

Stella spoke up in a quiet voice. 'Can I go now?' Without waiting for an answer, she rushed towards the door.

Stella had to run to catch up with Jack, her heels clicking across the timber floor of the building's lobby. 'Jack, stop, please stop. We need to talk about this.'

'I can't believe this, can you?' He stopped and waited for her to catch up.

'No. But what I don't understand is why Milly has stitched us both up? It was me she hated, not you. It makes no sense.'

'She's a fucking lunatic—why would she make any of these accusations? I'm her boss and you are her colleague, what was she hoping to gain from starting all this trouble?'

'We need to get to the bottom of this, but I don't know how,' she said and shrugged.

'Well, I do.' He got his phone out of his pocket and found the number he wanted. The person on the other end of the line answered, and Jack's voice was gruff as he spoke. 'We need to meet, no don't blow me off. You will meet with me *now*.' He hung up and stuffed his phone back into his pocket.

'What's going on Jack, who was that?' Stella felt frightened listening to him. Who was he going to meet?

'Never you mind—this is my problem and I'll sort it out.'

'Jack, it is *our* problem. I can help you.' They were standing at the door to the building now.

'Please don't block me out, we need to get through this together,' she pleaded.

'I will not have you impacted anymore. Just go home and let me do what I need to do.'

'Don't dismiss me like that, it is very condescending and I won't stand for it.'

'Milly is my EA and as her boss, and yours, it is my duty to fix this.'

'Your duty? For god's sake Jack, can you hear yourself? This isn't the 18th century. I don't need you to ride in on your stallion and save the day. I am perfectly capable of fighting my own battles.'

He ignored her, looking over his shoulder to the street beyond. 'I need to go. We'll talk about this later. Just stay out of it.'

'Fine Jack, you go and sort it out.' Tears prickled behind her eyes and she turned away from him.

'Stella, please don't be like that.' He stepped towards her, moving as if to take her arm. She took a step back. 'I see, it's like that now is it,' he turned and headed out of the building.

❧

The silence was deafening now he had gone and she crept back to her desk, dodging as many colleagues as she could along the way. She collapsed into her chair and called Jaz. 'Stella this is crazy, get out of your office and come over—now.'

CHAPTER 41

Jack was furious. The argument he'd had with Stella had been going around and around in his head since he had left her at the office. And now he couldn't find a parking spot.

'Why is there never any parking in this fucking suburb?!' he yelled. Anytime he had to come to the inner western suburbs of Sydney it riled him up. The street he wanted to park in was full so he ended up about a block away. The walk from his car to Eleanor's apartment did nothing to cool his temper.

He rang the buzzer, not even sure if she would let him in but the door opened and he took the stairs two at a time. The door to her apartment was open and she was standing there waiting for him.

'What is this Jack, how dare you demand to come here?' Eleanor said as he pushed past her. 'Hey, what the hell?'

'What I want to know Eleanor is *why*?'

'Why *what*, Jack?' She glared at him with her hands on her hips.

'Why have you and Milly stitched me and Stella up? We have done what, *exactly*, to you both?'

'What are you talking about Jack, you come barging in here making no sense at all—how should I know what Milly has done and why is it any of my business?'

'That crazy bitch has made all sorts of allegations and I think you're in on it too.'

'What the hell are you talking about? What allegations? You're the one who is crazy here Jack.' He proceeded to tell her everything and her face paled as he spoke.

'Jack, you have to believe me, I had no idea. Why the hell would I ask her to do any of this? It makes no sense. You and I broke up ages ago and I admit I handled it badly and I should have never gone on that hike, but I'm certainly not after any sort of revenge.' She rolled her eyes. 'God, you have to give me more credit than that. Get over yourself, you aren't the only man out there and I'm sure as hell not sitting around here pining for you.'

'I don't know. Maybe you're jealous and trying to screw with me.' He couldn't deny that Eleanor's bark of laughter stung his ego just a bit.

'I have some self-respect left.' Eleanor shrugged, holding the door open. 'I said what I needed to say on the hike. Messing around with an employee was always going to catch up with you, Jack.' This conversation wasn't going at all how he'd expected. He ran a hand through his hair, his mind whirling.

'She's taken *photos* of us, and accused me of threatening her.' Eleanor chewed her lip and looked like she was taking his concern a little more seriously now.

'Please, Eleanor, if you have some other explanation for why Milly is screwing with us, I would love to hear it.' Just as Eleanor was about to open her mouth, she was cut off.

'Oh Jack, of course she wouldn't have figured it out, she is so fucking stupid just like you and Stella.' Milly, her hair dishevelled and eyes sparkling, had appeared in the still open doorway to Eleanor's apartment.

'Milly, what are you doing here and how the hell did you get in to my building?' gasped Eleanor.

'I got lucky. One of your neighbours was leaving when I got here and I slipped in.'

'How did you know I was even here?' Eleanor backed away from Milly, her eyes wide.

'Eleanor, I'm not stupid. I saw the lights on in your apartment.'

'What do you want anyway?' Eleanor spoke, her voice cold. It was as if she had regained some of her confidence and remembered that this was *her* apartment. Jack felt a prickle of guilt at having invaded it, now that it was clear Eleanor was just as in the dark about Milly's motivations as he was.

'To make you pay.' Milly stepped forward, blocking the doorway.

'Pay, pay for what?' Eleanor glanced at Jack, which only seemed to infuriate Milly further.

'Don't look at him Eleanor! I'm talking to you. I knew he wasn't for you and would never love you like you loved him. I would have loved you and still love you but no, you were never going to be interested being my best friend were you, Eleanor? You just used me to get to Jack so you could find out what he was up to. Or what he was doing with Stella. You're a manipulative bitch.'

The colour had drained out of Eleanor's face now. 'I don't understand Milly, you did all of it just so we could be best friends?'

'You must have known. All the kind things I did for you, gifts I bought you, but it was never enough, was it? All I ever wanted was a best friend, someone who always had my back and wanted to hang out with me. I've never had that. No one has ever liked me my whole life and then I met you and I really thought that you liked me and you would be different. But no, you just used me like everyone else.'

She then turned towards Jack. Her eyes were round, in mock surprise. 'Well, well, well, what a bonus you being here.'

'Milly I—'

'Shut the fuck up Jack and listen to me, just for once.' She pointed at him and he felt silenced by her fury. 'Why didn't you stand up for me or see how horrible Stella was being to me? No, you just took her side and left me hanging. Then I get hauled into HR and told my job is on the line. I've worked for you so much longer and yet you took her side the instant she walked into our office.'

'Milly, please can we all sit down and talk about this?' Jack had finally found his voice. The girl was out of her mind and he needed to calm her down before things escalated.

'No, it's too late for that, way too late.' She started crying then, heaving sobs that seemed to come from some place deep inside her.

'Milly, stop, please talk to me. It isn't too late I'm here now,' he pleaded with her, taking a step toward her, palms raised.

'I have nothing more to say to either of you. Nothing you can say or do will ever change how you have made me feel. You two make me sick. You go through life taking what you want, never caring about who you hurt along the way. HR is just the beginning, soon you'll regret every time you dismissed me.' She sniffed and wiped her nose on her sleeve as she fumbled for the door. Then she was gone, slamming the door behind her.

'Oh my god Jack, what just happened?' Eleanor trembled.

'Look, let's sit down for a moment—' Jack felt like his legs were going to give up on him. They both sat at the little table in her dining room and Jack took a few steadying breaths. 'She is angry but I don't think she would ever harm either of us. Perhaps she will feel better now she has got it all off her chest?' Even to his ears the words seemed hollow.

Milly had always seemed quite highly strung and emotional, but hadn't raised any real concerns.

'I hope she's okay and heading somewhere safe to cool down,' Eleanor said, looking back towards the door, as if expecting Milly to burst through it again.

It was getting late now and Jack said he would head home.

'I'll check in with you tomorrow. Try not to worry too much about this. I think it's mainly Stella and I she is trying to punish. By putting in this complaint to HR I think she thinks she will be able to keep her job and see us out the door.' Jack grimaced at the thought. 'That is never going to happen, especially once I tell Dylan and Tyler what just happened here. They may even call you in to verify the story, are you happy to do that?' Eleanor appeared to still be dealing with the shock of this evening, but nodded her consent.

CHAPTER 42

Rage pulsed through Milly as she left Eleanor's building. *Bastards, I hope the three of them all rot in hell.* She jogged down the street and then turned into the main road. Pushing past people, she didn't care who she bumped in to.

'Hey, watch it girl,' someone snapped as her bag hit them on the shoulder.

She didn't apologise or make eye contact, she just kept on moving forward. Fumbling around in her bag she found her phone and started to type out a text to Eleanor. She let loose with a tirade of abuse and then deleted that and wrote something nice and then deleted that. Why couldn't she ever get things right? The tears poured down her face as she thought of the lost friendship.

'Oh god what's the point.' She threw her phone into a rubbish bin on the side of the road.

It was raining heavily now and she couldn't tell what was tears and what was the rain. Wiping at her eyes, she looked down the road and could see a bus headed toward the city. Perhaps she would take it and go into the office. No one would be there and she could use the place to come up with a plan. Despite all her threats, she hadn't thought through what she would do next. Beyond the complaint she'd already made to HR, what options did she have left?

The bus was getting closer so she decided to make a dash across the road. Keeping her eyes firmly on the approaching bus she stepped out between a parked car.

Brakes screeched and Milly felt herself flying through the air.

It actually felt quite peaceful. She closed her eyes.

With a thud, she hit the wet road and horrified onlookers came running. From the awkward angle she was lying in and the blood trickling from her mouth, they knew right away, she was gone.

⁊⟡

Some hours later, Jack received a call from the local police station. They had not been able to contact any family and had found one of Jack's business cards in Milly's bag. He had the grim task of going down to the city morgue to identify her. The whole thing had seemed surreal. He had nodded as they had pulled the sheet back, revealing the face he knew so well.

Back at the station, he gave a statement on the events as he knew them up to her accident. Eleanor was also called in and gave her version as well. It was a sombre moment as they both sat afterwards on the plastic seats waiting to be told they could go.

'I don't believe it, she's gone.' Eleanor started crying.

'I know, it is a huge shock.' Jack took her hand, offering a tiny bit of comfort was the least he could do.

'Do you think she did it on purpose? Did we upset her that much?'

'No, there were other witnesses who saw her run across the road without looking into the path of that car. It was so wet, even if the driver had seen her earlier, there was no chance they could have stopped.'

'Do you think she suffered? Was she lying there all by herself as her life slipped away?'

'Don't do that to yourself. From what they told me, she died instantly.' He hoped it was true.

'Oh Jack, this is awful. I just want to go home.' She took a shuddering sigh and rummaged in her bag for some tissues.

'It won't be long now I'm sure.' He looked up and down the hallway, hoping to see the officer who was on this case.

❧

Eleanor had been given a ride home by one of the police on duty. When Jack finally turned into his driveway, he sat in his car with his head in his hands. What a truly awful situation this was and he shook his head.

He replayed the events over and over. Could he have handled the situation with Milly any differently? He wasn't sure. Despite what he'd said to Eleanor, he felt guilty. Oh God, how would the rest of the staff feel when the news was broken to them?

When he thought back even though he had been annoyed with her prying into his private life he had never thought she was any more than just over protective or a bit nosey. No wonder she'd felt like she did when she had sat back and watched him form such a close bond with Stella in such a short time. *She must have felt so hurt,* he thought. He had never taken the time with her, or thanked her for her service over the years and for this he would always feel guilty.

He knew he had to call Stella but just didn't know how to tell her what had happened and he still was struggling to process it himself. As the new day dawned, he realised he was still unable to pick up the phone and call her.

CHAPTER 43

Stella, Jaz and Liz sat up all night talking about Jack. She filled them on everything. And when she got to the part about being hauled into HR and told them about the photos, they were stunned.

'Really?' said Liz eventually.

'Yep, can you believe it?'

'Surely not?' said Jaz. 'How can this Milly be so vindictive?' What did you ever do to her to deserve this?

'Oh, trust me, she's a piece of work, I can tell you.' She was sick of thinking about Milly, Jack and everything. 'Look, can we just change the subject? How's your holiday going Liz?' asked Stella.

'Well to be honest with you both, I'm thinking of extending it. I really have nothing to rush home for now Colin is gone.' Tears formed in Liz's eyes as she thought of her husband and Stella patted her friend's knee. 'I miss him so much and wandering around our place by myself, well, it's so hard. I keep thinking he's still in the hospital and will be coming back and then it hits me that he has gone for good.' Her face crumpled and she rubbed her hands across her eyes to wipe away the tears. Liz took a steadying breath before she continued, 'I've booked a trip to Queensland and I'm planning on staying up there for a few weeks. Any chance either of you would be free to join me?'

Jaz shook her head. If she could have taken the time, she would have in a heartbeat, but she knew it was pointless asking her boss due to her current work load. Stella regretted having to decline too.

'Nothing would give me more pleasure than to escape for a couple of weeks but with this whole HR thing hanging over me, I have been told to work from home and there is no way I could ask for time off. But my friend Tim is living up there Liz, he used to work with me. I'll give him a call and perhaps he can show you the sights. I'm sure he wouldn't mind a visitor.'

It was late and Stella decided to stay at Jaz's. Getting into the bed in her friend's spare room, her mind drifted back to the last words she had had with Jack. It had been their first argument and she had seen how stubborn he was. *Just like me*, she thought ruefully.

At 7.00am her phone rang. Half asleep, she fumbled and picked up her phone.

'Hi Jack,' she said sleepily.

'Sorry to wake you so early but you need to come into the office. Can you be there by 9.00am?' he asked in a terse voice.

'Yes, sure, I will be there. Is everything okay? You sound weird.'

'I can't get into it now.' He sounded so dismissive that she felt her hackles rising.

'You can't just call me and then order me into the office.'

'Look something has happened and I can't get into it now.'

'I don't want to walk in unprepared—I don't like ambushes. Just tell me, is it something to do with Milly? Is she okay? Are you okay? You have to give me something,' she pleaded.

'I will see you at 9.00am,' he said firmly and hung up.

She was alternating between fear and anger now. How dare he treat her like this? The more she thought about it the more it riled her up.

She started getting ready for the day, helping herself quietly to Jaz's extensive tea collection in the kitchen.

'Where are you going?' Jaz asked, yawning as she came into the room.

'Sorry, I didn't need mean to wake you up, I just had a call from Jack, I have been ordered to be in the office by 9.00am.'

'Ordered?' Jaz arched an eyebrow.

'Yes, I was told in no uncertain terms that I had to be in there by 9.00am.'

'Why? Did he tell you anything?'

'No, not one single thing. I can only assume it has to do with the case Milly has against us, but I'm not sure. I'm scared Jaz—I have never heard him like this before.' Stella's stomach turned in knots.

'I have to go but I'll call you later,' and with that she hugged Jaz goodbye and headed for the office.

CHAPTER 44

The office seemed to be deserted as Stella arrived. Looking around, she wasn't sure where to go. Her phone pinged with a text: *We are in the board room, come straight here when you arrive.* We? Who would be there? Jack and Dylan, would Tyler be there? Oh my god, perhaps Milly was there as well. Stella was shaking like a leaf as she headed in that direction.

Pushing open the door she looked around and saw Jack, Dylan and Tyler.

'Take a seat, Stella.' She sat where Dylan had indicated. She crossed her legs to stop them shaking.

'I'm sorry, but there is no easy way to say this, last night there was a terrible car accident and Milly was killed.' Stella gasped and put her hand over her mouth. Milly was dead? 'I know this has come as a huge shock but I wanted to let you know before I tell the rest of the staff,' Dylan said.

'There is something else Stella and it isn't easy for me to tell you this...' Dylan swallowed. 'When the police went to her house, they found something quite disturbing. It appears that the photo's Milly took of yourself and Jack in Fiji were just the tip of the iceberg.'

'What do you mean?'

'Now these photos,' he opened his laptop and pulled up a picture of Milly's room.

'Oh my god, there are so many of them,' said Stella. Her stomach felt like it had been doused in ice. There were photos of the day she started working here, her and Jack down at the park having lunch, the gala dinner, and Fiji. How had she managed to take so many photos without her and Jack noticing?

'I still don't understand,' said Stella blinking at Dylan.

She could hear Dylan talking but she couldn't focus. All she could think about was the fact that Milly was gone due to that awful accident. She had so many questions and knew that a lot of them would remain unanswered which made this so much harder to process.

How can I stay here? thought Stella. There was no way she could just keep working here like nothing had happened. Every day she would have to look at Milly's desk knowing that she was never coming back. Just last night she'd called the girl a "piece of work". She couldn't bear it.

Stella stood suddenly, her chair squeaking against the board room floor. 'I can't continue working here. It is just too much for me to deal with, I'm sorry. I know I have to give four weeks' notice, but I hope under the circumstances you will let me finish up earlier than that.' She couldn't breathe and was anxious to get out of this room. She avoided Jack's gaze as she spoke.

'I don't want you to leave,' said Dylan. 'Is there any way we can convince you to stay?'

'No, I am sorry but I have to leave. It will be impossible for me to stay here, given these circumstances. Now if you will please excuse me.' She left the room and headed straight to her desk.

❧

She planned on working from home up until her last day and started packing her things. Throughout the day as she looked up and saw Milly's empty desk, she felt dreadful. Out of the corner of her eye, she saw Jack approaching.

'Can't you give it a try for a little while? This feels like a rash decision.'

'I can't stay here Jack, I'm sorry.' She continued to put things into her bag.

'Well, what does that mean for us?'

She paused her packing and looked at him. 'I'm not sure. I need to take some time to figure it all out.'

'Can I at least call you later?'

'Probably best you don't. Let's just put some distance between us for a while please, I just need some time alone.'

'I don't want to do that. We need to talk about all of this.' He'd stepped close, and she could feel the warmth of his body against her back, but she didn't dare turn and face him. Seeing his expression could break her resolve.

'For God's sake, Jack, Milly is dead. I need to process this, okay? There can be no "us" at the moment.'

'Who do you think they called to identify her body, Stella? Me. Try processing that. There was no one else, she died alone and the person who had to identify her was her boss. Do you have any idea how incredibly sad I felt when I looked at her lifeless body that night at the morgue? It broke my heart that she had no one else looking out for her, no one.' and he dropped his head. 'Despite everything she has done to me, to us, she was a very mixed-up young girl and I will feel guilty for the rest of my life that somehow, I let her down. All the awful things I said about her, they go around in my head constantly.' Jack took a deep breath. 'Did Dylan tell you the whole story?' She shook her head. 'She confronted Eleanor and I at her place. She was in a bad way.'

'That was where you went that night?'

'Yes, I went to talk to her, confront her and see if she knew why Milly had it in for us. She had no idea but then Milly barged in and told us that we had all disappointed her and let her down. All she had wanted from Eleanor was friendship—said she had never had a best friend, someone who truly had her back. She was pissed off with me because when you started, we struck up a friendship and I had never offered her that. That's why she hated you, because I had become friends with you and had never tried to get to know my own EA. Next thing I know, the police ring, telling me she has been run over. Eleanor and I got called in to make statements—it was horrendous.'

'How is Eleanor taking all of this?' Stella had turned around by now and couldn't help but feel concerned about her.

'She's a bloody mess and blaming herself. Both of our lives have been fucked up now by the events that played out that night. I'm really worried about Eleanor's mental health. I'm going to call her and check how she's going later.'

Stella blanched, 'This is exactly why we need to take some time out. You need time to deal with all of this ...' She pulled her box of desk supplies into her arms. 'Look, I have to go. I'm sorry. Goodbye Jack.'

CHAPTER 45

When she got back to her place she collapsed on her bed and cried her heart out. She couldn't believe that Milly was gone. Then she thought of those photos. Some of them were quite disturbing. Milly had cut many of them up and placed them into a grotesque collage. It made her shiver just thinking about it. Her phone buzzed and it was Jaz. She really didn't want to talk but knew that there was never going to be a better time so she picked up.

'Stella, what's happening? I've been waiting for hours to hear from you.'

'Milly is dead.' The words sounded hollow even to her own ears. There was a deafening silence.

'What do you mean she is dead?' asked Jaz.

'There was a dreadful accident—she ran out in front of a car and was killed.'

'Oh god. How awful.'

'It gets worse,' said Stella.

'How can it get any worse than this Stella?'

'Apparently Milly had been taking photos of Jack and I for months and had them displayed in one of her spare rooms.'

'More photos?' asked Jaz.

'Yes,' Stella's eyes felt hot with tears. 'She had placed them rather creatively into a collage,' she closed her eyes to hold it together as that vision rushed past her eyes.

'So, what's happening now?' asked Jaz.

'I just had a meeting with Jack and Dylan and I resigned.'

'Why would you do that? You loved that job,' said Jaz.

'I did love it, but there is no way I can stay there with all of this mess.'

'What about Jack, what's going on with all of that? asked Jaz.

'I told him we needed to take a break. Process what has just happened. I just can't talk to him at the moment. I'm going to be working from home up until I leave so may be that will give us both some breathing space. Look Jaz, I'm exhausted I have to go; I'll chat to you later.' With that she hung up.

CHAPTER 46

Stella had returned to the office to drop her laptop off and hoped to get the hell out of there before she saw him.

The phone buzzed on her desk and she could see it was Jack's line.

She didn't want to answer the call but as he could see her desk from his office, she really had no choice.

'Hello, how can I help you?'

'As it is your last day, I thought we could have lunch, perhaps down in the park? For old time's sake,' Jack said. Part of her wanted to say yes and the other part was saying no. There wasn't going to be a happy ending no matter what she said. He must have sensed her indecision, so he made the choice easy for her. 'I'll take that as a yes, Stella. I'll come past your desk at 12.30pm.'

Watching the time tick past for the rest of the morning, she was so churned up and was pretty sure she wouldn't be able to eat a thing. Why was he asking her for lunch? All she wanted to do was just slip out at the end of the day and never see him or anyone else from this place ever again.

'Ready to go?' She jumped at his voice.

'Um, yes, as ready as I'll ever be,' she mumbled to herself.

They picked up sandwiches and then headed to their favourite spot. Neither of them knew what to say and they both just pretended to be focussing on getting their food out. Looking at him out of the corner of her eye she could see that clearly he wasn't hungry either.

'Can I get you to change your mind, Stella? It isn't too late. Please stay.'

Shaking her head, she told him that the answer was still no, she had to have a clean start. He sighed and set his sandwich aside, the pretence of eating abandoned.

'I'm going to miss you. You know that right?'

'I will miss working with you too Jack, we made a great team.' Her smile felt forced.

'I like to think that it wasn't just at work. For a minute there, didn't it feel like we had a future together?' She hated the pain in his eyes, knowing she was responsible for putting it there.

'I thought so too there for a while.' Her voice was soft, but firm. 'But I just don't think it is meant to be.'

'Why? Help me to understand.'

She had hoped to avoid all of the ugliness from her past but then decided to tell him as by now she really had nothing to lose.

'Jack, I'm a disaster when it comes to relationships. I always seem to choose the wrong men and then I get hurt. I can't keep doing this.'

'How do you know it will happen with me?' he asked.

'Because this is just how it started with Marcus.' There, it was out in the open now. 'We met at work and dated. Eventually, we got engaged. He was younger than me, just like you. It ended up being a disaster. We grew apart and then my mum finished it off like she always did with any of my relationships.'

'Your mum? What's she got to do with this?'

'She has everything to do with it.' Her voice rose as the pain rolled through her and then it all came tumbling out. 'My mum never loved me, Jack. She hated me from the day I was born. She told me on a daily basis how much she hated me, no one could ever love me, I would always be by myself. She told me I would never have any sort of job because I wasn't clever enough. Jack, I couldn't even have a pet—I had a kitten and she took it away from me.' She was crying now.

'Jesus, I'm so sorry to hear all of this.' He shuffled along the bench to be closer to her, but she was relieved he didn't touch her. Right now, she felt too raw and even the thought of a kind touch made her recoil. She swiped at the tears falling down her cheeks.

'I don't deserve you. Look at you and look at me. How can you possibly find anything to like? I'm too old for you. Stop wasting your time and go and find someone else.'

His hands bunched into fists, his knuckles white. 'Despite what your mum did, look at the person you turned into. You are kind, clever and I want you in my life.'

'You know nothing about my mum and I.'

'I know she destroyed your confidence; you need to let her go Stella. It's eating you up and you can't keep pushing me away.'

She stood up. 'You'll never understand. Please, just leave me alone. Whatever this was, it's over now.' Her heart was loud in her ears as she left him sitting in the park.

She didn't go back to the office, she just couldn't. Besides, it was her last day, it wasn't like they could fire her.

When she got home, she called Jaz and told her she had ended things once and for all.

'Stella, you need to slow down and think this through,' said Jaz.

'No, it's done now. I really think it's for the best.'

CHAPTER 47

It had been three months now since Stella had ended things with Jack and Lindy worried about her. She wished one of them would break the ice and contact the other, but the way it was looking, that was never going to happen. They were both as stubborn as mules.

Taking things into her own hands, she had lunch with Stella.

'It's good to see you Lindy,' Stella said as she gave her a hug. 'How're Paul and the kids?'

'They're okay but missing you. We all are.'

'I miss you guys so much, you know that, right?'

'Of course I do. Still, you should come around to the house and see us some time.'

Stella fidgeted with the cutlery on the table as she spoke, avoiding meeting Lindy's eyes. 'I would love to but it feels weird doing that without Jack. Plus, I'd worry that he'd show up there too and I just can't face him.'

'Look, it's been ages now since you have seen him, why don't you call him?'

'How can I, after everything I said to him? I'm sure I'm the last person he'd want to hear from.'

'How do you know that? Perhaps a catch up to try and clear the air would be good for your both.'

'What's the point? It's done now and we just both have to move on with our lives.' Stella sighed and their food arrived as a welcome distraction from the heaviness of the moment. Once the waiter had left, Lindy leaned forward, not willing to let this drop just yet.

'After everything you went through, why would you give up so easily?'

'What else can I do? It feels like if it was meant to be, it wouldn't have been so hard.'

'Oh Stella,' Lindy's heart ached for her friend. 'What you said couldn't be further from the truth. From the moment Jack met you his heart belonged to you and yours to him. Don't even try and deny that.'

'Perhaps that was once true but I don't think that anymore.' She frowned down at her potato rosti. Lindy shrugged and turned to her own food, a plan formulating in the back of her mind.

'I still think you should call him. Or… do you want me to speak to him and get him to call you?'

Stella's eyes flashed. 'Don't you dare do that—promise me Lindy. I will never speak to you ever again if you do.'

'Okay, I promise,' Lindy said, crossing her fingers beneath the table. 'What else has been going on? Are you working yet?'

Stella seemed relieved by the change in conversation, her shoulders relaxing. 'Yes, I am actually, I managed to get a temp role so that's keeping me busy.'

'Temping? Are you still hoping to go back to McGregor and Bailey?'

'I loved that job but that ship has well and truly sailed now sadly.'

'Would you go back if Jack wasn't there?'

'Is he leaving?' Stella leaned forward; alarm clear on her face. Lindy patted her hand reassuringly.

'No, he isn't, but I just wondered if that would change anything.'

'It would make no difference, way too many memories there.'

'Yeah, I guess so. That whole business with his EA was dreadful. Well, I hope this new role works out and maybe you'll decide to stay on.'

'Maybe...' Stella said uncertainly.

'Well, the kids will be home in a couple of hours so I guess I had better go.'

'Thanks for today, Lindy, it was great to see you.'

'Don't be a stranger Stella, call me or pop over anytime, you are always welcome. In fact, I may call you should we ever get stuck and need a babysitter. It's getting harder to lock in my parents now, and the kids love you.'

'Of course, anytime, I would be happy to help out'.

⚜

Jack knew that he'd been shutting everyone out, especially Paul. He had wanted to contact him but every time he did, he couldn't help but think about Stella. She was such good friends with Lindy now so he assumed they would still be catching up. Did Stella still think about him? Or talk to Lindy about him? It wasn't like he could ask Lindy, or Paul, for that matter—he didn't want to appear desperate.

He knew damn well he could pick up the phone and call Stella and he almost had, many a time, but her last words to him still haunted him so he would put his phone down again.

A few days later, he had had a really awful day so decided he would finally reach out to Paul.

'How the hell are you? I had begun to think that you had dropped off the planet,' he laughed.

'I know, I've been slack mate. I should have called but, well, you know, things have been crazy with work...' and he petered off before he said what he really wanted to—that things were still crap with him and Stella.

'I was hoping we could catch up for a beer, any chance you are free tonight?'

'Your timing couldn't have been better. Lindy is going out tonight with the kids so I am at a loose end. What time do you want to meet up?'

'I'm still in the city so how about in an hour? I'll meet you down at the usual pub.'

'Sure, sounds great.'

❦

Traffic was bad but when Paul arrived, he soon spotted Jack at their usual table.

'Do you want one?' Jack offered.

'No, I'm good.'

Jack headed to the bar and then pulled up a stool, beer in hand.

'Cheers mate—it's good to see you,' said Paul.

'I know it's been a while and I'm sorry about that. Just haven't fancied any company.'

'Yeah, I know, things have been pretty messed up.'

That was an understatement. Jack took a long pull from his beer. 'What have you been up to? Hopefully not just working 24/7?'

'I've been throwing myself into work, I must admit but also doing some renovations at home. Between both of these things, I don't have a lot of down time.' Paul put his beer down and quirked a brow. 'How's things in the office?'

'Settling down again—it was pretty rough there for a while. Everyone was so shocked and then there was the funeral…'

'Yeah, it was pretty full on about Milly, I still can't believe what went down.' Paul shook his head.

'Have you found a replacement for Stella's role yet?' He looked over the rim of his glass before taking a sip.

There was a slight pause and Jack swallowed. 'Ah, we have a temp at the moment, nice bloke and he fits in well with the rest of the team.'

'Is he temping because you think Stella may come back?'

'No. She made it clear she won't be back.' Jack took a sip of his beer.

'Have you thought about contacting her?'

'And say what exactly? She made it clear that things were over between us. She doesn't want the job and she sure as hell doesn't want me. Can we just leave it?'

'That was months ago mate, and after what you had both been through, surely it was to be expected in some way. It was a lot to process for the both of you. Perhaps she was right and you needed some time out?'

'What I don't understand is why we couldn't have worked through it together? I would have been happy to try that but she shut that idea down straight away.'

'Perhaps that was just her way of coping—not everyone deals with things the way you do. Stella is strong, but everyone has their breaking point. Even you. Ask her out, meet up for a drink, someone has to make the first move.'

'Nah, I don't think she'd be interested now, too much happened. It's too late for us.' Jack took the last sip of his beer. Paul watched the beads of condensation run down Jack's beer bottle and puddle on the tabletop.

'That's bullshit. From the moment you guys met there were sparks. You know deep down that she's the only woman for you. Why let that go so easily? Fight for her, win her back. It isn't like you to give up this easily mate.'

Jack ran a hand through his hair. 'If she rejects me again, I don't know if I can handle it. It nearly broke me when she walked away from me that day in the park. I've barely survived losing her once, to lose her again, I just can't take that risk.'

Paul left it there. Clearly, he was broken and he had no idea on how to help his friend out. There was no way Jack was going to make the first move, he was well and truly defeated. It all looked so hopeless.

CHAPTER 48

'This is nuts Paul, he has to shake himself out of this depression,' said Lindy after Paul had got home and told her Jack was in such bad shape.

'I know, I tried to get him to ring her and I'm out of ideas.' He shrugged and turned back to his videogame. Lindy stood in front of the TV, hands on hips.

She gave him the look.

'Oh no, please tell me that you aren't thinking of interfering?' he groaned. 'You know what happened last time you did that. That BBQ was almost a disaster. Jack was less than impressed with you. You put them both on the spot and I'm not sure either of them has ever forgotten that night.'

Lindy sighed and flopped next to her husband on the couch. She rested her head on his shoulder. 'No, maybe, I don't know, but I can't bear to see them like this. I feel like we need to do something to help. If neither of them will make the first move perhaps we need to?'

'Whatever you're thinking, please be careful.' He didn't want Lindy pushing their friends over the edge with one of her harebrained ideas. From the next room, he heard the sound of kids squabbling and dropped a kiss on Lindy's head as he went to sort it out.

⁂

After he had walked away, Lindy picked up her phone and dialled. Job done, she couldn't help but feel pleased with herself. A prickle of guilt stirred in her stomach, but she quickly dismissed it. This was not interfering. She was just looking out for her friends… right?

'Paul, where are you?' Lindy called.

'Here,' and he came in the back door, looking slightly exasperated after what she assumed had been a more severe fight between the siblings.

'I've just had a brilliant idea, let's go out next Saturday night? We could do with a break and perhaps have a romantic night ourselves.' She wiggled her eyebrows suggestively.

'Sounds good but what about the kids? Didn't you say your parents are still away?'

'I've just arranged a babysitter which is great news isn't it?'

'Who is coming over?' Paul's eyes narrowed in suspicion.

'Just a friend,' she never mentioned a name and nor did he ask, the kids calling for their attention once more. They both headed for the backyard.

'I've booked us a table at our favourite place. We need to be there by 7.30pm so the sitter will be here by 7.00pm.'

'Great, it sounds like you have it all sorted. It'll be nice to have a night out by ourselves.' He kissed her on the cheek.

⁂

Saturday night rolled around and when the doorbell rang, Paul answered the door. He stopped in his tracks when he saw who it was.

'Mate, this is a surprise. We are actually going out.'

243

'I know, that's why I am here. Didn't Lindy tell you? She asked me to babysit.'

'She told me she had arranged a babysitter but didn't say it was you.' Paul felt a little uneasy and prickles ran up and down his spine. Jack didn't seem to share the sentiment, stepping inside the house and slapping Paul on the shoulder.

'Lindy mentioned her parents are still away and that it's been difficult to find sitters, so I offered. You guys should have said something, you know I would always come over and help out.'

'I know, but with everything going on, we didn't want to bother you. You have enough on your plate without having to look after our kids.'

Jack grimaced. 'Sorry I've been such a sad sack. Having friends like you has been a lifesaver. I'm actually starting to feel a lot better now so expect to see a lot more of me.'

Paul showed Jack through to the lounge and the kids came running in. Lindy hadn't told them who was babysitting and when they saw their uncle Jack there were bear hugs all around. Paul loved to see how good his friend was with his kids, maybe this would all work out fine.

The doorbell rang again and Jack raised an eyebrow.

'I'll get it,' called Lindy, breezing through the room, affixing her earrings. They could hear muffled voices at the door. Paul felt the prickle of unease grow. What was his wife up to?

※

Jack nearly fell through the floor when Lindy re-entered the lounge room and following behind her was Stella. Their eyes locked and kudos to her, she hid the shock well.

The kids missed all the tension in the room. 'Stella!' They ran towards her engulfing her in big hugs.

'Hi guys, how are you?'

'We didn't know that you were going to be babysitting us with Uncle Jack.'

'Neither did I,' she mumbled. 'Isn't it a lovely surprise?' Stella's eyes burned into Lindy's. It didn't seem to bother her.

'Well, now you're both here, Paul and I should go or we will miss our reservation.' She herded Paul quickly to their front door, 'Have a great night and be good,' she called out to the kids and then they were gone. Jack and Stella stood there then in the middle of the lounge staring at each other neither knowing what to say or do.

❧

As Paul and Lindy drove away, Paul turned to Lindy and chuckled.

'What have you done?'

'What was needed Paul,' she said primly, but then grinned. 'Now, let's get to the restaurant, I'm starving.'

CHAPTER 49

'Hello Stella,' Jack said. His mouth felt like it had been filled with cotton, and he was aware of the sweat beading on the back of his neck. He tried for a bit of lightness, but his laugh came out too high. 'Well, this is awkward, isn't it? I didn't expect to see you here tonight.' He clasped his hands together so they weren't just hanging uselessly by his side.

'I never expected to see you either. Quite a surprise, I must say.' Stella crossed her arms.

'Well, I guess we are sharing the responsibility tonight then,' he smiled at her, but she didn't return it.

'Looks like it.' She headed towards the couch. He caught a glimpse of her hands, despite her apparent composure, they were trembling. He sat down on one of the chairs facing her.

'How have you been?'

'Good thanks and you?'

'I'm good.' It was hard to look at her, she was so gorgeous, so he looked at a spot above her head.

'I guess you've been busy at work?' she asked.

'Work is busy as always, well, you know that first hand.' He laughed nervously. Where were the kids when you needed them?

A buffer would have been most welcome, but Paul and Lindy's children had become absorbed again by their toys in the next room.

'Ah yes, never a dull moment at that place.' Her laugh seemed nervous too.

'So, what have you been up to? Have you found a new job yet?'

'Yes, I have, just a temping role but it's going okay. They may ask me to stay.'

'Well, that's good to hear.'

There was an awkward silence between them now and Jack found himself wishing even more that the kids would reappear and demand attention soon.

'Oh, I'm doing some renovations at my house so that's also keeping me busy,' he offered feeling like work was a dangerous topic to focus on for too long.

'Renovating, what are you doing? I don't remember you mentioning you were planning on that?'

'Just a few bits and pieces.'

'Oh well, keeps you out of trouble then.'

'Perhaps I like trouble.' The words escaped before he could snatch them back. Had he overstepped? But from the beautiful blush spread over her cheeks, it would appear not.

'Well, you do seem to attract it.'

'Yes, I do. It isn't always bad, you know.' He felt a subtle shift, as the mood in the room lightened.

With typical perfect timing, the kids interrupted them and they spent the rest of the night playing games with them until it was time for them to go to bed. Jack helped Neil get ready for bed and as he left his room, stopped outside the girl's room where Stella was reading them a story.

The younger girl, Mia, asked, 'Are you going to marry Uncle Jack?'

Through the gap in the doorway, Jack could see Stella's face flush bright red.

'We think he likes you,' piped up the older girl, Bree. She giggled.

'Do you now?' Stella smiled at them.

'Do you like him?' Mia asked, undeterred and both girls sat there, waiting for her answer as did Jack who found himself holding his breath.

'Yes, I do. He is great, isn't he?' Both girls nodded.

'So, are you going to get married? asked Mia.

'Well only if he asks me.' Stella seemed surprised by the words herself and closed the book. 'That's enough questions. It's time for bed,' she said.

Jack hurried back to the lounge so she wouldn't know what he had heard. He couldn't seem to wipe the smile from his face. She liked him, more than that, if she would hypothetically be willing to marry him. For the first time in months, hope flared to life in his heart.

❧

As they left Paul and Lindy's that night, Jack gathered up the courage and asked Stella if she would have dinner with him soon.

'It's a great place, you will love it,' he added.

'That sounds great, I would love to.'

'Are you free next Friday?' he asked.

'I am. Do you want me to meet you there?'

'No, I'll come and pick you up, if that's okay? It seems pointless for us both to take our cars.'

Stella smiled. 'Okay then it's a date. Oh sorry, that sounded presumptuous of me, didn't it? Perhaps you just meant dinner.' Her cheeks turned pink and she stared down at their feet. Gently, Jack tipped her head back with his finger under her chin so they could meet eyes again.

'Stella, it's definitely a date.'

⁂

Over the following weeks they spent more and more time together. Neither of them had actually come out and said they were now "exclusive", it was just assumed, but deep down they thought it would be nice to know where they stood with each other.

The question was verbalised one lazy Sunday afternoon while they lay in Stella's bed. 'Stella it's been four months now since we started dating so can I officially say that you're my girlfriend?'

'I was wondering what this was?' Before he could question her, she said, 'Just kidding.' He grumbled but kissed the top of her head. She wound her fingers through his, musing, 'So, I guess that means that you're my boyfriend?'

'Yes, it does, and you aren't going anywhere,' he tugged her closer and kissed her lips. 'I'm hoping you can come over this weekend, I have something special planned.'

'This sounds exciting,' she teased. He was the master of mystery dates and she adored him for it.

'Look, do you want to come on this date or not? Yes, or no?'

'Yes.'

Jack winked, 'It's a sleepover, but I doubt there will be a lot of sleeping. Oh, and pack light.'

'Any other instructions?' Stella asked.

'No, not really, though perhaps get a few early nights in before. I expect you this coming Friday night at my place for dinner and I might consider letting you leave… on Sunday night, after dinner.'

'Mm, I'm liking the sound of this long date,' said Stella.

⁂

Stella started mentally going through her current underwear collection and sighed. Nothing seemed quite right for this date so she decided she would pop into Victoria's Secret.

'Why are you smiling?' he broke into her thoughts.

'No reason, just happy to be here with you.' He leaned over and took her hand and squeezed it. Something better came into her mind then and she wondered if she had the guts to pull it off! Victoria's Secret could wait.

CHAPTER 50

That weekend, Stella pulled into Jack's driveway. As she picked her bag up and started walking towards the front door she was suddenly rocked with a bad case of nerves and stopped.

What the hell am I doing? she thought. She half-turned back towards her car, catching a glimpse of her reflection in the dark tinted windows. Self-doubt tendrils probed her brain. The familiar doubts about her age had come creeping back in these last few days. How did her body compare to someone younger? *Things aren't taut and don't sit where they used to when I was younger,* she thought.

Then again, he had already seen what she had on offer, a few times now, and he'd still asked her to stay for the weekend. Things couldn't be that bad! She shook her head and then walked with a new spring in her step, up to the front door and rang the bell.

❧

Jack had been watching her from his lounge window and wondered what the hell she was doing. It had looked like she was going to make a bolt for it and go home. What had rattled her? Maybe she didn't like him quite as much as he liked her. They'd been together a few times now and maybe she was losing interest in him. He was conscious of their age gap but it didn't matter to him at all. Perhaps it bothered her?

He shook his head to stop himself going down that path and when he looked out the window again, she was heading to the front door. When she knocked, he quickly opened the door, not wanting to give her time to change her mind and leave.

'Hey, beautiful. I'm so glad you're finally here.' He leaned in and kissed her. Her lips were warm and welcoming, tasting like the vanilla ChapStick he'd learned she was so fond of. Jack reached out and took her hand and pulled her into his hallway. As she shut the door, he spun her around so her back was up against the door and leaned in close. Kissing Stella was going to be the death of him, he was sure.

She was wearing a sexy black dress, low cut in the front and back. The high heels that accompanied the dress were impossibly high and showed off her calves. Jack loved a woman that had great legs in some killer heels—all he wanted to do was just rub his hands up and down those legs.

As he slipped his hand into the front of her dress something was on the edge of his mind and he couldn't quite grasp what it was. Like a bolt out of the blue, it hit him. He hadn't felt a bra! *Hmm*, he thought, *this is interesting*. As he ran his other hand up the side of the dress it started to ride up so he thought he would check out what kind of underwear she was wearing. He hoped it was black.

As his hand slid up from her thigh to her hip, it didn't connect with anything. His hand hit her waist and he slid his hand back down. *Oh, dear lord*. It had suddenly become very obvious that she wasn't wearing any underwear at all!

He looked at her and she smiled. She knew she'd got him. Jack said nothing, not one single thing. He simply slid his hands up her body and slowly turned her around so she was facing the door. He kissed her neck and continued kissing down her back to where the zip started. Stella thought she was going to pass out.

As Jack slid the zipper down and her dress dropped to the floor, Stella nearly lost it. She still had her back to him and could feel him pressing up against her and she could feel how hard he was and his breathing had increased as had hers, but still, neither of them spoke.

The only thing she still had on were those killer heels.

This whole thing was driving Jack crazy. He needed to get naked, now, so he could feel her skin on his. He let go of her briefly and tore his shirt off. Somehow, he managed to remove his jeans and boxers in one sweep. He was barefoot so now the two of them were naked, except for Stella's standing there in those damn heels.

'We need to get to my bedroom now or I'm going to slip in to you right now.'

He grabbed her hand and started backing her towards the stairs up to his bedroom. There seemed to be so many more stairs than Jack remembered. He wasn't sure he was going to make it there. He wanted her now.

He finally couldn't stand it anymore. Jack carefully lowered her down onto the stairs and straddled her. They inched up another couple of stairs and then had to stop again. It was torture. Surely they would never make it to a bedroom. At this stage he would have been happy just to make it to the landing. Somehow, someway, they did make it to the top of the stairs. Jack picked Stella up and burst into his room. He pushed her down onto his bed and entered her. In moments, they both climaxed. Desire satisfied, they both lay there trying to catch their breath. They had been together before, but not like this. With the barriers that had kept them apart finally crumbling to dust, their passion was growing in intensity.

Stella snuggled into his chest and said, 'I really like the way the weekend has started. I can see why you said clothing would not be required!'

CHAPTER 51

As they lay together on Jack's bed, Stella started laughing. 'What's so funny?'

'I was just thinking about how many bedrooms you have in this house and all the potential places to have sex this weekend,' she said.

Jack rolled towards her and caressed her breasts. 'I'm so looking forward to it.' Then he started moving both of his hands down her body. She grabbed his hands and pushed them away.

'Look, I know you're a fit young guy but you need to save your strength and pace yourself!' she laughed. Jack knew she was teasing him but he still took the bait.

'Don't worry about my stamina,' he said as he rolled her on to her back and started kissing her again.

❧

Sometime later, they hit pause and both declared that they needed food. Jack went downstairs and returned with a bottle of wine, a wedge of brie, and the fancy kind of crackers she'd always wanted to try. They cuddled up in his bed listening to some music while they ate and drank. Great wine, food and company, what else could you possibly want?

Jack traced his fingertips along her arm, his voice soft. 'Do you want me to cook something? Are you still hungry?'

'No, I'm fine. The cheese and biscuits have filled me up,' replied Stella.

'Are you sure? I don't want you going to bed hungry,' insisted Jack.

'I can assure you, I'm quite satisfied in so many different ways.' Jack kissed her and whispered that he was *very* pleased to hear that.

Stella yawned which in turn started Jack yawning. 'I think I need to go to sleep now, I'm exhausted.' She stifled another a yawn. Jack agreed. He had a big day planned for them tomorrow and they would need a fairly early start. Stella snuggled into the pillows and soon drifted into one of the most peaceful sleeps she'd had in a long time.

Jack smiled as he lay beside her. He knew he wanted Stella there, in his bed, not just for the weekend, but every single night. Sometimes it scared him just how much he had fallen in love with her in such a short period of time.

⚹

The next morning when Stella woke, Jack was nowhere to be seen. She looked around the room and couldn't see any of her clothes either. Spotting a T-shirt of Jack's lying over a chair, she got up and put that on. *God knows where my bag is,* she thought, *I can't even remember what happened to it after I came through the front door last night.*

Stella headed downstairs and Jack was in the kitchen.

'Good morning gorgeous,' he said and greeted her with a lingering kiss. 'Love that tee on you by the way.' She laughed and replied that it was the only piece of clothing she could find. He pointed to his lounge room and there lying on the floor was her overnight bag.

'Right. Thanks for that, I should go and have a shower and get changed then.'

'No, hold that thought, breakfast is ready so let's eat it while it's hot,' Jack suggested.

Stella sat at his dining room table. He had set it up so nicely—he had even put a tablecloth on the table. A warm glow flared to life in her chest as she saw right in the middle of the table was a vase full of sunflowers, her favourite. He really had gone to a lot of effort.

'Oh Jack, the table looks lovely,' she gushed.

The breakfast was amazing. Jack had cooked bacon, eggs, hash browns and little sausages along with lots of toast. He even had made a plate of pancakes with whipped cream, maple syrup and some strawberries. It was quite the feast.

'I'm not going to be able to move after all of this food. I'll be in a food coma for days!' Stella groaned.

'Well, I guess this is the time to tell you what I have planned for today and then you will understand why you needed a big breakfast to get your energy levels up. We are going on a bike ride.' Stella hadn't been on a bike for years, but thought it sounded like fun. They finished eating and got cleaned up. Jack hadn't made a huge mess, but Stella was still thankful he had a dishwasher.

'Now, shall we go and get ready?' Stella nodded and went to get her bag so she could finally get dressed.

They left Jack's place and she settled back and watched as the city disappeared behind them. As they started heading up into the mountains the scenery changed and it was gorgeous.

'Wow, this looks pretty cool,' she said as they pulled into the carpark. They got out of the car and proceeded to get the bikes off the rack and get the rest of their gear out. Stella was happy with the bike Jack had hired for her, it was just the right height. She put her backpack, helmet and some sunscreen on and she was ready to roll.

Jack led the way and they started down one of the tracks. The sign said it would take an hour and was a relatively easy ride. She hadn't ridden for years so he knew she wouldn't want anything with too many hills.

They settled into an easy rhythm and the time flew by. The track was a bit rough in places and there were some inclines but they managed to get through without having to stop. There were a lot of trees so it was quite shady and on one side of the track was a gorgeous river that followed alongside them.

In no time at all, they rode around a corner of the track and arrived at their final destination, the lookout. Thankfully there was only a couple of other people there.

They sat looking around enjoying the tranquillity. Jack leaned in and whispered to her that it was just as well there were a few other people there or she would have been in all sorts of trouble. Stella laughed and agreed with him: with their history it was just as well they weren't alone!

She moved closer to him and he put his arm around her. Stella smiled at him and he arched an eyebrow in silent question. She leaned toward him and started kissing him and as they pulled apart, she whispered to him, 'I love you so much.'

And he whispered back, 'I love you too.'

Lunch was yummy. It is amazing how hungry you get when you're out in the great outdoors—the food always tastes so much better when you're on a picnic.

After a few hours of lying there in the sun, Jack suggested they should head back so packing up all their gear they started the ride back. By the time they got back, Stella could feel all the muscles she hadn't used for a while protesting and groaned as she got off the bike.

'Gosh, I'm not sure what has happened to my fitness but I will definitely need more exercise before I attempt another ride.' She stretched out her legs and felt the muscles cramp. 'Ow, that hurts a lot.'

'How about I give you a nice massage when we get home?'

'That sounds wonderful. You really are the best boyfriend.'

⁂

Stella dozed off during the car ride home and woke up with Jack rubbing her arm and saying, 'Wake up sleepy head, we're home now.' She yawned and stretched.

'I'm so sorry. How boring for you having to drive home with no one to talk to.'

Unpacking the car, Jack suggested she head in and have a shower if she wanted to. After doing as he suggested, Stella dried her hair and popped some make up on and was standing there trying to decide what to put on. Looking at what she had packed and decided to wear her halter neck sundress. It was lovely and light; she had made the purchase with Jaz, on a day when she hadn't even planned on buying anything.

Normally, this dress wasn't a colour she wore but something made her try it on and it looked stunning. It was a real sunburnt orange colour and had tropical flowers all over it. Jaz had also talked her into buying some orange beads, bracelets and sandals to wear with it, but today, she just popped the dress on and headed downstairs.

Jack watched her walking towards him with a smile on his face.

'Wow Stella, you look like sunshine.' He poured her a white wine and he grabbed a beer and they headed into his lounge room.

For their dinner he had made an entrée, a main, and a dessert. It all smelt divine and Stella couldn't wait to try what he had prepared. The sunflowers were still in the centre of the table and he'd added some yellow napkins that matched. Stella was glad she had her lovely tropical-coloured dress on, as it went very nicely with the theme. Jack was wearing a pale yellow shirt with some denim shorts which made him look very sexy. The meal was superb, everything was cooked to perfection and they both ate way too much—especially the dessert.

'Oh my god Jack! I'm so full I don't think I can actually move. I think I need to go and lie down and try and digest all of this food,' she said to him.

'Go and relax in the lounge then and I'll clean up,' offered Jack.

'No, that's not fair—you did all the cooking. I will not let you do all those dishes on your own.' She stood and started clearing the table before he could protest.

With both of them cleaning, they had the kitchen spotless in next to no time and returned to the lounge room. Within seconds they both collapsed onto the chaise, still so full of the wonderful dinner.

Jack made a move to get up and Stella shifted to make it easier for him. He was gone for a while and she was just about to get up herself and see where he was when he reappeared. He held out his hand and she took it and he pulled her to her feet.

His arms went around her and he held her tight and kissed her softly and then said, 'Follow me.'

No sooner had they turned out of the lounge and into the hallway when Stella noticed the rose petals. There was a trail of them all the way down the hallway and they continued up the stairs. There was mix of red and white petals. Stella felt her heart racing.

'What is this Jack, what is going on?'

'Just keep walking and you will find out soon enough.'

Walking up the stairs, she expected the trail of petals to lead into his bedroom but they didn't. They continued down the hall past one of the other bedrooms and stopped at the bathroom door. She had never been in here before as they always used his ensuite. Jack wrapped his arms around her waist as he stood behind her.

'Close your eyes,' he instructed. After moving her into position, he whispered, 'You can open them now.'

Stella couldn't even put into words how beautiful the room looked. It was illuminated by candlelight, so many candles, she couldn't even count them. They were all red and white and there were roses lying over the vanity and still more petals on the floor.

The bath was recessed and had steps you walked down to get into it. Behind the tub was a massive window that looked out into his garden, so it was very private. A large shelf ran around the bath with an ice bucket with a bottle of champagne and two glasses, plus a bowl of strawberries sitting on it. Loads of green plants in hanging baskets cascaded towards the bath and it felt like you were in a tropical garden. She turned around and put her arms around his neck and kissed him. Tears welled in her eyes. It was really too much to take in. In the end, all she was capable of saying at that moment was how much she loved it, and him.

They got undressed and she felt like she was in one of those posh spas and half expected someone to come in and give her a facial and a massage. Stepping into the massive tub she slipped into the water. It was incredibly warm and there were plenty of bubbles and Stella groaned with the sheer pleasure.

Sitting on the little seat along the back of the tub, listening to the hum of the jets, it felt like they were the only two people in the world.

Jack opened the champagne and poured some into a glass and handed it to her, along with a strawberry. 'Cheers,' he said and their glasses touched softly.

After taking a sip, Jack took her glass from her and placed it next to his on the shelf.

'Now, didn't I promise you a massage?'

After a considerable amount of time, the water was starting to cool so they decided it was time to get out. The towels were just as Stella had imagined, soft and fluffy, like floating on a cloud. They put on their robes and headed back to Jack's room.

Passing by the spare room Jack made a crack about breaking that room in next but for now, she was perfectly happy to be heading back to Jack's bedroom. They dropped their robes and climbed into bed.

The next morning, they just lazed around at Jack's. They toyed with the idea of going out for a good old Sunday drive but couldn't agree where to go, so in the end they just sat in Jack's lounge room watching a movie on Netflix. It got to late afternoon and she announced it was time to go home. He pulled her back down and lay on top of her. 'I don't want you to go, just stay with me.'

It was hard for Stella to resist him and say no to anything he wanted, but she remained firm and pushed him up and jumped up to her feet. She quickly headed upstairs to grab her bag and Jack was hot on her heels.

He grabbed her and pushed her down on to this bed. Her arms were pinned by her side so she couldn't move an inch. She laughed and started wriggling around to try and get free.

Jack groaned, 'Please don't do that Stella or you definitely won't be leaving anytime soon!' She offered him a wicked smile and wiggled some more. 'Okay woman, you asked for it.' He started to take her top off.

She slapped his hand away, 'No, I have to go Jack,' and she sat up and put her top back on.

'Another time,' Jack sighed.

She packed up her gear and he walked her to her car. 'Guess this is it then.' He leaned into her car window and kissed her goodbye.

'Thanks for a great weekend.'

He kissed her again and whispered, 'I'm sure going to miss you in my bed tonight.'

'Don't even go there, I'm trying not to think about how hard it is going to be to sleep without you in my arms tonight,' she said and blew him a kiss and drove away before she could change her mind.

CHAPTER 52

As Stella pulled into her driveway, she could see something on her front porch. *That's odd,* she thought, *I don't remember leaving anything there when I left on Friday.* As she got out of her car and got closer she could see a big bouquet of sunflowers. Reaching down she picked up the card.

Stella, you came into my life when I was least expecting it. I have never met anyone like you before and I know I never will. I will love you forever.

All my love Jack xx

She reached into her bag and pulled out her phone. She pressed Jack's number and he answered straight away.

Before he could say anything, she said, 'I love you, Jack. The flowers are gorgeous! When on earth did you have time to come to organise all this?'

'That's my secret—I don't want you to know all my moves now, do I?' He laughed.

After she hung up, she headed into her house and into her room to unpack.

The evening dragged being on her own and she picked up her phone a couple of times to text Jack and then put it down. She didn't want to seem too needy and clingy but she really wanted to hear his voice. *Stop it she thought,* you're acting like a lovesick teenager, pull yourself together.

She had tried to call Jaz and Liz, but, neither of them picked up so she had a nice long shower and slipped on her pyjamas. She decided to try what it felt like to sleep on the other side of her bed— Jack's side. She plumped up the pillows and picked up her book. Minutes later, she was squirming around, no, this wasn't working. With a sigh, she moved back to 'her side' as it felt so wrong. She had just turned the page when her doorbell rang. It gave her such a fright she dropped the book. Her heart was pounding. Who the hell could it be at this time of the night?

She got out of bed and peered out of her window. She couldn't see much as her bedroom didn't face her driveway but she checked as much as she could to make sure there was no one lurking on her property. Slipping on her dressing gown she headed downstairs and tiptoed to her front door and nervously called out, 'Who is it?'

There was a pause and a deep voice answered. 'Stella, it's me. It's Jack.' She opened the door and sure enough, he was standing there. Her heart rate began to recover.

'Why didn't you call and say you were coming over?'

He shrugged and said, 'I don't know. It seemed like a good idea when I thought of it.'

She hadn't been expecting anyone so hadn't bothered to put her porch light on. Stella reached into the dark night and pulled him inside. She shut the front door and spun him around so his back was up against the front door and then she started kissing him. The passion was a repeat of Friday night, in the best way possible.

She reached up, took his shirt off and then undid his belt and his jeans hit the ground seconds later so did her pyjamas. They were both standing there now at the front door naked.

As Jack picked her up and started carrying her to her room he murmured, 'Here we go again. What is it about us and front doors?'

Stella answered, 'Don't know, and I don't care. Just move it and get to my bedroom as fast as you can, please.'

❧

The next morning, Jack got up early and headed home. His phone rang as he got to the end of her street. It was Paul asking if him and Stella were free, did they want to have dinner with him and Lindy next Friday. She had found an Italian place and was keen to try it out. Jack said he would check and let him know. He messaged Stella later in the day and she was keen so he let Paul know so Lindy could make a reservation.

Friday night traffic was a nightmare in the city. But eventually they got into a carpark.

Jack took her hand and they walked towards the restaurant. As Paul and Lindy approached from the other direction, they could see the satisfaction on their friend's faces as they held hands.

Meeting up at the door, they all hugged each other and headed in. Obviously, the girls couldn't get into the 'nitty gritties' with both the guys sitting there, so they excused themselves from the table and headed to the ladies room. Once they got in there, Lindy turned to Stella and said, 'Okay, spill! I'm dying to know what's going on with you two.'

Stella filled Lindy in on everything (well not *everything*). Lindy was a little envious, she hadn't realised that Jack was such a romantic and joked that she'd need to give Paul a bit of a rev up.

When they returned to the table, the guys had ordered some entrees and wine. The food was great, none of them could remember eating such great Italian food. It really was to die for! But, of course, they all managed to save some room for dessert and coffee.

They all headed home early as both Jack and Paul were heading away to Andy's bucks weekend and it was going to be an early start. Stella remembered Andy from the hike, a friendly guy with a wide smile and was happy to hear he was engaged.

CHAPTER 53

Jack dropped Stella off at her place and then headed home to finish packing for the bucks weekend. He wasn't looking forward to the early start, but at least he wasn't driving so he could have another few hours' sleep in the car. Knowing these guys as he did, he knew it would be a big weekend of drinking and not much sleep. Best to get some while he could.

Jack had had some of the best times in his life with these guys. Some of the stories he could share with Stella… but there were others that were probably best kept to himself. He hadn't seen Andy since the hike to Plumpton Ridge so was looking forward to catching up over a few beers.

❧

Stella watched Jack drive away and then went inside. *Gosh it feels so quiet here when I'm on my own now,* she thought as she headed to her bedroom. She flicked on the light and glanced at her bed. A pit welled up in her stomach as she thought about sleeping in it by herself.

But she didn't want to dwell on the empty feeling inside her. She actually had some plans of her own for the weekend. She text Jaz to confirm their get together for tomorrow. Stella was excited to finally catch up with her and couldn't wait to fill her in on the latest with her and Jack.

She changed into her pyjamas and climbed into her bed. She had thought about reading some more of her book but was too exhausted, so she flicked off her side lamp and lay there for a while thinking of Jack. She picked up her phone and sent him a quick text. Seconds later she got one in return.

He sent something suggestive which made her smile. A bit more sexual banter passed between them and then they decided that they had better shut this down before one of them had to drive over for a booty call.

Stella got up to get ready for her day with Jaz. They had arranged to have an early breakfast and then go to a day spa. Facials and massages were just what was needed, along with a good old chat.

Stella pulled up outside Jaz's place and tooted the horn. Jaz opened her front door and called out that she would be there in a minute before she disappeared. Re-appearing with her bag she walked down towards the car.

'Hi there stranger, long time no see or hear,' she said and reached over to hug Stella.

'I know, I know, I've been a very slack bestie lately, but I promise I will make it up to you this weekend.'

Arriving at the day spa, they were ushered towards their room and were swaddled in fluffy robes and slippers. They sat there sipping glasses of champagne and eating the nibbles that were laid out on a platter. This really was the life—they both sighed with pleasure.

Once they were lying on the tables next to each other, there really wasn't much time to chat, they just closed their eyes and listened to the relaxing music. There were birds chirping and water running, authentically replicating the atmosphere of a forest next to a flowing river.

The massages were divine. Stella hadn't realised how tight her shoulders and back were from that bike ride. She felt her muscles softening up with each stroke and when the masseuse put the hot rocks on her back, it was heavenly.

After their massages and facials were finished, they sat in the spa pool. More drinks were provided and they chatted. Thankfully there was no one else around so they could talk quite freely.

Stella told Jaz about the night at Jack's and the other dates they had been on. She obviously didn't tell her everything—but Jaz got the general idea. She commented with a grin that she had never seen Stella so happy.

Stella told Jaz that Liz was having a ball up north and she had called the other day to say she had made it up to the Daintree Rainforest and was actually up there with Tim. That bit of news had Stella speculating on what was going on there!

At 5.00pm they decided that it was time to get dressed and head back to Stella's. By the time they got there, they had decided they didn't feel like cooking so felt like placed an order for Chinese take away. They put their pyjamas on, opened a bottle of wine and got comfy on Stella's lounge. Jaz started scrolling through Netflix to try and find something they both hadn't already seen. No doubt it would be a romantic movie and they would both end up crying. They really should start watching some movies from other genres but couldn't help themselves; they were both suckers for a good romance.

As soon as their takeaway arrived, they dished up and started the movie. It was a typical chick flick and they both sat back and watched the story unfold. It didn't take long before they'd thought they'd figured out what was going to happen to this couple. But it took a direction that neither of them had seen coming—the girl got sick and was diagnosed with cancer. It ended up that the couple decided to still get married and did so with her terminally ill in the hospital. Then she died and that was the end of them. They cried their hearts out and used up all of Stella's tissues. By the time the movie ended they were drained, but they agreed that it always felt good to have a good cry with your best friend.

Stella chose the next movie—a comedy—while Jaz dug some ice cream out of Stella's freezer. They needed that after the last movie. When it had finished, they decided to call it a night.

Jaz popped down to Stella's room to say goodnight. 'Thanks for today. I had a ball,'

'Yes, it was a fab day,' agreed Stella.

Jaz rolled off the bed and stood at the door. 'Stella, it sounds like you have met the perfect guy. Jack is pretty amazing and you're amazing, so you make an amazing couple!' Stella blew her a kiss and told Jaz how much she loved her.

Stella read a few chapters of her book and switched off her lamp. What was Jack was doing at this moment? He was most likely getting into all sorts of mischief with Paul and Andy. She could imagine the hangovers that they would all have when they woke up in the morning.

He'd said he'd have no phone coverage while he was away but she hoped he would call or send a text when he got home tomorrow night. It had only been a few hours since they'd last seen each other, but she already missed him so much.

CHAPTER 54

J ack was indeed having a great time away with Paul and Andy. The cabin they were staying at was pretty basic, but it suited their purpose and more than likely they would all just end up crashing around the fire anyway.

The beers came out and they all settled in for the afternoon. They cranked up the fire as the temperature dropped and a couple of the other guys got some meat cooking.

The night wore on and the stories got more and more raunchy. Some of the guys were still single so they were giving Andy a hard time and had planned a few pranks for later in the night. *It was going to be a messy night*, thought Jack and he shook his head.

Someone asked Jack about his love life and some light banter erupted.

'Look you buggers, I have met a great woman.'

Grabbing another beer, he sat back by the fire and told them all they had met at work and he had been on a few dates with her. He told them he was going to bring her to Andy's wedding and they could all meet her then. They latched onto the detail that she was older than him and of course he got hammered then. He knew this would happen, so wanted to let them all get it out of their system before he introduced Stella to his friends. If any of them dared to call her a cougar to her face, they would live to regret it.

Eventually, it was just Jack and Andy sitting side by side having their last beer.

'Cheers mate,' said Jack. 'Bella is great, you've got a good woman.'

Andy nodded and said, 'Mate, meeting her has been the best thing in my life. So, what I want to know, is what is going on with you? I'm "assuming" that this lady you have met at work and have been seeing is Stella, from the hike? After all that drama at Plumpton Ridge, I wasn't sure if anything was going to happen there.' He laughed.

'Well mate, prepare to be blown away with what has been happening in my life since then.' Jack quickly brought him up to speed.

'Wow, you have been through a lot since we last caught up.'

'Yeah, it's been pretty full on but things are settling down now.'

'Sounds like things are pretty serious between you two. Perhaps you need to propose to her—you don't want someone else swooping in, now do you?' He gave him a good-natured shoulder nudge. 'A good woman is so hard to find so when you do find one, pop the big question and settle down. Well, that's my two cents worth anyway.'

Jack mulled over what Andy had said as he sat by the fire. There was no way he could go to sleep now. Andy was right, what was he waiting for?

He was going to propose to Stella.

CHAPTER 55

Stella's phone rang late on Sunday night.

'I just wanted to say I'm home now,' Jack said, his voice a warm rumble in her ear.

'Good to hear. Did you have a great weekend?'

'Yeah, it was good, but I drank too much so still feel a bit ordinary,' and he laughed.

'I knew you would feel like crap, but it was a bucks so I wouldn't expect anything less.'

She told him about the spa and that her and Jaz had an enjoyable day together. She had even managed to find the perfect outfit for this wedding, during some late night online shopping. The dress she had found was gorgeous and she had managed to find the perfect little bag and matching shoes. As it was a fairly casual wedding that was going to be held outside, so with Jaz's counsel, she had also bought a cute little hat that would help keep the sun off her face.

❧

The weekend of Andy and Bella's wedding finally arrived. It was being held at a great little winery—Cooks Retreat. Jack got out of the car and went and checked in.

'All sorted?' she asked when he got back into the car.

'Yep, all good.' They followed the road around to their cabin. Piling their luggage inside, she admired the tall ceilings and plush bed. The room was gorgeous and her eyes lit up upon spotting the spa bath in the ensuite.

'Don't even think about using that spa now, Stella. It's late and we have a big day tomorrow.'

'Party pooper,' moaned Stella and poked her tongue out at Jack. She hadn't any intention of having a spa now.

'I'm so tired,' Stella said and yawned. 'I can't wait to go to sleep. I'm pretty sure as soon as my head hits that pillow, I'll be out like a light.' She turned around so he couldn't see her smiling. She waited to see if he would take the bait. But he didn't fall for the act—he knew exactly what was going on.

'No sleep for you just yet.' He gathered her in his arms and kissed her deeply. Jack sighed, 'Oh, how I have missed kissing you.'

Stella murmured something similar against his lips and they both moved towards the bed. Clothes came off left, right and centre, and they found themselves completely naked on the massive bed as Jack slowly explored her body as she did the same with his. They just couldn't seem to get enough of each other.

❧

Later, as they lay curled up against each other, Jack reached down and pulled up the blanket to cover them both. Stella snuggled into him, content, and they both fell into a deep sleep.

They woke just as the sun was rising and went out to the balcony. She hadn't noticed it the night before, too distracted by her lover. Speaking of Jack, he joined her and stood behind her, wrapping his arms around her. They watched the sun come up in all its glory.

To fill in time before the wedding, they wandered around

chatting to other wedding guests and sampling wine. They tried some of the cheese that was produced onsite and it was divine— Stella fully intended to purchase some (lots!) before they headed home on Monday.

There was also time to try out that spa bath. It was nowhere near as good as the one at Jack's, but it was still relaxing to lie in there with a glass of wine. When Jack got out, Stella stayed in a little longer and read some more of her book. She stretched her legs out and sighed. 'This really is the life,' she said.

The next time she looked at the clock, it was nearly 2.00pm. Gosh that time had slipped away quickly. Jack was still nowhere to be seen but she knew it wouldn't take him long to get ready. She was pleased that she had this time alone to get herself ready as she knew he would distract her and she definitely didn't want him to see her new lingerie and ruin the surprise.

By the time Jack came in through the door, she was dressed and was putting the finishing touches to her hair and makeup. He came up behind her and slipped his hands over her shoulders, trying to touch her breasts.

'Hey, no touching the merchandise buddy.' She laughed at him.

'Spoil sport,' he retorted and walked away huffing to get dressed. Every time she glanced over at him, he was mock glaring back at her. Stella found it quite funny, and even more so very cute.

☙

The wedding was lovely. Bella looked stunning and the expression on Andy's face as she walked towards him brought a tear to most people's eyes. Jack held Stella's hand and squeezed it when the bride and groom said their 'I do's.'

After the ceremony, Stella and Lindy stood chatting about what a beautiful wedding it was and how gorgeous Bella looked. Jack drifted away towards the bar, with Paul.

'Mate, I'm going to propose to Stella.' *Wow it felt good to say that out loud.*

'It's about bloody time. Don't let Stella get away, she's a keeper! We all adore her and she obviously makes you happy. You two are soul mates,' Paul said with a grin.

'Watch it mate, you're starting to sound like Lindy.'

'I know we normally laugh about this kind of bullshit when Lindy tells us that there is someone out there meant for everyone, but I guess all her talk has rubbed off on me over the years,' replied Paul.

'Stella is into all the stuff with the universe—no wonder the two of them are as thick as thieves,' said Jack.

'Two men talking about fate and love, what the hell has happened?' said Paul and he changed the subject and they started talking about the latest NRL game—a topic they felt a lot more comfortable with.

⁊

Re-joining the girls, they made their way to the dining area. All the food had been produced here at the winery and it was an appetising spread.

After the cake was cut and handed out to anyone who was still able to squeeze a piece in, the dancing started. There was a four-piece band and they started off with a slow dance for the happy couple before everyone else wandered onto the dance floor.

'Care to dance?' asked Jack and she took his hand and followed him out on to the dance floor. He took her in his arms and they swayed from side to side.

'Happy?' he whispered into her ear.

'Very, very happy,' she replied and kissed him on the cheek.

Sometime later, as they were just about to step off the dance floor and sit down the band started playing their song. Jack couldn't believe it—of all the songs that the band should choose to play at the wedding, they chose this one. What a happy coincidence.

The universe smiled as she knew it was no coincidence…

Jack looked deeply into Stella's eyes and said, 'Looks like they are playing our song,' and took her in his arms. He remembered when it had played in Fiji and how much had changed since then. As they slowly circled the dance floor Jack quietly sang to her. This would be the song they would have their first dance to as a married couple, he'd have to insist on that. Stella's eyes sparkled with happy tears as she looked up at him.

They spent a lot of the time on the dance floor and as the music got faster and everyone relaxed, there were some dance offs. The good old chicken dance was played and they all had so much fun doing that. It was a brilliant evening.

As the night wore on, Jack decided he wanted some alone time with Stella. He had found a track that wound through the dense vines when he had been out for a walk earlier in the day and he led her there now.

'There's something I want to talk to you about. A surprise,' he said. She smiled and wrapped herself around him tightly and pressed into him.

'I think it's my turn for a surprise,' she said, a sultry look in her eyes. He groaned as she stepped back, sliding her hands up her sides, drawing his attention to her figure and evaporating the speech he'd had prepared.

'You drive me crazy Stella. I just want to take that dress off you right now.' Sliding the zip down it fell into a pool around her ankles.

Standing in the moonlight she looked like a goddess. She let her hair down and it tumbled around her shoulders. She was wearing a sexy corset and he could see her breasts through the sheer lace. It was laced up at the back and Jack untied the ribbon as fast as he could and then he gave up and dragged it down, his hands grazing her hard nipples which made her groan. She had suspenders on as well and if he had known that the stockings she had on were connected to these, she would have been in trouble a whole lot earlier than this.

He watched as she unhooked the stockings and started rolling them slowly down her legs.

She walked around him, provocatively rubbing herself up against him.

'Oh, stop Stella, please,' he begged. He couldn't stand the sexual tension that was building up between them.

'I don't think I want to,' she danced around, enjoying teasing him.

'You do realise that we can't stop now, there is no way I can make it back to our cabin.'

'Ah ha, I do and I have no intention of leaving this spot, well not until I get what I want and,' she rubbed her hand over his groin, 'I need you now.' He looked around for somewhere to lay down with her. Spotting a grassy area, he threw his jacket down and dragged her down on top of him. He slipped into her and tried to pour all the love he felt for her into every movement, every touch. Their lovemaking was hot and frantic and when they had finished, they lay there in each other's arms, utterly spent.

As the sweat cooled on their bodies, they noticed voices carrying over the night air. It was then they realised just how exposed they were and it was probably time to get dressed. Dragging their clothes on as best as they could in the dark, Stella laughed and hoped her dress was on properly and not inside out. *Gosh, imagine if I'd left a stocking lying here,* she thought as they ran off hand in hand back to their cabin.

They caught up with Andy and Bella before they left on their honeymoon and thanked them for a great weekend and wished them well. They were heading to Fiji for a week and were looking forward to lying on the beach and drinking lots of cocktails and recovering from their wedding day.

The trip home was subdued. They had only been officially dating for ten months and it had been wonderful. But so many thoughts were going through her mind. Would he eventually get bored with her like Marcus had and cast her aside? She had passed the age where she could have children—did he even want any? This had never come up and she knew she'd have discuss this with him eventually. If he wanted kids, well that would probably be a deal breaker.

Jack held out his hand and she took it—just touching him gave her so much comfort and she couldn't imagine her life now without him in it.

CHAPTER 56

Jack had been thinking a lot about the ring he wanted to give to Stella. He had a rough idea on what he wanted but hadn't seen anything in the local jewellers that suited. So, after doing some research online he found a manufacturing jeweller and made an appointment for later in the week.

He had drawn a rough picture of the design he wanted and the jeweller fine-tuned it. It was going to be stunning, a unique ring. Stella loved anything that was different and was actually very easy to please. Quirky, thoughtful gifts gave her so much pleasure. He knew it was a risk buying a ring without any input from her, however, something told him that she was not going to be disappointed.

He was glad now that he hadn't proposed at the wedding. It had been Andy's day, and he hadn't wanted to steal the limelight—though he'd almost done it anyway, when they'd gone for that walk.

It was a miracle that Stella didn't sense Jack's mood and start to suspect something. He was trying to play it cool but he was sure she would be able to feel the excitement coming of him in waves. But so far, so good, she didn't suspect a thing.

Five weeks later, Jack got the call he had been waiting for. The ring was ready so he arranged to go and pick it up the next day.

He could hardly concentrate on work and spent the rest of the day looking at the picture he had drawn of the ring—hoping it looked exactly like he had visualised.

Stella had wanted him to come over for dinner but he made up an excuse, one that she brought thankfully. There was no way he was going to be able to spend the evening with her and contain his excitement. He was sure that he would end up blowing the surprise somehow. He was so close—he just couldn't take the risk of her finding out now.

While they were on the phone, he asked her if she was free next weekend and pretended they were going to be camping. *I must remember to put the tent in the car,* he thought or she would find it strange that they were going camping without one!

❦

He could feel the ring burning a hole in his jacket pocket. Over the last week, his anxiety had taken over and he'd found himself checking and double checking the safe where he'd kept the ring. Even now, he found himself touching the pocket where it was kept just to check it was still there. He did *not* want to lose this ring after all the trouble he had gone to getting it made. The jeweller had done a fantastic job and he couldn't thank him enough. The ring was absolutely beautiful and looked even better than he could have possibly ever have imagined. His rough drawing didn't do it justice!

Every time he opened the tiny velvet box he smiled. The ring was inlaid with a purple, heart shaped stone. It was just perfect for his Stella and he couldn't wait to see her face when she saw it.

Pulling into her driveway, he thought how much her place was starting to feel like home to him. That was going to be an interesting discussion to have down the track—where would they live? There were pros and cons for both places. Perhaps they could sell both of their houses and buy one together, incorporating the best parts of their current houses into the new one?

Stella came to her front door and waved to him. Jack could see she already had some bags sitting out so he got out of the car, grabbed them and popped them in the boot. *Let the weekend begin!*

'Where are we going Jack?' she asked, barely even saying hello to him.

'We are heading out to a property that belongs to a friend of mine.'

'How far is it?'

'Only a couple of hours.' He turned away so she couldn't see him smiling. He knew not knowing their destination would be driving her crazy.

⁂

When they eventually turned off the main highway, they travelled another five kilometres and then Jack turned into a dirt road. Bumping along that for another kilometre they arrived at a gate and Jack jumped out and unlocked it and they continued on.

As they came into a clearing there was the cabin. Stella loved it instantly and in fact it reminded her of something, but she couldn't quite place it.

Looking at the cabin and then at him she said, 'Camping, are we? Obviously we won't be using that tent.' She nudged him on the arm.

'We can, if you would prefer it. I don't mind,' he replied with a twinkle in his eye.

'No, the cabin will do just fine thanks... provided there are no spiders or snakes lurking in there?'

Jack winked. 'I'm such a gentleman, I'll go in first and check it out for you.'

'I can come in with you, I'm not that much of a wuss.' Secretly, she hoped there would be nothing in there as she hated any kind of creepy-crawly.

Jack walked in first and called back to her, 'It's okay. You're going to love this.' Stella walked in behind him and looked around. There was a small table with a couple of chairs, a basic kitchen and near the window there was a two-seater couch and another single chair.

Stella pushed open the leadlight window to let the breeze in and she could smell jasmine and lavender. She noticed there was a little veggie garden so decided she would check it out and see if there was something she could add to their dinner. She thought she could see some mint which would be perfect for the salad she was planning.

'Thanks for bringing me. You do realise that I'm never going to want to leave now.'

'I knew you were going to love it. If you're anywhere near the bush or water, well, I can't go wrong. I know these are your favourite things, Stella.'

Jack went back out to the car and brought in their bags. They unpacked and sorted out the food and then decided to head out and check out the rest of the property. They walked to the edge of the land and took in the view of the mountains. If it had been winter, they would have probably been shrouded in fog, but today you could clearly see their majestic outline. Jack told her there were some great hiking tracks all around them so they planned to go out there one day soon.

'Are there any glow-worms out here by any chance? She had not forgotten that amazing night and being out here had reminded her of it.

'No, but I've seen plenty of kangaroos and even a couple of koalas.' They went and checked out the veggie garden and Stella was delighted to see that there were lots of things she could use. Jack assured her that the Airbnb hosts had said they were welcome to help themselves. She picked a couple of tomatoes, some beans and took some of the mint she had spotted earlier.

They headed back to the cabin and she curled up in one of the chairs on the balcony. Jack came out with a beer and a glass of wine for her.

'Cheers. This is the life, isn't it?'

'It is stunning out here, so peaceful.' She closed her eyes, soaking it all up.

⁂

After dinner, Jack headed out to the fire pit so he could get the fire going before it got too dark. Stella picked up the blanket and grabbed their little Esky and headed down to join him.

Lying there together in front of the crackling fire was so relaxing and Stella yawned.

'Time to go to bed?'

'Yes, I think it is. I'm exhausted.' She yawned again.

'Me too.' He started kicking dirt over the fire to make sure it was completely out.

As they walked back up towards the cabin, Jack looked back at the fire pit and smiled. He could hardly wait for tomorrow.

CHAPTER 57

There was a spectacular lookout nearby so once breakfast was done, they packed up some sandwiches and drinks, loaded up their packs and headed off.

Now and then through the trees she could see the mountains they'd admired yesterday. They looked glorious today with the sun reflecting off the dark trees. The track had a few ups and downs and they crossed over another part of the river that connected with the one near their cabin. There was a canopy of trees they were walking under and it was refreshing to be out of the sun for a while.

Reaching the lookout, the view took Stella's breath away. You could see for miles and miles. They found a nice spot to rest and eat their lunch. Stella closed her eyes, listening to the sounds of the bush. Jack was lying down beside her and he reached out for her hand.

'I love you, Stella.'

'I love you too, Jack Turner, with all my heart.' She leaned over and kissed him.

It was late afternoon by the time they got back to the cabin and Stella decided she was going to go and have a rest.

❧

Once she had disappeared Jack got busy setting up for their evening. He could get lots done that she wouldn't notice until it got dark He snuck into their room and looking into his bag patted the pocket of the shirt he planned on wearing tonight. Yes, the ring was still there!

࿐

Sometime later, Stella stirred and it took her a minute to remember where she was.

'Hey there sleepy head,' he said when she appeared.

'How long have I been sleeping for?'

'Only a couple of hours.'

'You should have woken me earlier. I feel bad for sleeping the rest of the afternoon away.'

She blinked. Jack was dressed pretty smart. He had on a pair of black jeans and a nice white shirt. He had even shaved! What was this all about? Feeling underdressed in her activewear, she went back into the bedroom and rummaged through her bag to try and find something suitable. She finally decided on a pair of jeans and a nice lilac top. She swept some makeup on and gathered her hair up into a bun. *What a pity I don't have some pretty sandals to put on,* she thought as she put on her hiking boots again. They didn't quite go with the outfit but were a lot more practical than sandals.

She walked out and Jack whistled.

'You look lovely.' Stella blew him a kiss and told him that he looked pretty flash himself.

'So, are we heading outside?' She made to move towards the door. He reached out and grabbed her arm stopping her in her tracks. 'What's going on?' she asked slowly.

He grinned. 'You'll see soon enough. For now, close your eyes.' As she did, Jack came up behind her.

'I'm going to walk behind you, so don't worry, I won't let you fall,' he assured her. She felt him start to move her forward with his hands braced on her hips. She heard the click of the door and felt the cool night air on her face.

'Open your eyes, Stella,' Jack whispered to her.

⁂

Stella opened her eyes. When had he done all of this? It didn't seem possible that he could've done this all by himself. Something was niggling away in the back of her mind but she still couldn't quite grasp what it was. Why did this all seem so familiar?

There was a path out to the fire pit and all along this he had set up candles. In between the candles were flowers; sunflowers, wisteria, bunches of lavender, and white roses.

Stella wandered down the path towards the fire pit and the flames on each of the candles wavered as she walked past them. They were purple and white and looked stunning and the scent from the flowers filled the air. Stella kept breathing in deeply to take in the glorious aroma coming from them. There wasn't a breath of wind and even the birds had stopped their singing for the day. The silence was only broken by the crackling of the fire as the branches burned away slowly.

Once she reached the fire there was a picnic basket, a bottle of champagne and two crystal flutes. She turned to him her eyes full of tears. 'I really don't know what to say, I really don't.' She turned to him and smiled, then leaned forward and kissed him. 'What is this Jack, are we celebrating something?' Jack took her hand and they both sat down.

He poured champagne in to both of the glasses and handed her one. They were looking into each other's eyes so deeply that Stella really felt like she was looking into his soul.

Jack's eyes filled with tears as he said to her, 'Stella, I fell in love with you the very first moment I met you. Our eyes met and I felt our souls collide. I knew then that you were the one for me and I love you now and I always will. You make me smile every single day and you always laugh at all my jokes. My life began the day we met and I can't imagine living the rest of my life without you in it. I know things haven't always been easy for us, but I honestly think I have been waiting for you my whole life.' Her heart jumped as he pulled a little heart-shaped box from his pocket. 'Stella, will you make me the happiest man in the world and marry me?'

He opened the box and nestled inside was a ring. It was a square cut diamond with some tiny little amethyst stones placed around it. The dainty band was gold with a diamond on each side of the central stone. It really was the most exquisite ring Stella had ever seen.

'Jack, that day we met... I-I-I too felt the connection between us. I believe my soul had been searching for you my whole life and... I feel like I'm finally complete. You make me smile every day and you're my best friend. I had thought that the love I feel for you was never going to be returned and was one that I could never have.' She took a deep breath. 'I love you so much. Yes, I will marry you. I can't wait to spend the rest of my life with you.'

Jack let out a shaky laugh. 'Thank goodness you said yes.' He slipped the ring on to her finger. 'I wasn't sure what you were going to say for a second there!'

Stella smiled and moved her hand from side to side, the diamonds twinkling in the firelight. She really couldn't believe that they were now engaged. They belonged together now, forever.

The moon was shining so brightly, the stars twinkled in the night sky and the fire crackled away. Jack leaned over and threw another log on to the fire and the embers flew up and danced above the flames before settling down again.

Jack and Stella lay there curled up on the blanket in each other's arms and neither of them could remember a time when they had been as happy as they were right now.

EPILOGUE
SIX MONTHS LATER...

'I can't believe we are married Stella,' said Jack. Neither could Stella, but as she looked down at her hand, at her ring, she knew it hadn't all been a dream. She was finally his wife and he was her husband. Gosh, that has a lovely sound to it! she thought—my husband! The last few months had gone by in a blur with all the planning that led up to their wedding day. There had been so much to organise in such a short time, but the day had been absolutely perfect and she wouldn't have changed one single thing.

The venue they had chosen was stunning and of course, outside. They both loved the outdoors so much that there was no way they would have been married anywhere else. The weather was perfect and all of their friends and families joined them. There were plenty of tears when they both said their vows to each other.

The reception had been set up in a large marquee, with a dance floor and a band. The food was divine. Naturally, the best part of it all was the dessert table. Stella was worried she would burst out of her dress after they finished the meal!

Stella had asked Jaz and Liz to be her bridesmaids and Jack had asked Paul and Andy to be his best man and groomsman respectively.

Paul had a wonderful speech that had everyone in tears of laugher as he told them all some stories of Jack's life. They had certainly shared so many good times together over the years and the memories would last them a lifetime.

Jaz also said a few words, and she too told some stories that made Jack raise his eyebrows more than once or twice. *How well did he actually know his wife?* he thought and he chuckled. He would be asking for more details of these stories later, that was for sure!

Liz had decided to stay on in Australia. To Stella's delight, Liz and Tim were engaged and expecting a baby. Stella had been thrilled especially when they asked her and Jack to be the godparents.

After they had cut the cake, it was time for the happy couple to have their first dance together as husband and wife. And it goes without saying what song was played that night. Once again, as he always did, as he always loved to, Jack sang it to her as they moved around the dance floor in each other's arms. They both had tears in their eyes. They couldn't believe they were now married.

Later that night after everyone had gone home, they were sitting together out in the garden by a little pond. They had both left a note for one another in the rooms they were using to change into their wedding outfits and had decided to read them to each other after they were married.

Stella had tucked her note from Jack under the bodice of her dress and it had lay there right next to her heart as she said her vows to him. And Jack had put his note from Stella inside his jacket pocket, so it lay there right next to his heart when he said his vows to her.

Stella opened Jack's, and her eyes welled up as she started reading what he had written to her.

My dear Stella,

Today you made me the happiest man alive when you took my hand and became my wife. I have loved you from the moment I saw you.

You're one of the kindest people I have ever met. You're funny and smart and gorgeous inside and out. My soul was searching for you my whole life and now we are together I don't wish for us ever to be apart. I will love you as long as I live and I will protect you and try and make you happy every single day. I choose you Stella and you're my forever love.

All of my love.

Jack xx

'Oh, Jack,' she cried, 'I love you so much.'

Jack took Stella's note out of his pocket. He had such a lump in his throat he wasn't sure if he was going to be able to read it to her. Stella took his hand and smiled at him and he started reading.

To my darling Jack

Today you made me the happiest woman alive when you took my hand and became my husband. You're my soul mate and my best friend and now I'm proud to call you, my husband.

I fell in love with you on that first day that our eyes met and I knew without a doubt that you were meant for me. I love your passion and your enthusiasm for life and we have already had so many adventures together and I know we will have many more as we travel life's journey together.

You make me smile and laugh every single day and I thank you for that. I can't wait to spend the rest of my life with you and I can truly rest now knowing that my search is over and I have found you, my darling. Our souls are now finally united for all eternity and I will love only you. I choose you Jack and you're my forever love.

Love you always.

Stella xx

Stella smiled. She had finally remembered what it was that had bugged her about the night Jack had proposed up at the cabin. The whole setup with the candles and the flowers and the cabin had been so much like that recurring dream she'd had so long ago. It had to be a coincidence that he had just about replicated what she had dreamed about, there was no way he could possibly have known, was there?

The universe smiled and knew her time with these two was done. It hadn't been easy but finally they had stopped fighting their destiny and accepted that she really did know what was best for them.

ACKNOWLEDGEMENTS

To my husband Ross and sons Luke and Liam – thank you for your support. Through the tough days you were there listening as I procrastinated over the story! I am sure that you have all heard enough about romance to last you a lifetime now!

To my best friends Julie, Marie and Ros, I can't thank you enough for your support and friendship. Gosh we have had some adventures together and I know we will continue to! I am so glad that the universe ensured that we all met!

Special thanks to Judy Ballinger – the best mother any daughter could ever wish for. You always believed I could do it and your faith in me kept me going. When you think where this story started and where it ended up, it really is quite remarkable and I thank you for bearing with me as I bounced ideas of you! I love you Mum x.

Thank you to all my Scouting friends who listened to me as I pondered over this story on a daily basis! Your support and friendship means the world to me.

Thank you to the team at Shawline Publishing for helping me bring this story to life – working with you all is an absolute pleasure!

Shawline Publishing Group Pty Ltd
www.shawlinepublishing.com.au

More great Shawline titles can be found here

New titles also available through Books@Home Pty Ltd.
Subscribe today - www.booksathome.com.au